ABOUT THE AUTHOR

Bisi Daniels is the pen name of the prolific writer, Bisi Ojediran. A graduate of the University of Ghana, Legon, he is now the Chairman of the Editorial Board of *This Day* newspaper. Prior to that, he was Business Editor of two of Nigeria's most influential newspapers, including *The Guardian*, before he started work in the oil industry. He joined Elf Petroleum as Media Relations Manager in 1995, moving on to Shell Petroleum, and has recently returned to journalism.

He has written over 20 books, including eight novels.

THE GIRL FROM NIGERIA

BISI DANIELS

THE GIRL FROM NIGERIA

AUSTIN & MACAULEY

A CIP catalogue record for this title is available from the British Library.

ISBN 978 1 905609 38-3

www.austinmacauley.com

First Published (2009)
Austin & Macauley Publishers Ltd.
25 Canada Square
Canary Wharf
London
E14 5LB

Printed & Bound in Great Britain

DEDICATION

To Ayodele

CHAPTER ONE

Peter Abel stared down at the two bloody severed ears. The last time he had seen them, they were on either side of Tunde Picketts' head. Now they were sealed in a plastic evidence bag, held casually by a stocky policeman. Abel had no difficulty recognising the ears as Tunde's. Each sprouted distinctive wiry hairs. He often wondered if Tunde's pretty wife noticed them and if she cared that Tunde never bothered to groom them.

As he continued to stare, they reminded him of the imported dried apricots he bought in the marketplace on special occasions. Abel was embarrassed by the idea. What on earth was he thinking? Thank God he hadn't said it out loud. He looked sheepishly at the policeman who had introduced himself as Sergeant Fakorede.

"What happened?"

"Mr. Picketts' wife received a parcel this afternoon. She opened it and found these. She recognised them as her husband's. She called us. She thinks it is a kidnapping with a ransom note to follow."

"Jesus is Lord!" Abel whispered. Suddenly, he felt his legs begin to give way under him and he leaned against the wall. "When my publisher told me to come over here, he only said this was something about an accident."

"Tunde Picketts is your colleague, yes?"

"Yes. We are both on the paper."

"You are the investigative journalist?"

Abel nodded.

"A dangerous profession these days."

Abel looked back at the evidence bag and wondered what Tunde was working on that could have prompted such a response. Ears. The message was clear. Hear no evil. And if you do, don't write about it.

Only an hour before, Peter Abel had been standing on the third floor balcony of *The Zodiac* newspaper's headquarters in downtown

Lagos. The five-storey marble edifice, with a luxurious penthouse for its publisher, Chief Alade Benson, reflected the paper's overwhelming success. The same hard work and sweat that financed the building made *The Zodiac* Nigeria's most respected newspaper.

Abel was in Ikeja, a suburb, on the northern end of the boisterous city of Lagos, which defies a clear-cut description. It used to be an agricultural centre in the 19th century. No more. Over the years it transformed rapidly into the residential and industrial hub of Lagos City. In the mid 1960s an industrial estate was established there, a precursor to its emergence in 1975 as the capital of the newly formed Lagos state. The political face of the suburb made it a choice residential area of the high and mighty in politics, which was quickly followed by an influx of other people. Abel stood there, amazed at the suburb that had become an intricate mix of commerce, industry and politics.

As Abel watched, Lagos was thrown into a damp partial darkness by angry rain-bearing clouds. He knew the city's collapsed drainage system, chronically in need of repair, would soon turn major streets into streams and rivulets, snarling traffic in the evening rush hour.

All along Awolowo Road, hawkers and stall owners abandoned their stations and scampered for shelter from the mounting assault of large raindrops. Abel amused himself with the sight of impatient drivers cutting each other off, honking horns and shouting abuse. The familiar chaos created by these sudden storms brought him comfort. It was all so predictable.

Standing here, as he often did, Abel felt above the fray, an observer for his own amusement instead of a requirement for his work. Abel didn't know it then, but he was himself about to enter the storm. Soon he would find himself drenched and frustrated, sitting in the "go slow" traffic jam he now watched like a detached deity.

His publisher's call couldn't have come at a worse time. Unknown among his friends on the newspaper, Abel was about to give up journalism. Tonight he was to meet with an investor who would help him establish a think-tank. Abel was eager to get to the meeting. He had even planned his route home so there would be no delay. He would take the out-of-the-way third mainland bridge to his Ikoyi home, adding kilometres but avoiding snail traffic.

As the rain picked up, Abel ducked away to cover, protecting his expensive clothes. He had picked his outfit carefully for the think-tank meeting that evening. He was all in black: black pin-striped suit, a shiny black silk shirt and black shoes. Creeping age had produced a receding hairline, so he had scraped his head clean and shiny. It gave him an unintentionally yuppie appearance and took 10 years off his chronological 48. He hoped he projected a confident self-assurance.

As Abel stood on the balcony watching the city, a raindrop splashed onto his polished shoes and he retreated toward the doorway. As he turned, his cell phone sang Bob Marley's *Natural Mystics*. A glance at the phone's digital readout indicated it was his publisher. How ironic. Abel had been hiding his decision to leave journalism from Benson. It made him wonder if Benson had gotten wind of his plan. Was this why he was calling?

As the cell phone repeated Marley's musical phrase, demanding to be answered, he was tempted to ignore the call. But of course, he couldn't. You didn't ignore Chief Alade Benson.

"Yes, Sir," he said into the cell phone, trying to keep annoyance out of his voice. The emotion grew from more than the potential disruption of his evening plans. It was borne out of the guilt he felt for leaving the paper.

Benson was on his mind when he dressed for work that morning. He had observed his image in the full-length mirror his late wife brought home one rainy day. It was one of her endless bargains. He loved teasing her about her inability to pass up a good price, even if they had no use for the object.

As he had regarded himself in his wife's mirror, Abel saw a man slightly over six feet tall with an athletic build threatened by middle-aged fat in the tummy and cheeks. His skin was becoming sprinkled with light brown spots. The real attraction remained his face, his warm brown eyes, pointed nose and thin lips. The slight overbite to his teeth, an imperfection some people said made him look sexy, was still there. He had nodded, satisfied.

That's when he had remembered his boss's description of him as having a sweet personality. It had made him playfully blow a kiss into the mirror. He felt light-hearted this morning. He had finally made the decision to leave journalism. He felt free of a burden he had been carrying around. Not the burden of his work, but the burden of uncertainty.

He had spent the past decade in what he thought of as "the valley of the shadow of death," his special brand of James Bond-like investigative journalism. But he wasn't young any more. With slower reflexes, creaking muscles, and the deep desire to remarry and raise a family, running a think-tank would be equally challenging but far less risky.

"Yes, Sir," he said again to prod his boss who had gone into a long pause.

Abel began to suspect that Benson's silence was an indication that he had in fact discovered Abel's plans and was furious. He imagined an apoplectic Benson, rendered speechless with anger.

But his fears were allayed in the next second when Benson finally broke the silence and spoke.

"Sorry, Abel. Please go immediately to Tunde Picketts' home. The police just called. There must have been an accident."

"Yes, Sir," Abel said. Something in Chief Benson's tone alarmed Abel. So much so that the disruption of his evening plans never entered his mind as he ran back to the office for his briefcase.

As he ran, he wondered why Chief Benson was sending him on this errand instead of the editors under whom Tunde worked. As a features correspondent, Tunde reported to the Features Editor, who would have handled some routine problem. All the more reason to believe this problem wasn't routine.

Peter Abel's status on the paper freed him from dealing with the hum-drum issues that arose almost daily. Not only was he a star deep-undercover reporter, but he sat on the editorial board during his free periods. He was Chief Benson's most trusted employee. It was the combination of Benson's funds and managerial acumen, and Abel's skills as the country's number one news-breaking journalist that made *The Zodiac* Nigeria's leading paper soon after it was established some 11 years back. Success did not blind Chief Benson to the magic of that combination. And, grateful, he had continued to treat Abel the way he would treat a favourite first-born son.

Which in Abel's mind, made this unexpected errand that much more worrisome. He was being sent because of his personal connection with Tunde. And this meant the situation was serious. Abel felt a pang of affection for Tunde. He had grown fond of his colleague during the time they had worked together on the paper. The younger man had been a kind of protégé. And they had become friends.

As Abel reached the garage of *The Zodiac* building, he pulled out his car keys. Looking at them, Abel was suddenly overcome by a wave of inertia. He couldn't abide the idea of driving himself through the flooded Lagos streets. He was too unsettled to deal with snarled traffic and obnoxious boisterous drivers. So, he opted for one of the official unmarked Honda SUVs in the company's fleet. As the paper's star, he only had to wave his hand at the attendant to summon a car and driver.

The driver, a short and stoutly built man of about 40, arrived five minutes later, his wide frame crammed in behind the Honda's steering wheel. He extracted himself from the car and held the door as Abel slipped into the back seat.

Abel recognised the man as one who had driven him before. He was glad to see a familiar face. The driver was a friendly sort, known for always having a bawdy joke he picked up in one of the beer and pepper soup drinking joints he frequented on paydays. But this evening, the driver wore a solemn look and licked his thick, black lips as he hit Awolowo road in a hail of heavy raindrops. The wipers fought a losing battle against the onslaught. As Abel anticipated, the road was flooded, and traffic flow reduced to a pace slower than that of the people who waded through the ankle-deep water.

Abel leaned forward so he could speak to the driver. He wanted to ask what the man knew about Tunde. Drivers always heard things. They listened to radio calls and exchanged gossip with colleagues returning from runs.

"Have you heard anything about Tunde Picketts?" Abel said. He had to shout over the clattering noise of the raindrops assaulting the car's roof.

"Yes, *Oga*, (meaning Boss). Word is that Tunde was attacked."

Abel's heart pounded. "How badly is he hurt?"

The driver shrugged. It was a piece of information he didn't have.

"Do they know why he was attacked?"

"Most probably because of the story he wrote for today's paper," the driver said. "I just hope he is alive, *Oga*. He exposed too many people. Read for yourself."

Abel saw tears well in the driver's eyes as he handed him a copy of the day's paper. Abel felt a chill. This is why Benson had wanted him on the scene.

He had seen Tunde's story entitled, "Visa, the Serpent and God," on the front page of the Metro Section, but he had not read it. He had been too busy preparing for his meeting on the think-tank he was planning to set up. Abel held the paper up to the window so he could read the story in the murky light:

It is a strange world indeed when a renowned racketeer turns to voodoo and religion to fulfil illegal contracts. But oftentimes truth is stranger than fiction. And for racketeer Sunday Ola, a very strange truth entered his world.

The story broke through the discovery of a headless snake on Saturday on a suburban Lagos road by a famished hunter, who rushed home with his saliva flowing for a snake soup. But to his dismay, the snake carried a dozen visa applications stuffed inside its belly. Visa applications! Tracking the origin of these applications led to the aforementioned Sunday Ola.

The snake was an "Embassy" of sorts for some 15 visa hunters. The applicants had paid Sunday Ola a goodly sum of money to obtain illegal visas for them, visas they would use to travel to the US or the UK.

But when Sunday could not make good on the visas and could not refund the money to his angry clients, the desperate criminal sought spiritual help.

He approached his pastor, a certain Pastor Majayi, seeking divine intervention to obtain the visas. In turn, Pastor Majayi consulted a local Prophet, practised in powerful voodoo arts.

The Prophet showed Pastor Majayi a plastic drum that contained a large snake and water. Pastor Majayi was reportedly shocked, but he said the Prophet assured him God works in mysterious ways.

At midnight, Pastor Majayi said the Prophet woke him up for a special prayer. As part of the voodoo ritual, the snake had been killed and its belly stuffed with passport photographs of the angry applicants. The two men spent the night in prayer over the dead snake. At dawn, the Prophet handed Pastor Majayi the long snake and ordered him to bury it down the road. Pastor Majayi was assured that Sunday's clients would not be disappointed..."

Abel quickly scanned the rest of the story. When he finished, he swallowed hard. From his long experience in undercover reporting, he had learned caution. Never jump to conclusions. But the facts here seemed clear. Tunde had written about certain people who would not take his accusations lightly. He had paid a price for reporting this story. But what was that price? Abel prayed it wasn't the ultimate one.

Shaken, Abel handed the paper back to the driver and said, "We will know what happened after an investigation."

"Yes, the drivers all expected Chief Benson to send you, so you can get to the truth."

Abel was even more eager now to reach Tunde's home. He strained to look out the fogged window and was dismayed to see in 15 minutes they had covered less than 200 metres on Awolowo Road. Only the floodwater and commercial motorbikes, locally called *Okada*, were moving quickly. Okada meandered dangerously through the stream of cars, their riders drenched.

Normally cautious when it came to such things, Abel decided to risk hopping aboard an Okada. He ordered his driver to stop so he could flag one down.

"The fastest way for admission into an orthopaedic hospital with broken bones," the driver warned.

Abel waved him off.

"Stop!" He ordered as he removed his jacket and tie, putting them on the seat. "It will be a short ride. Ogba is not far from here."

Before the driver could protest further, Abel had opened the door. Seeing he couldn't dissuade his passenger, the driver lifted a raincoat from the front seat. "*Oga*, take this. You will need it."

Abel took the coat, exited the Honda hurriedly, and flagged down a young man riding an Okada. The driver rolled down his window to watch as Abel climbed aboard the bike. Abel said something to the young man who nodded.

"Ride carefully, my friend," the driver said, his voice filled with concern.

The bike squeezed into the small space between the two lines of traffic and sped away. Abel tried to balance himself uncertainly, water from the street spraying up all around him.

CHAPTER TWO

The rains had stopped by the time they arrived at 10 Williams Street, an unpainted block of flats with a foreboding feeling of death in the air. Ogba is a high-density area of decidedly low-income population. A medley of industries and residential settlements, it is very busy in the evenings.

Two policemen stood guard inside the small lobby leading to the flats on the first floor. Abel folded the raincoat, hung it on his left hand and moved towards the flat on the right. One of the policemen, a stout fellow in his thirties, approached him.

"Can I help you, Sir?" he asked politely, both hands on the rifle hanging down on a strap from his shoulder. His short-cut hair exaggerated his oval face and big brown eyes.

"Peter Abel from *The Zodiac*," Abel flashed credentials as he put the raincoat on one of the two straight-back chairs that stood against the wall.

The policeman nodded in recognition. "I am Sergeant Fakorede. We have been expecting you. You have come to see the victim's wife. But she is asleep. Her younger sister is in…." Fakorede reached to open the door to the flat.

"Hold on. I need to talk to you first," Abel said as he tried to dry himself with a sodden handkerchief.

Fokorede nodded deferentially. Abel was a well-known figure to the police. He had helped them uncover many crimes. Perhaps the policeman wanted to make an impression so that Abel would one day write about him.

"Tell me, Sergeant, what really happened?" Abel took a second handkerchief from his left pocket to mop his face.

And this prompted Fakorede to show Abel the pair of severed ears in the plastic evidence bag. When Abel had asked about the origin of the ears, he knew he looked ill. He felt ill. The sergeant almost smiled, probably pleased that he had impressed the reporter.

"Well, I need to get these to the station, Mr. Abel," Fakorede said. "They are evidence, you know. My people are combing the Tagry Road and environs for the body." A dramatic pause. "While the victim's wife still holds hope for her husband, I believe he is dead."

Abel saw Fakorede watching him closely, to see how his statement would affect the reporter. Abel nodded weakly.

"Yes, that is a reasonable conclusion," he said. "Any suspects yet?"

"No, Sir. The Commissioner of Police has briefed your publisher, and I hope you know that we will be helpful in any way we can. We are not unmindful of the status of your paper or of yourself."

Abel's attention was drawn by the voice of the second policeman who guarded the door to Tunde's apartment. Abel noticed him when he first entered the lobby. Armed. Humourless. Sinister. The man was speaking into a Motorola walkie-talkie. He signed off and then approached Fakorede.

"The body has been found…"

"Oh my God!" Abel said, an involuntary response.

The speaker ignored him. "Those mentioned in the snake story are being questioned."

The door to the flat burst open just then. A young lady in her 20s stepped out. She regarded them, her eyes red and wet, her hair shabby. This didn't stop the men from taking note of her appealing curvaceous build. Despite her demeanour, she looked smart in a pair of jeans pants and a black blouse.

"My sister wants to know if Mr. Peter Abel has arrived," her voice was strained, unsteady.

"Yes, I'm here," Abel stepped towards her. "What is your name?"

"Bimpe."

Abel heard Fakorede whisper from behind him, "Don't do it," which he understood to mean, 'don't tell her about the body'. Although he was no stranger to breaking bad news, Abel knew word of Tunde's death should be delivered by a priest.

After a brief introduction, he followed the lithe young woman into the living room. He immediately took a seat opposite the bedroom. Abel knew Lola, still unaware she was a widow, lay resting behind the closed door.

He glanced around, nervous. Many times he had visited the couple as their friendship grew. They had shared such good times here. And now it was full of sorrow.

Unlike the bare walls of the block, the room had been carefully decorated with cream-coloured Spanish tiles. A pair of leather settees helped fill the space. As he sat on one of the settees, Abel told himself to remain professional. Act as he would on any job. Do not become sentimental. *Keep your presence of mind. Keep alert. You still have a job to do. You still must investigate the crime.*

He thought of Tunde Picketts. He had been a diminutive young man in his late 20s, yet he packed so much energy into whatever he was doing. He had worked at *The Zodiac* for only two years, but Abel remembered that when his promotion had been discussed at a management meeting, his editor described him as a "bundle of initiatives." He also was the friendly butt of newsroom cracks. His colleagues teased that his wife was twice his height, even though she was only about a foot or so taller. Abel smiled sadly at the memory. He glanced toward the closed bedroom door.

On the other side of the door, Bimpe was telling Mrs. Lola Picketts that Abel had arrived. Tunde's wife struggled to her feet and cried, "That is the man he wanted to be like." Then she slumped back on the bed. She held her head in her hands and could not stop the flood of thoughts that came to her. Thoughts of Tunde's dreams and ambitions, castles in the air she and her husband had built together.

A graduate of English, she appreciated good writing. She had noticed Tunde's by-line when he first began at the paper. She admired Tunde's beautifully written feature stories. But she never thought she'd meet him.

Then she saw him at a cocktail party given by the bank for which she worked. He was there with others from the paper. She wanted to approach him and saw her chance when she noticed that he kept to himself, away from his colleagues who busied themselves consuming the hors d'ouvres and free booze their hosts offered.

"Good evening, Mr. Picketts," she walked to the corner where he stood alone nursing a glass of Coke. "I'm Lola. I work at the bank."

"As an officer?" Tunde inquired.

Lola laughed at the notion.

"No. I'm not that important. Just a teller. You sometimes come to my window."

Tunde smiled, recognising her. "Of course. How could I forget such a pretty face?"

Lola blushed but thrilled at the compliment. "You don't want to be alone at a pleasant cocktail party like this, do you?"

"Thanks, Lola. But my height," he tapped the top of his head. "I easily get lost in the crowd, so I keep a distance from it." He broke into a grin.

"You speak just the way you write. You put so much fun into your stories, that one hardly gets bored reading two pages of them."

"Thank you," he said with a good-humoured bow, and then a laugh that rocked the glass in his hand.

His strong, white teeth caught Lola's attention. He was elegant, dressed in a rich red-striped Eton shirt and perfectly pressed black trousers. His shoes were Italian. He had more style than any of his colleagues.

"Tunde, it is your taste and not your height that sets you apart." She ran her eyes from his shoes up. "You are dressed like one of our bankers."

"Yes, but my ambition is to become a very successful journalist. Do you know Peter Abel?"

"Of course. Everyone knows him."

"He perhaps earns more than your managing director," he whispered, "and everybody, from the President down to the common man, fears him." He took a sip at his Coke.

"They ought to. At least those who don't keep clean cupboards."

"When I achieve Peter Abel's status, I will come back to see you."

"Till then, Tunde." She offered her small right hand, which Tunde took with a bow. Then, "Goodbye to the next Peter Abel," she said and left.

He told her much later how great an impression she had made on him. He had stared at her as she waltzed away. At nearly six feet two, she was one foot taller than he was. A mismatch, except she sounded as intelligent as he felt he was. He had noticed she wore a wig, but her heart-shaped face, thin lips and mesmerising eyes had impressed him. As had her perfect figure.

For her part, Lola went home that night thinking of the determined young man who dressed so well and spoke so beautifully. And who had such beautiful teeth.

A week later, when Tunde invited her out for dinner, she felt her heart dictate, "Yes." They were married three months later.

Lola lay in the semi-darkness thinking about how the day had begun so routinely. She had to leave for work early, and Tunde was still in bed. His right foot peeked out from under the covers as it always did as he slept on his back. Knowing that he had to travel to Tagry to follow up on the snake story, she had tiptoed to him and whispered "Peter Abel" into his ear. They were the last words she ever spoke to him.

Lola opened her eyes, tears staining her cheeks. Her sister stared down at her, concerned.

"Lola, please don't be sad. We don't know what has happened. Do not think the worst."

Lola ignored her plea. "Where is Peter Abel?" she asked simply.

"Come. He is outside." Bimpe helped her up.

In her black blouse and piece of cloth tied below it, *buba and iro* as it is locally called, Lola felt fragile and older than her years. She leaned on Bimpe, too distraught to walk alone. As they entered the living room, she saw Abel. He was sitting with two members of her church who had just arrived to lend support and sympathy.

As Abel rose and started forward to take her hands, Lola flung herself at him hysterically, "He wanted to be like you! He wanted to be like Peter Abel."

Abel gathered her into his arms and hugged her firmly, whispering to her, "Please be calm, God is in control, be calm." She sobbed heavily as Abel led her to the settee.

Before Abel could say anything more, the door opened slowly.

Police Commissioner, Fred Datti, a tall, burly man, and Chief Benson entered. They were accompanied by a woman Abel did not recognise.

There were pro-forma expressions of concern for Tunde's fate. Platitudes people say on such occasions. Platitudes Abel had heard when his own wife died. After a lengthy appreciation of Lola's strength and reliance on God, the Commissioner said the one thing Lola had most wanted to hear. There were indications that Tunde might be found.

Abel knew of course that Tunde had been found already. Dead. The Commissioner was hiding the truth until the family priest could deliver the news. Until then, he could only say soothing things and lie. Kind lies, perhaps. But lies nonetheless.

Then Chief Benson, who was dressed in a flowing blue gown, promised Lola that *The Zodiac* was going to take care of her "until the family found stability." Referring to the lady Abel had not recognised, Chief Benson said, "We brought a nurse to take care of you overnight."

"And we are going to beef up police protection here," the Commissioner added. "It is good to have sympathisers, but I would suggest only close relations and church members who come to pray for you should stay overnight. We will be back to see you tomorrow morning."

As they all stood to leave, Abel felt a heavy, crippling guilt. Lola's admonition, "He wanted to be like you!" echoed in his head. The pain deeply etched in the faces of those around him added to his discomfort.

Lola slumped in her seat, her face wet with new tears. Impulsively, Abel moved over to her, bent over slowly and whispered in her right ear, "It will be all right. Believe me."

He was compelled to say this. And in making this promise, he had dedicated himself to solving the mystery. To finding Tunde's killer. And to unravelling the mystery which underlay the killing. He would finish telling the story Tunde had begun. This was Abel's mission.

It was at that moment that Abel recognised the truth about Tunde's severed ears. They were not meant as a message to his wife.

They were meant as a message to whoever might pick up Tunde's cause: *This could happen to you, too.*

The message was meant for Peter Abel.

CHAPTER THREE

The visitors streamed out of Lola's apartment to find several additional policemen standing guard in the courtyard. Abel saw his boss separate himself from the Police Commissioner. He knew it was a silent signal that Benson wanted to speak with him privately. Abel moved swiftly to his side.

"You know Tunde is dead?" Benson said.

Abel nodded.

"It is bad, but we can't break the news," the publisher added, obviously upset.

"Yes, Sir. I understand," Abel said, his voice raspy. He swallowed to clear it. He felt the pressure of tears behind his eyes and saw his boss shake his head.

"You must work on this, Abel. The Commissioner and I are going to meet with Tunde's editors to see what they know. But you are to follow your own road."

Abel nodded, understanding the charge he had been given. Benson turned and hurried after the Police Commissioner who was talking to his men beside the open door of a black Peugeot 607.

Fakorede approached Abel.

"My Commissioner and your publisher are working together," he said. "Nice to have this collaboration between the police and journalists."

Abel saw Fakorede suppress a smile breaking around his thick lips.

Fakorede reminded Abel of the mortician who is no longer moved by corpses. He had the ability to remain untouched by tragedy. Abel never got used to seeing the pain of others. And he considered it a blessing. It allowed him to empathise with the victims, thus made his reporting better. But on this occasion, he envied Fakorede for his detachment. The Sergeant would have been pleased to know he had made an impression on the famous reporter.

Abel thanked the policeman and moved towards the road looking for *The Zodiac* driver whose car he had abandoned earlier. Abel wasn't sure the man had waited for him until he heard his familiar voice.

"*Oga*, I waited for you," the driver said as he came out of the darkness. "I finish the job even if I am left alone in the rain." Abel smiled and nodded his gratitude, then followed the driver as he led the way to the car.

"The office," Abel said, hurling himself into the back seat. He would have to pick up his car, then drive home.

As they drove through the streets, Abel remembered when Tunde had first introduced him to his wife. It was on a Sunday afternoon. He had run into them in the newsroom. They were passing through on the way home from the church. Tunde had simply said, "*Oga* Abel, Lola is my wife."

Abel had never heard such an elegantly simple introduction. It could only have come from someone with Tunde's charm and grace. Abel shook Lola's hands. Her dimpled smile was warm, and Abel had said, "Welcome to the crazy world of journalism. He needs your support."

Abel sat back and closed his eyes, remembering his earlier schedule for the evening, now impossible to keep. He would have to call the man who was investing in his think-tank and put him off. His dream of starting another business had to be suspended until one more assignment was completed. When exactly it would be, he did not know.

An hour later, after picking up his car, Abel arrived home. His white seven-bedroom bungalow, set among the rich and mighty in the swanky Ikoyi area of Lagos, always gave him comfort. The one safe place in his world.

He declined the dinner offered by his house-help, Thomas Ikomma, and headed for the bathtub with a glass of beer in hand.

Abel felt Ikomma's eyes on his back, watching him go. Stocky, fair-skinned, Ikomma wore a permanent grin. He was a warm, neat and intelligent man, whom poverty had denied a formal education. Only three months into his stay in what he called the QWH, for Quiet White House, he come to understand the solitary lifestyle of his boss and his moods. Abel was grateful that this night, Ikomma suppressed his usual good cheer, realising perhaps that his boss was terribly sad.

In the tub, partly buried in the soothing foam of the bath, Abel searched for motives for Tunde's murder. He knew Tunde's story had something to do with it. It crossed his mind that people in the church, whom Tunde had exposed as practising voodoo, might be responsible. They probably did not want any further investigation into their unorthodox, secret and heretical practices. But he immediately ruled that out as plain stupid. It was, after all, still a church. The House of God.

Similarly, he ruled out the visa racketeer. Tunde might have embarrassed the criminal, but he revealed nothing new about Sunday Ola. The police knew him and his illegal business well. Abel sipped his beer and theorised that there could be a third force that feared exposure as a result of Tunde's ongoing investigation. It was a puzzle whose pieces did not fit together, and which offered few clues.

Abel wondered about the suspects the police had already, the pastor and the criminal, Sunday Ola. What did they know? And would they be willing to talk?

He took a sip of beer and tried to clear his mind when the phone on the wall opposite him rang.

Abel knew it had to be Chief Benson. Nobody else would call at this hour. He scrambled out of the tub, dripping wet, and answered the line.

"Boss?"

"Yes, boy, you have any early thoughts?" Chief Benson's voice was strong now, and harsh, like an editor demanding a story from his reporter.

Abel stood on the cold tile, a puddle gathering at his feet. "I have not got anything yet, Boss. Still putting the pieces together."

"Okay, listen. The police released some details of Tunde's death. They found Tunde's body behind a deserted school building. Whoever it was, drove a knife into his heart. From time of death it must have happened in broad daylight."

Abel knew what this meant.

"Now, we cannot keep the story out of the media tomorrow morning," he said. "It is probably already all over the place."

"Yes, and our competition will love to splash it. So, the news editor has crafted a copy with all the police details ..."

"Lola!" Abel cut in.

"The doctors are going to keep her sedated, and she won't see the story until she has been told by her priest. They didn't have kids, so it becomes easier to manage. Later in the afternoon, the police will address a press conference, but her parents and in-laws would have arrived from Ondo State by then. We will make sure that soon after the autopsy, the body is buried."

Chief Benson's voice was quaking now. Abel never had heard such emotion from Benson. His boss must be in great distress.

"And her benefits are ready, Sir?"

"Yes."

"I suggest the tourism editor arrange for Lola and her sister to travel to the UK to get away for a while."

"I am depending on you, Abel. We must unravel this mystery. I will not get scooped on our own story."

"I will begin my investigation as soon as possible."

"I know I didn't have to tell you that," Chief Benson said and hung up.

Abel returned to the bath to rinse off. The flood he had created on the white tile floor reminded him of the Lagos rain and of his afternoon in the car, reading Tunde's article.

And then it struck him.

He dried off quickly, threw on some clothes and hurried downstairs to his desk where he had left the paper with Tunde's article. There had to be more to the story than mere voodoo and garden-variety corruption. Tunde wasn't killed over such trivial matters.

The visa applicants' names were listed in the article. He re-read the names and ages, which he had only skimmed that afternoon. And then he knew for certain.

Of the 15 applicants whose photographs were in the snake's bowels, 13 were females. Young women. Under the age of 18. It all made sense. The trafficking and prostitution of female children stared him in the face. That is what this was about.

Re-energised, he asked Ikomma to bring him coffee. Then he sat down at his computer and immediately engaged the Google search engine. It was to be a long night.

CHAPTER FOUR

Lagos woke up on Tuesday morning overwhelmed with the stench of death and fear. Every paper, every radio and television station, led with the story of Tunde's shocking murder.

Killings by robbers and ritualists were so common in Lagos they hardly made news. But this was different. Not since the gruesome bombing of the editor–in–chief of a news magazine nineteen years before, had a journalist been killed. The public clearly were unnerved. If the institutions the people depended upon came under attack, the illusion of order crumbled. They demanded the mystery be solved. And the easy deduction that Tunde was killed because of his story put the police and *The Zodiac* itself under immense pressure.

No one knew this better than Peter Abel, who had spent most of the night researching the names of the visa applicants on his computer. Some were not to be found. Others had minor arrest records. All seemed to be anonymous children picked, he suspected, precisely because nobody would care if they disappeared. Illegally shuffled off to some foreign country to work as prostitutes and slaves and to die as anonymously as they had lived. No public outcry for them. No major paper putting all its resources into finding those responsible. No Police Commissioner visiting the girls' families to make assurances or post guards outside their doors.

But somebody had to speak for these girls. And Abel was determined to be that somebody. Just as soon as he discovered who had killed his friend. Abel knew that solving Tunde's death would lead him to whoever was marketing and then discarding human flesh.

A few minutes later, the editor from his paper called with an update. He had been receiving them all night. Lola had been told about the death of her husband by her priest. She fainted at the news and had to be revived by the nurse. Was Abel going to visit the grieving widow?

Yes, at some point. But not today. The best thing Abel could do for Lola was to find her husband's killer.

Things began to move swiftly. By noon, the autopsy result had been issued, and an hour later, the Police Commissioner himself addressed a press conference. Here he announced that the visa racketeer and Pastor Majayi were suspects. They had not been charged, but they were in custody and being questioned.

Abel did not attend the packed press conference. It would only draw attention to him. Reporters from other papers and TV outlets would want to know if he was investigating the case. Abel preferred to fly below the radar. So, while the press conference was on, Abel took the opportunity to visit Pastor Majayi's church. Thus he entered the storm that raged over Tunde's death. There could be no turning back now.

The church was tucked away about a kilometre from the Lagos-Tagry road. Abel made note of the building, a hut with dwarf walls and incongruously luxurious new steel roofing sheets. When Abel entered, he saw two young men kneeling before the high wooden pulpit, praying. They did not notice their visitor. Or perhaps they simply chose to ignore him. Abel wasn't sure which.

As he waited, he studied the men, noting their clean white robes and dreadlocks. Finally, one of the supplicants reached up and clanged a bell thrice after a shout of "Amen" bringing the prayers to an end. The two devotees shook hands and then acknowledged Abel's presence.

"Welcome to the Central Christian Church, brother. You are more police?" said the one who had rung the bell. Both men were tall and remarkably thin with high cheekbones and sunken eyes. Abel guessed they were in their late 20s.

"No. I am not a policeman."

"So, what do you want here?" A hint of hostility crept into the young man's voice.

"I am a reporter." Abel saw the men react, slightly alarmed. He had to put them at ease and give them a reason to talk to him. "I apologise for intruding on your service. But given what's happened to your pastor, I thought you might want to tell me your side of the story. You can talk to me without disclosing your names, if you would prefer."

"Speak on the condition of anonymity," the shorter of the two offered cynically.

"Yes. As you say. And the sooner you speak to me the better."

"And why is that?"

"People become biased against you if they only hear the other side of the story. You know your pastor has not been allowed to talk to anybody ..."

"True. None of our three leaders has been allowed to see him at the police station," the other acknowledged.

"So you see, it is as I said. Only the police are telling their tale. Giving the public reasons to suspect your pastor."

The other man nodded, softening. "Shall we sit down?" He led the way.

"Thank you, Mr. ... ?" Abel said.

"Junior Pastor Joshua. My colleague is Deacon Samson."

"And your newspaper?" Samson asked quickly.

"*News Breaker.* It is a new weekly magazine," Abel had prepared for this question and was already rummaging in his pocket for a phoney ID. If the men knew he was from *The Zodiac*, the paper that employed the dead reporter, they surely would have recognised this visit for what it was - an attempt to gather intelligence, to determine what role the church played, if any, in Tunde's death.

Deceit was part of Abel's job. He played many parts. And after all these years, it came naturally. A chameleon, his publisher dubbed him.

"First let me say I am sorry about what has happened to your church for merely offering spiritual assistance to a desperate man," Abel said as he took a seat on the wooden bench opposite his hosts.

Most people have mixed reactions when a reporter confronts them. They are thrilled by the attention, the possibility of getting their names into the paper. And they fear what they might expose about themselves. But Abel had become a master of disarming potential sources.

"Thank you," Samson said, smiling in gratitude. "That is why we are here praying. Our church is just recently taking hold, gaining new members every day. Publicity like this could be devastating."

The other added proudly, "You see, this is our new site. The old church in Agege is far too small for our growing congregation."

"A shame if this all hurts your ministry," Abel said. He waited a moment before continuing. "So, how is it the church became involved in all this? Are you often asked to pray for people with visa problems?"

"Yes. But it is with the best of intentions. This murder is quite shocking."

"You had no idea there was anything illegal about this man trying to get visas for so many young women?"

"Of course not. You see, over the years, we have helped a lot of people with exactly this kind of thing. People come here, we pray for them, and they get their visas just like that," Joshua snapped his frail fingers. "Even those who are already out of the country, we pray for them so their lives may prosper."

Abel regarded them. Did these men really believe the vulnerable young girls who came to them were going abroad happily or that once there, they would lead prosperous lives? Samson and Joshua were either lying or stupid.

Samson appeared eager for this reporter to think well of the Church.

"So I don't know why they suspect the pastor," he said. "How can a man of God cut off someone's ears and send them to the wife? Eh, don't people think?"

Abel wanted to discuss something else.

"I wonder," he said. "These girls, do they come alone? Or do others pay you for the prayers?"

The two men glanced at one another and shook their heads.

"We could get into trouble seeing such girls," Samson said.

"I don't follow," Abel told them.

Joshua chuckled. "You don't keep attractive girls like that too close if you don't want to fall to temptation," he said. "The devil is smart. He uses no guns. He manipulates the mind and the heart."

Samson added, "Lust. We do what we can to avoid the temptation. We are, after all, vulnerable men. Weak."

"So you don't ever meet the girls themselves?" Abel asked.

"They have agents who bring us their names and photographs for us to pray on."

"For how much?"

"Ten thousand naira for visa applicants and twenty thousand for those who are there."

"By 'there', you mean girls who have gone abroad?"

The men nodded.

"And these girls keep paying you even after they are out of the country?"

"Yes. For our continued prayers so they will be protected by God from whatever harm they fear."

Whatever harm they fear?

Abel was horrified. These girls were sold into hideous, miserable lives. And then this Church took what little money they managed to earn as payment to "pray" for better lives. The money the girls made, money they might use to make a better life, was handed over to these so-called "men of God."

Despite his revulsion, Abel nodded as if the men had described a perfectly reasonable business transaction.

"For the money these girls make overseas," he said, "I think that is too low a price to charge. But please don't say I said it, o? They will hate me and my magazine."

"Considering what our pastor is going through, we may have to ask for more," Joshua said sternly.

"And please remember I didn't say this, o?" Abel reminded them and feigned a smile.

He rose from his seat, knowing if he didn't leave he might let his true feelings show. It took all his self-control to keep from attacking these two self-satisfied hypocrites. Instead he merely said, "I have many places to touch before nightfall. The Lord will give you strength and courage in this ordeal."

He left, never offering his hand. The men might have noticed or not. Abel didn't care.

As he drove off, Abel wondered what he would have done if *the agents of the devil*, as he thought of them, had offered to pray for him. *It would have meant a curse*, he said to himself and shook his head.

Apart from the dirty revelation, he had found nothing to link the church to Tunde's death. The encounter made him regret that he had not taken a serious look at human trafficking before this. He had realised, during his night-long computer search that the topic was worth an in-depth investigation. He knew the dangers. They were all too clear.

After all, they had cost his friend his life.

CHAPTER FIVE

Abel arrived at the State Police Headquarters in Ikeja to get an update on the official investigation. He found Fakorede in a small, crowded office. Unlike the night before, when the Sergeant had been alert and focused, he now looked exhausted. Abel signalled Fakorede to follow him outside. He wanted a private conference.

"What have you learned, Sergeant?" he asked.

Fakorede shrugged. "An important man like you, Mr. Abel, you must know more than a humble policeman such as myself," Fakorede said when they stopped under a mango tree by the fence.

"I am a bloody civilian as they say in the military," Abel said, knowing he sounded testy and not caring. "Now what have you got?"

"But your people were at the press conference. We held nothing back." Fakorede said, his voice defensive.

Abel sighed. This was the last thing he needed. A cagey policeman protecting his investigation.

"Collaboration between the police and journalists, remember?" Abel said and moved closer to him. "I am looking for motives."

"Maybe you should check with one of the detectives working on the case." Fakorede had become increasingly tense. Abel had isolated him outside and was standing close, watching his every expression. The reporter would not give up until he heard something. If he didn't already, Fakorede soon would understand why Abel was such an effective investigator, how he got people to tell him things. Abel suspected that Fakorede wanted to help him but didn't want to get into trouble with his own superiors.

Abel knew the Sergeant was privy to information. And he preferred getting it from people like him, men lower in the food chain. It helped Abel do his work more anonymously. But he would have to give the man a reason to talk. He had to show him how cooperating would be to his own benefit. It was simple human nature. Everyone operated from his own self-interest.

"Remember, Fakorede," Abel said, "if we share information, any big break will help your career. I would even mention you quietly to Chief Benson. You saw how close he is with the Commissioner?"

He had judged Fakorede correctly. He was ambitious. This had become obvious the day before, the way he reacted to Abel's celebrity.

"Exactly what do you want, Mr. Abel?"

"Just a copy of the visa racketeer's statement. Nobody will know I have it. And here is my private cell phone number." Abel thrust out a piece of paper in his open palm. Fakorede smiled as if a great misunderstanding between them had suddenly been cleared up.

"Oh, my God. But why didn't you say that? Wait in your car." Fakorede walked away quickly.

He returned five minutes later with a folded document and handed it to Abel through the car window. Abel nodded his thanks and drove off.

After a few kilometres, Abel pulled off the side of the road to read the statement. It disappointed him. He found nothing really interesting related to Tunde's death, except the revelation that Sunday Ola had been in the visa business for six years. It made Abel suspect there was a connection with a foreign embassy. The perfect front for obtaining fake visas.

As Abel pondered the report, he glanced into the rear view mirror. Some sixth sense made the hairs on the back of his neck stand up. A car was parked a hundred metres back, too far to tell much about the driver except it was a male. Age unknown.

Abel put the report on the passenger seat and started the engine. He eased the car into the flow of traffic, keeping one eye on the rear view mirror. He saw the other car move into traffic too. Was this a police escort provided by his new friend, Fakorede? Or had someone discovered he was taking up Tunde's investigation? More likely the latter. Abel headed for home. He lost sight of the car once he left the highway and travelled through the lush tree-lined streets of his neighbourhood. But this meant nothing. A sophisticated tail would use two or three cars, one taking over from another. And the traffic was heavy at this time of day. Too many cars to keep track of.

When Abel reached his house, he parked and waited. Several cars passed by. He recognised none of them. And no one stopped.

Abel went into the house and tried to reach Chief Benson. Instead, he was put through to a news editor. Chief Benson had gone home to escape the stream of sympathisers arriving at the paper's headquarters. Benson, he was told, did not want to be disturbed.

Abel did not normally call his boss outside the office, especially at night. But there was nothing normal about any of this. Abel picked up the phone and dialled a private number he had for Benson. After two rings, his boss answered, his tone short.

"Can I see you, Boss?" Abel glanced at the clock in his VCR. It was a little after nine p.m.

Benson sighed. Abel knew he was irritated. And the few words Benson deigned to say ruined what was left of Abel's night.

"Have you found the killer?"

"No," Abel admitted. A long silence, clearly meant to relay Benson's disappointment.

"I know you have been working hard, Peter. But all that means nothing unless you solve this case."

Abel admitted he was stumped.

"This is also about the image of *The Zodiac*, Peter."

Abel asked the Chief if he was all right. He sounded odd.

"My doctor is here to manage my blood pressure." The words were harsh and impersonal. They expressed a mood Abel had not seen in him since the early days of *The Zodiac*, when they had to work all day and night to find space in the highly competitive media in Lagos. He couldn't help but feel badly for his boss.

Abel had wanted to tell Benson about being tailed, but now he didn't want to cause him any more stress. So he simply apologised for the lack of progress and promised more hard work. The conversation ended abruptly.

Abel asked Ikomma to make him some coffee and headed for his book-lined study. As Ikomma served him, the phone rang.

"Hello," Ikomma picked up the receiver.

Abel saw him strain to listen, his eyes widening with horror, then "Hello, hello." He stared briefly at the dead receiver and then put it down. "He has dropped, Oga."

"Who was that?" Abel said, somewhat uneasy.

"Ah, *Oga*. I don't know who he is. He just said, 'Tell your boss to back off. We are many where I come from'."

As Ikomma tried to pick up the coffee pot his hand trembled.

"Forget the coffee and sit down, Ikomma. Your boss is okay."

"All right, *Oga*." He struggled into the seat across from the writing table.

"Now, Ikomma, you are a very keen observer of things. You pick up on details like a good reporter."

Ikomma knew his boss's methods. The elaborate compliment was delivered in the service of getting something from him.

"You do not need to smooth talk me, Boss. Just ask me what you want to know."

Abel smiled, caught at his own game.

"Very well," he said. "Think carefully. What kind of English did the caller speak? What was the accent like?"

Ikomma smiled wryly, nodding. "I picked it up right away, Boss. I was going to tell you. He spoke with a heavy African-American accent. The slang of the American street culture."

"Any word he stressed or repeated?"

"'Back off, back off.' He was almost shouting it."

"Okay, Ikomma. Thank you. I'll have my coffee now."

As Ikomma poured the steaming brew, Abel reached for his satellite phone. He began to dial Lola but stopped. He didn't want to speak to her until he could give her real news. All he had now were suspicions. So instead, Abel dialled Fakorede's number, which he got out of the small notebook he carried with him everywhere. When the policeman answered, Abel told him he might have a lead.

"Ask Tunde's wife if someone called for Tunde the night before he was murdered."

"Why? What's this about? If you get a lead I was to know. Remember your promise?"

Abel smiled sadly. People never failed to disappoint him. Fakorede's first thought wasn't about breaking the case and bringing a killer to justice. It was about his own advancement. Well, at least he wasn't trafficking in young girls.

"I just got a threatening call," Abel said. "Someone warning me to back off the investigation. Ask Lola if Tunde had such a call."

"The woman is too distressed to talk, Mr. Abel."

"Then ask the sister, Bimpe."

"Okay, I will come back to you shortly," Fakorede said.

As he waited, Abel sipped his coffee and read one of the many computer printouts on the criminal trafficking of women. He became absorbed in the story of a Nigerian woman who had been found murdered in Turin, Italy. She had entered the country on a false visa and was working there as a prostitute. Nobody attended her burial or contacted the police about the case. No family member came to visit the grave. The killer got off with a light sentence, because nobody objected when the authorities allowed him to plead guilty to some lesser charge. Disposable people, Abel thought as the phone rang. It was Fakorede.

"Yes, Mr. Abel. Tunde received a similar call."

"Did she have any idea who it was? Did she recognise the voice?"

"No. It was a stranger to her." Fakorede sounded agitated.

"Easy, Fak," Abel used a familiar address now with the policeman. He was getting somewhere and therefore needed him. "Did she say anything in particular about the way the caller spoke? Maybe an accent?"

"As a matter of fact, she did. She thought he sounded African-American."

Excited, Abel gulped some more coffee and stole a look at Ikomma, who seemed to be enjoying the exchanges.

"Fak, listen carefully. You may be on your way to your next promotion…"

"I am listening," he said, excitement growing in his voice.

"I think I know how to find our killer. Go to the station where they are holding Sunday and Majayi. Take them to an interrogation room. Tell them you have identified the killer as an African-American. Study Sunday's body language. If it is positive, tell him you know he has met the man. And if he cooperates you will do him a favour."

"What favour could I do him, then?"

41

"You won't destroy Majayi's church for trafficking in human flesh."

"Can you prove they are doing such a thing?"

"No," Abel admitted. "But he doesn't know that. And I visited the Church of the Prophet in Tunde's story today. They are terrified of being dragged down by this scandal."

"And what if his reaction to my assertion is negative?" Fakorede said, always cautious.

Abel was becoming irritated with this bureaucratic policeman. Must he be told everything?

"You guys know how to make people talk."

Fakorede laughed, as if Abel had somehow just granted him permission to do whatever he wanted.

"I will pull all his fucking nails off, trust me," he said, and sounded as if he might mean it.

"I don't need to hear the details," Abel said. "And Fak, I suspect the killer might be an American diplomat, or at least work at their embassy."

"No problem, Mr. Abel. If he turns out to be a diplomat, I will consult the Commissioner."

"If you need any help just call. The paper has powerful connections, which Chief Benson will be more than happy to use."

The conversation ended.

Abel had given up smoking shortly after he was widowed. He didn't know why. He supposed it was a way of imposing self-discipline at a difficult time. Whatever the reason, his good efforts crashed that night. He needed something to relieve the tension and pressure.

He asked Ikomma for more coffee and a pack of cigarettes, which he had kept hidden away. Ikomma gave him a disappointed look. Abel scowled and repeated his request. "Please, just do it." Ikomma brought the cigarettes to his boss, delivering them with a cold glare.

Abel ignored him and lit up, enjoying the familiar taste. Then he got down to work. Like a football coach, he sketched his strategy on a piece of paper, smoke enveloping his head.

Arresting the killer was only the beginning. He was about to

42

start a war with a much bigger enemy. And he needed a plan. So he scribbled away. Names and places, people to interview, records to search through, neighbourhoods to canvass. The article about the murdered girl in Italy gave him another set of leads.

Thirty minutes into his strategy session, he was convinced he was dealing with a powerful international syndicate. Ties to foreign embassies and churches – and God knows – what other upstanding organisations. So much hypocrisy. He would sink them all. He finally dismissed Ikomma, sending him to the boy's quarters as he continued the vigil.

Two long hours later, Fakorede called.

"We got him after one nail," he said.

Abel didn't know if Fakorede was serious and didn't care. He had only one question. "Who killed Tunde?"

"He's a returnee from the U.S., lives in Yaba. Must have picked up the accent in America. The irony is he hails from Tagry."

Abel understood. "The town noted for its history in the slave trade."

"We are headed to Yaba now."

"Will there be any trouble with the embassy?"

Fakorede laughed. "I doubt it. The Commissioner is going with us."

"And then you must make this man talk, give up the whole syndicate of traffickers."

"He will. When he begins to lose nails, too. I will let you know when he is in custody." The policeman hung up.

Abel immediately decided to inform his boss even though it was well past midnight. He felt Benson needed the good news to help relieve the stress on his ailing heart.

Benson answered, clearly having been roused from a deep sleep.

"Sorry to wake you, Boss. But you'll want to know."

"You got him?" Benson was suddenly wide awake.

"Yes. I provided the police with some information. They used it to get Majayi to talk. That and some old-fashioned persuasion."

"Whatever it took. I don't care."

"Majayi identified a man who earlier this evening called to threaten me. He is most probably Tunde's killer. A heavy battalion of the police, including the Police Commissioner, is headed to Yaba."

"You did a good job, Abel. What would I do without you? " His voice was deep but very weak.

Before Abel could say, "Thank you," Benson had hung up.

Abel suddenly felt exhausted. He hadn't slept the night before, and today had been gruelling. He lay down on the couch, intending only to rest his eyes.

When the phone rang, it was after two a.m. Benson's voice boomed from the other end of the line.

"Abel, boy! I have stopped the press. The Commissioner called."

"They got him?"

"At his home. And without resistance. He is the mastermind. But some embassy staff are also involved. The Commissioner is going to see that this is handled quietly. That way, the Americans will cooperate."

"You must be relieved, Boss."

"Aren't we all? Listen, I need you to write a short piece about the arrest for the front page of the paper. Keep it brief because the Police will address the press tomorrow. Thank you again, Abel. Good night."

Unbelievable! Abel shouted with a pump of the air then sat down quickly to write the story. As he did so, an excited Fakorede called to supply all the details of the encounter. His four-paragraph story, entitled: POLICE ARREST PICKETTS' KILLERS, was mailed to the newsroom a little before 3 a.m. Now Abel could sleep. Without fear of interruption.

CHAPTER SIX

The thick cloud of gloom that had hung over *The Zodiac* lifted gradually on Wednesday morning once people read Abel's story. The mood of *The Zodiac* staff matched the clear, sunny Lagos weather. And they had additional reason to feel happy. Management had pledged ongoing financial support for Tunde Picketts' family. It sent everyone a clear signal that Chief Benson took care of his own, that the paper's employees would be supported should tragedy strike.

By noon, TV and radio stations were already broadcasting the police press conference, which had taken place an hour before. There, they had paraded the suspect, Jimmy Jay, before a curious and angry but relieved public. Jimmy Jay, the police spokesman informed his listeners, had lived 15 years in New York. He had confessed to killing Tunde to protect his business.

Against his lawyer's advice, Jimmy insisted on making a statement. He spoke in a heavy African-American accent, rationalising that he had been pushed into this evil business by the "devil who dwells in drugs." He said further that he surrendered without a struggle to protect his lovely wife and children. Dozens of heavily armed police had surrounded his home while he and his family slept. Through a megaphone the Commissioner himself had ordered Jimmy's surrender, threatening to pull his house down if he resisted.

When booed over his concern for his wife, the increasingly distraught criminal turned to the sea of attending journalists, imploring them to convey his deepest apology to Mrs. Lola Picketts.

Asked to explain how he operated, and who his collaborators were, he said he had given the names to the police, insisting that he was himself a target for elimination as Sunday Ola was.

The Police Commissioner took time to commend Sergeant Fakorede and the investigating team, promising that appropriate commendations would be presented soon. As Abel watched, the whole affair struck him as surreal. It seemed more like a circus than a press conference. Everyone acted their parts for the amusement of a curious and ghoulish public. Jimmy was at last led away, ending the spectacle. But not the story as far as Abel was concerned. For him, it was only beginning.

Later that evening, Tunde's remains were committed to mother earth in the presence of a large group of mourners from all walks of Lagos life. Residents praised the police for their quick efficient action in solving the case.

Abel did not attend the burial rites. He couldn't take another spectacle. Besides, his strategy was to stay out of the public eye. Which allowed him to work on the story in anonymity. At some point, he would call Lola to reiterate his promise. He would get to the bottom of Tunde's murder. The capture of his killer was only the first step.

While the entire staff of the paper attended the ceremony, Chief Benson met privately with Abel in his office. When Abel entered, he noticed the bright yellow curtains had been changed to black. Benson explained his secretary had suggested it to reflect the mood of the company.

Chief Benson nodded for Abel to sit as he swallowed *Norvasc* and *Moduretic* tablets for high blood pressure. He had abandoned his desk for the comfort of the black leather settees where he received visitors. A glass of water still in his hands, he looked at Abel with admiration and nodded his head.

Abel settled into a seat to his right. His boss appeared pale and tired.

"Chief, I am sorry about all that has happened. You must know that I share your pain."

"Thanks, Abel boy. This has been hard on all of us. Especially senior citizens with weak hearts." Benson paused.

"What is it?" Abel said.

"What pains me more is the story we failed to do. Had we attacked this trafficking earlier, Tunde might be alive. As the leading paper in Nigeria, we shirked our responsibility ..."

Abel nodded. That very thought haunted him, as well. He and the boss were always on the same page. This was the reason they worked so well together.

"I came out of my research on Monday night feeling the same guilt," Abel said. "We have to expose not only the prostitutes, but the syndicates that manipulate them."

"It is dangerous work, Abel." Benson set his glass down and stretched. "Age is catching up on me, so I have to slow down."

"You need some more rest. Delegate some of the work, Boss."

Abel had the sudden impression that Benson was about to talk to him about stepping into management. But Abel also knew this wasn't the time. They were discussing an urgent project, which Abel had to complete before any change of assignment could be discussed.

"So apart from Tunde's murder by a man who has no balls, what have you found?" Benson said.

"We hear and see most of these stories daily, but we ignore them. In a country groaning under so many other problems, we tend to overlook trafficking in innocents. That is where I go next. I have spent too much time investigating government scandals. This is a much greater one when you consider the cost in human lives."

"Go on," Benson said. Abel knew the Chief loved to listen when Abel became passionate about something. It always signalled the beginning of an important investigation.

"The average age of women trafficked from Nigeria to Europe is fifteen," he said. "There are about eighty-thousand prostitutes in Italy and neighbouring countries. Out of these, sixty to eighty percent are Nigerians. Think of the implications for HIV and AIDS and other sexually transmitted diseases."

"Time bomb," Benson said with the nod of his head.

"Chief, the trafficking begins when a recruiter goes around looking for girls to take overseas. Now, because the recruiters are known members of the community, they even find willing accomplices in parents, who pressure their daughters to go abroad and make money. The daughters send money home, and their families use it to build modern houses and set up businesses. It is all about getting out of poverty. But at what price? Some of them don't see their children again."

"Go on," Benson said. "This is getting interesting."

"The U.S. State Department says someone who recruits and

47

transports a woman to a madam in Europe is paid about twelve thousand dollars for every victim. The madam then seizes the girl's passport so she cannot run and pushes the victim into the streets, into prostitution, to repay a debt of about fifty thousand dollars. These girls are forced to commit disgusting acts with anyone, or anything, they are told. Bestiality is not uncommon."

"Good God."

"There has never been any serious prosecution of these traffickers," Abel said, wound up now. "The laws aren't effective, witnesses can't be protected, and families are often involved."

"Like the drug business."

"Yes. Exactly. And like the drug barons, these madams are never caught. That is the problem, Chief."

"So, this will be your next assignment."

"I will do it for the Picketts."

"Good luck, my boy. As usual, you have all my support." He offered his hand.

Abel rose and took it. "I told Lola it would be all right, Boss."

"Then fulfil that promise."

Chief Benson broke the handshake.

CHAPTER SEVEN

Abel threw himself into the investigation. He spent his days researching certain police files to which he was given access. Chief Benson had paved the way with the Commissioner. These files contained the names of suspected traffickers, interviews, surveillance records, and correspondence with police agencies abroad.

At night, Abel became a "regular" at various notorious spots in Lagos, establishments which were known to be frequented by prostitutes and their clients. These were not the expensive restaurants and clubs where high-priced call girls could be seen on the arms of rich men in business suits. The places Abel stalked were low-end dives, dark, anonymous and wretched. Places where the downtrodden and the poor came to play. Along nearby streets, young girls hung out waiting for customers. These were the girls traffickers preyed upon.

In a short time, Abel learned the players, recognising the teenage prostitutes and their scummy pimps. The locals thought he was some down-on-his-luck salesman because this is what Abel led them to believe. He had turned down more than one offer of sexual favours at a fair price. But so far, Abel had not met anyone who dealt in trafficking.

After days of putting up with sawdust floors, dirty cutlery served by uninterested waitresses amid the stench of fish, urine and beer, Abel became discouraged. He needed a night off. So, one cool Friday evening, he drove himself to the high-end La Scala Restaurant tucked in the centre built by the Musical Society of Nigeria.

The restaurant was known for its fresh sea food, inviting atmosphere and affluent clientele. Abel looked forward to the starched, pressed, white table cloths and delicious food served on shiny, clean, delicate china plates.

He had dined here often over the years. In fact, he was so well-known that even the managing director could predict his order of *crab diable, fried prawns with potatoes and red wine.* A steward seated him at a table for two opposite the entrance.

As Abel reached for the intricately folded napkin placed just so between the gleaming silverware, he casually observed new arrivals checking in with the maitre d'. Abel enjoyed watching people come and go, and he especially enjoyed the sight of elegantly dressed women with lush figures. Some would throw a glance in Abel's direction, wondering at this well-groomed handsome man sitting alone. If they made eye contact, Abel would smile, fantasising about taking them home with him. It wasn't just for the sex. He missed the warmth and companionship.

Abel hadn't been with a woman since his wife died two years before, and he felt he was ready to venture out again. But such pleasures would have to wait until he had completed this assignment. It was too all-consuming, allowing him no time to start an affair. And because of the danger, he could not risk causing pain to a woman who might become his wife. So, Abel was content to flirt from a safe distance with these lovely women on other men's arms.

Tonight especially, he was here to relax and get away from the investigation. When his food arrived, he dug in eagerly. He was so busy enjoying the fresh crab, he barely noticed when a couple took the seat in the corner to his left.

But observation was his life's blood. Reading people and taking their measure was Abel's default position. And so he could not help but notice that throughout the entire meal, the couple had not said a word. He was attracted by their silence and so continued to study them.

The man, plump, clean-shaven and middle-aged, exuded an arrogant confidence. His cream jacket made him look dignified. But his taste for alcohol was a little strange. The man had consumed three bottles of stout and was ordering another when Abel switched his gaze to the lady.

She was a sharp contrast to the man, shy, jittery and very clumsy with the cutlery. Abel put her age at 13 or so and decided it must be a father and daughter outing. No wonder they didn't speak to one another. The girl probably had an iPod stuck in one ear.

Later, while Abel sipped his after-dinner coffee, the girl returned from a trip to the lady's room. He hadn't been able to appreciate her remarkable figure before. But now, as she swayed across the room, it was impossible to miss. The open dress revealed a long delicate neck. The girl was quite pretty. Her full black hair was tied in a ponytail to highlight heavy brows over big, round dreamy eyes. Her nose was straight like Abel's, her mouth wide with a stubborn jaw. Her chin had a decided dip right in the centre. *An intriguing face*, Abel thought.

The coffee finished, Abel paid for his meal and left the generous tip for which he was known. Once outside the restaurant, he moved to his beloved navy-blue Peugeot 406 car and got his key out.

The couple exited just behind him. In the glare of the street lights, it was even more obvious that the beauty on this older man's arm was a teenager. She looked elegant and even tempting in her black miniskirt and shiny blue blouse, cut low at the base of her pear-sized breasts. She was slim with curves in the right places, and her fair complexion shone.

Abel looked for body language between the two. *Poor*, was the verdict. The girl's otherwise attractive face was now masked in a mix of anger and fear. She walked behind the stocky six-footer, and not beside him. They remained silent. Abel decided he had been right, this was father and daughter and neither was happy. But something changed that impression just as they climbed into a big Toyota SUV. The girl protested and the man yanked her arm. This was not the gesture of a father. Abel sat in his car watching them as they continued to argue. When they finally drove off, instinct told Abel to follow.

Outside the centre, Abel saw them struggle violently in the SUV, with the girl trying to open the door. Soon they pulled to a stop by the national museum, and the girl jumped out. Abel parked behind them as the man literally tumbled out of the SUV, slammed the door and sprinted towards the girl who back-peddled as if expecting a blow.

"No! Please, no!" Abel heard the girl scream. The man grabbed her by her blouse, yanking her towards him. She pushed her attacker away, and the man stumbled, temporarily losing his balance. Abel leaped from his car and ran towards them.

When he arrived, he saw the girl's blouse had been torn in front, exposing her breasts. She tried to cover them with her elbows bent to cover her face with her palms.

The man came after her again, but Abel got between them, raising his hands in an appeal for calm.

That stopped the man in his tracks.

"What the fuck do you want?" he said with a snarl.

Abel was used to assuming roles, and he slid immediately into this one.

"I'm a cop. And this girl is under-aged!" Abel assumed a tone of authority.

The man watched Abel for a beat, unsure. "You don't look like a cop."

Abel reached behind him under his coat as if going for cuffs.

"You want to spend the night in jail, fine by me." Abel was bluffing. He figured if he had to he could win a fist fight. After all, he'd seen the number of beers the guy had consumed. But as with most bullies, this one folded.

"Shit," the man cursed as he quickly retreated. He got back in the SUV and screeched away, disappearing into the Lagos night.

The girl heaved a sigh of relief, looked up at Abel and fell into his protective arms. "Thank you, Sir."

"It's okay." Abel looked at his watch. "It's after midnight. You should go home."

"Nooo!" she shook her head mildly.

"Where is home? I will take you there."

"No!" she protested again.

Abel was thrown by her vociferous reaction.

"Come on. You can't stay here."

When she looked at him, the tears had dried up, the fear replaced by a suppressed smile around her over-painted lips. "I'm Alice."

Again, Abel was thrown. The girl had suddenly adopted a seductive air.

"It is too late to go home," she said. "Besides, I have no money for a cab."

"Where is home?"

"Yaba, but my Mum will kill me," she stamped her feet childishly.

The scene had started to draw a crowd. Street urchins, locally known as area boys, gathered around them. Abel knew they could cause trouble if he didn't get both of them out of there.

He made a quick decision: "I will take you home with me, but I will call your Mum later."

"Well, maybe you will change your mind and want to keep me for a while," she said cockily and went for the passenger door. The girl seemed incapable of relating to Abel in any other way than as a potential customer. It was disconcerting seeing this in someone so young.

As they sped along in Abel's car, it occurred to him that Alice's man might be lurking somewhere, waiting to take revenge. And at this time of night the usually bustling Tafawa Balewa Square was almost deserted, making it a threatening criminals' den.

Abel drove fast through the streets and tried to not let Alice see his concern. It was not until they reached the much safer Third Mainland Bridge that he could pay attention to the girl.

When he did finally look at her, he noticed she was holding the torn material from her blouse over her breasts. She wasn't having much success. Abel reached into the backseat and recovered a clean duster which he handed to her.

"Here."

The girl took the duster. "You are afraid people will think you raped me?"

Abel looked at her to see if she was smiling. She was so casual with the thought that it stunned Abel. She spread the duster around her neck.

"You are a kind man. I don't even know my saviour's name. You are a Pastor?" She cast a seductive glance at him.

"I am Peter Abel, a consultant and a writer. So why were you fighting the man? Who is he?"

She swallowed and looked out of the window. "I like Kingsway Road. See, it is all lit up and clean."

Abel knew she was avoiding an answer.

"Answer my question, Alice."

"They call him Sanko. He's a businessman, the importer and exporter type. A friend introduced him to me, but he has a monster cock, too long and big. He tore me up the first night, and after hospital, we agreed no sex. But he seems to have a high sex drive. Either that or he loves me too much. He wanted to tear my pussy apart again."

Alice had told her story casually, as if she were describing a typical teenage problem, like breaking up with a boyfriend or fighting with her parents. Abel had been so taken aback by both her tone and the facts she was relating that he had driven past the junction to his house. Alice must have sensed his discomfort because she had fallen silent.

Abel tried to decide upon a response to her. He wanted to express sympathy without approval. And he wanted to establish a relationship with her which did not make him a potential customer.

"Alice, you are a beautiful girl. Talking that way doesn't become you."

"You sound like my mother!"

For the first time, she was defensive and this made her more childlike. Abel saw an opportunity to find out more about this waif.

"You never mention your father, Alice. Is he alive?"

"Yes, he is there," she said with a tinge of hatred.

Abel made a mental note to explore this later.

"I'm hungry," the girl almost whined. She suddenly reminded Abel of his younger sister. She had died years before of congenital heart failure. She was always sickly, and Abel had spent many hours taking care of her. He wondered if this is why he was interested in Alice. In fact, it occurred to him child prostitution might be a sore subject with him because he once had a little sister. But this was amateur psychology, something Abel abhorred. He turned to the girl.

"You are still hungry after such a big dinner?"

"I was so afraid I didn't enjoy the food. I feel better now. At ease. And I would love a kebab."

Abel smiled at her. He liked this softer, more vulnerable Alice.

"My house-help will buy you a kebab. We are almost there. I

live on Queen's Drive."

"But Queen's Drive is behind us," she said. "We are almost in Victoria Island."

The girl was observant and clever.

"I wanted to confuse anybody who may be tailing me," Abel said.

"Like who? That man?"

Abel could have told her about the car that tailed him several weeks ago, on the day of Tunde's murder. But he didn't want to scare her. And he didn't want to explain what kind of a story he was investigating because he was beginning to think she might become part of it.

"He won't cause any trouble," she said. "I told him I will tell his wife if he tries anything funny." She paused and asked the obvious question, "Are you married?"

"I am a widower."

Alice didn't take note of this tragedy not, apparently, through callousness, but because, like most children, she was easily distracted. They had arrived at the gate to Abel's imposing house.

"You live in this big house alone?" Abel opened the gate with a remote control anchored to the sun visor above his head.

"Yes."

Alice's eyes widened as she looked around the grounds. Abel parked in the garage, and they went inside.

"Welcome to my home, Alice," Abel said formally as he gestured her into the spacious living room.

She sat slowly on a settee and studied her surroundings. There were eight settees in the room and all were finished in cream to match the long heavy curtains and thickly woven rug.

"Something to drink while your room is prepared?"

"Yes, a Fanta. I think I can do without the kebab."

Abel got her a can of Fanta from the kitchen. After handing her the drink, poured into one of the frosty beer mugs he kept in the freezer, Abel went through the courtyard to Ikomma's room. He asked him to prepare the guest quarters for "a girl I saved from an attacker."

Ikomma went off to do as he was asked without comment.

On his return, Abel saw Alice still looking around in amazement. He noticed she had not even touched the drink.

"Time to change, Alice. There is a robe for you in the guest room. In fact, there is everything a woman needs for the night." He was already heading for the guest room as he spoke, giving Alice no choice but to follow.

They went down a short staircase to a small comfortable bedroom where Ikomma was making up the bed. Abel introduced Ikomma and then the two men left, allowing Alice to change in private.

As Abel returned to the living room, he reminded himself to keep his distance from this child. In the past when he patronised prostitutes, Alice would have been a good dish served on a silver plate. No more. That she triggered an unexpected memory of his sister embarrassed and worried him at the same time, especially because he had responded to her sexually in the restaurant. He couldn't allow an emotional entanglement to grow here.

He also knew he might be using this young teenager in his investigation. If she provided a way into the world of trafficking, he would have to allow her to take him there. Ultimately, this was about avenging Tunde's death. That was never far from Abel's mind. But using a child in a dangerous mission made Abel uncomfortable nonetheless.

A final reason to keep his distance was his distrust of the girl. He knew she was perfectly capable of accusing him of rape if he did not treat her with tact. Bringing someone her age to his home was risky. The look on Ikomma's face when he saw her said as much.

Alice appeared beside him in a white robe she had tied tightly at her waist to accentuate her curves. On the thick, soft rug, her bare feet made no noise. Extremely beautiful after a bath, she looked delicious.

Abel turned to the coffee Ikomma had brought in.

"You drink coffee like you are from Brazil, where they grow it," she said. She drew closer to him and caressed his back.

Abel fought his emotions. She was the first woman who had been physical with him like this since his wife died. And he had to admit, it felt good. He stood.

"Your drink, Alice. I'll get some ice for you."

"No, I don't need it," she said.

"Then, let's sit and talk." He moved to the settee opposite her.

Alice sat coquettishly letting the robe part and then her legs. She was well versed in seduction. It was how she survived, he supposed. And probably the only way she knew to gain acceptance and affection.

Abel decided if he was to survive this encounter unscathed, he had to let her know he wasn't interested in sex. He looked at her impassively. She was able to match him in this game, too. With a smile dancing on her lips, she winked.

"Alice, close your robe."

"You don't like what you see?" She managed to sound hurt.

"Of course. But that's not why I brought you here."

Alice shrugged, sullen, and closed her robe.

"So, what do we do? Play drafts?"

The question was partly meant to cover the rejection, but also meant to put Abel on the defensive. He realised this was how she dealt with the world that had used her so badly. It gave her the illusion of control. And it allowed her to maintain an emotional distance. Who could blame her after the life she was forced to lead? Abel wanted to keep his distance, but not to hurt her feelings. So he decided to engage the young girl.

"Tell me your surname."

"Udor," their eyes were locked now and Abel felt intense heat running wild in his nerves.

"Tell me about yourself. Who is Alice Udor?" he took some more coffee.

"I am Alice Udor, my Mum is Mary Udor. We are originally from Edo, but I was born in Lagos, and we have been here since then. I am 15 years old and I have just finished from Yaba Mixed School. I am looking forward to an offer of admission from the Lagos State University, where I hope to read English." She crossed her legs slowly and sipped her drink. "Any more?"

"I was correct to have threatened your attacker that you are underage?" He stared hard at her. This time, she swung her face away in discomfort.

"It never stopped anyone before."

This sudden flash of vulnerability actually made it harder for Abel to keep from putting his arms around her. Did he want to comfort her or sleep with her? Did the girl even make that distinction? Abel sat up straighter.

"Okay, but what is Mr. Udor's first name. Obviously, you like your Mum more."

Life drained from her face. She put her glass of Fanta down and took a deep breath.

"He is Winston Udor, a retired civil servant. He says he was once well-to-do. But with irregular pension payments made valueless by inflation, today he is a poor man. I have two brothers. We all live on my Mum's foodstuff business."

When she finished speaking, Abel noted that the spark in her eyes was gone. She suddenly burst into tears.

This seeming total collapse moved Abel more than he realised.

"Cheer up, Alice," he moved into the seat beside her. "It may not have been a coincidence that I was the person to save you."

That put some life back into her. She rubbed her eyes and looked up at him. "So you love me? You are a good man."

This caught Abel off-guard. There it was again. Her immediate presumption was he wanted sex, and her eagerness was to provide it.

He reached for his coffee.

"You are a very beautiful girl," he looked up and saw her blush. "Now, if you think back, you would remember that many of the boys and men who said they loved you, really wanted you for sex ..."

"Yes, like that man you saved me from," she sounded cheerful. "Thank you very much."

"You are welcome. Listen to me, Alice. At my age, I know that love grows. Some people see a flower they admire, pluck it, smell it, hold it for a while and throw it away. Or even if they don't throw it away early, it soon withers and becomes unattractive, then they throw it away. Did you read some biology?" He saw her listening intently, her head cocked to the left.

"Yes," she said.

"Good, if the flower is not picked, it will stay attractive for a much longer time and in the end be pollinated to produce more flowers. Alice, you are very attractive, but my primary concern is to help you first."

She sighed and cupped her head in her hands. Abel could see she was crying.

"What is it, Alice?" he asked with concern.

"Since I was born, no man has treated me kindly like this." More sobs. "They all want to take advantage of me. Even my teachers. But you are different." When she looked up at him her eyes were red.

Abel decided to change the mood. "Come. Let's go to the kitchen where you can find something to eat." He pulled her up.

"I will take tea and some boiled eggs," she said.

She brightened as he held her hand, leading her to the large kitchen. Alice looked around then ran her hand admiringly over the smooth counter tops.

"With such a home, you don't think you need a wife, Mr. Abel?"

"A widower should not rush into marriage, otherwise, he ends up calling his new wife by the former wife's name. You women hate that, don't you?"

"Yes, we do," she broke up into ripples of laughter.

"Sit there," he pointed to a cushioned stool, "while I prepare everything."

"Your place is so fine that I don't want to break anything."

"I trust you." Alice smiled broadly at this.

Twenty minutes later they were eating and cracking jokes like old friends. Abel glanced at the clock on the wall. It was almost two.

"Help me clean up."

The girl happily began scraping the plates and washing them off, enjoying the familiarity. Sharing this most common of domestic chores created an unspoken bond between them. And familiarity bred, in this instance, friendship, and more importantly, trust.

"Do we agree that I will take you home tomorrow morning?" Abel asked as they cleaned the kitchen.

"No, that is not possible. You said you would call my mother."

"I thought I said your father," Abel lied for her reaction.

"No!" she protested, turning pale. "Please. You mustn't!"

Abel noted her distress. It was already clear that Alice's father was somehow the source of her troubles.

"Okay, we call your mother," he said, reassuring her.

Alice finished cleaning the counter tops, washing them carefully with a dishrag, then drying them with a towel until they shone. She wore a smile all the while, happy being the woman in the house.

"Thank you," Abel said as he drew closer to where she stood.

"You are welcome, good man."

"I think it's time you got some rest. My boy will get a nice dress for you in the morning, and then he will bring your mother here."

Alice seemed to acquiesce, and Abel turned and led the way to the guest room.

When they reached the bedroom door, Abel turned.

"I will leave you now. Goodnight."

She remained rooted to the spot, her mouth parted with surprise and hands akimbo. "So we are not sleeping together?"

"Alice!"

She responded in a stone silence. She was insulted in spite of what he had tried to tell her.

He took her hand and whispered in her ear. "Alice, remember all I said about love. Give me the opportunity to help you first."

It seemed to work. She nodded.

"I will not forget this night," she said simply. Abel was moved and gave her a peck on the cheek. "Goodnight, then."

After watching her shut the door, Abel retreated to his own bedroom and had a quick shower. But he didn't sleep in his own room, which was far removed from the central area of the house. Instead, he returned to the living room and settled down on one of the settees.

She sounded sincere, but I can't leave my house to a total stranger, he thought. He slept very lightly that night.

CHAPTER EIGHT

In the small neat guest room, sleep did not come easily to Alice. She was enjoying the luxury of the house and felt she sincerely loved its owner. But the comfortable surroundings could not stop memories of her terrible past from flashing through her mind. Her latest troubles began the day she visited *BOOKS and ALL* in Surulere.

The three-storey shop was heavily stocked with books and CDs and drew customers from all over the locality. For poor Alice, who had not bought a new book in her four years in secondary school, a highbrow bookshop was a painful reminder of her deprivation. On this particular day, she would have skipped entering the place entirely but for the insistence of her friends, Dupe Adeleke and Ngozi Okaro.

Instead of joining her mother at church, Alice followed her friends into the shop. As soon as she entered, her fears were confirmed. She watched as her friends dashed from one shelf to another to fill their baskets with books recommended by their teachers. Dupe and Ngozi were both rich. Or at least they were in Alice's eyes. Whatever they needed - money, clothes and food - they merely had to ask.

Plump and very hairy, Dupe was not naturally attractive; however, she made up for looks by being sly, fast-talking and fashionable. She had a way with men that amazed Alice. But she wasn't a good student. After failing the GCE examinations in her former school, her parents sent Dupe to Yaba to retake the test. This was a practice the students jokingly called *fighting the Second World War*.

Dupe knew she needed a more intelligent classmate to help with her studies, so she picked out Ngozi, a smart but not overly popular girl. Ngozi was an easy target for a conniving girl, and Dupe soon had a useful friend. Tall and curvy with large breasts, Ngozi was drawn by Dupe's taste for fashion and her ability to attract men.

Neither had anything close to Alice's beauty, but both had more confidence and better resources. Alice was constantly jealous of their means. She even joked occasionally about being Cinderella, while they were the spoiled wicked step-sisters.

As Dupe and Ngozi glided around the bookshop filling baskets, Alice became Cinderella once again, bereft, humiliated and angry. Where was her Prince Charming?

She deadened her pain by retreating to the fiction section and reading a paperback. Occasionally she looked up to track her friends. At one point she saw Dupe chatting with a middle-aged man in a shiny grey suit. He looked trim and warm and smiled confidently. Alice noted his perfect white teeth.

Alice was surprised when she found the man standing at her side a few moments later. He grinned at Alice and the Prince Charming thought passed through her mind again.

"You won't buy anything?" he asked with a smile playing around his lips.

"No," she said, and turned away humiliated.

"Is it because you do not have any money?"

She nodded her head but refused to meet his eye.

"Please allow me to help you. My name is Kehinde Lawal."

Alice knew Dupe had said something about her impoverished circumstances. Damn the girl!

"No, thank you," Alice said, embarrassed.

"Come on," Kehinde persisted, "however intelligent you are you can't do well without books. I have a little money here for you." He offered some fifty naira notes.

Alice took a quick look at him and jerked her head away.

"No," she said, growing more uncomfortable. But then she remembered the set of literature books her father had still not bought for her. The offer was very tempting, and would save her the embarrassment of borrowing recommended literature books from friends. He continued to hold the money out to her. Finally, she took it with a bow.

Had she realised then what that seemingly harmless decision would bring into her life, she might have demurred. But Alice could not guess the dark future she had, in that instant, chosen for herself.

Instead, she smiled, thinking only that now she could buy what she needed.

"Thank you, Sir," she said as Kehinde nodded and walked away. Alice ran to her friends on the second floor to tell them about her sudden good fortune. Dupe advised her to get what she needed quickly. It was almost closing time.

As Alice picked out the books, she kept a look out for Kehinde. She wanted to show him what she was buying with his largesse. But she didn't see her benefactor again.

On the way home, Alice began to have misgivings. Her friends' insistence that she was fortunate to have met such a considerate and generous gentlemen did not make her feel any better. Something was wrong here. It began to dawn on Alice that of course there would be a price to pay. Nobody gave something without expecting favours in return. Not even Prince Charming.

Her parents were not home when she returned at eight that evening. She went to her room and unloaded the small carton in which she carried the books. Safely home, she forgot her misgivings and felt a great sense of relief. In one short moment, she finally had gotten all the books her father had been promising her for six long months.

Then she thought of her benefactor, tall and slim, with a smooth dark complexion people called "black and shine." Kehinde was an attractive man.

Alice still nursed a lingering fear about his intentions, about the suspicion that favours such as his have strings attached. She tried to allay these fears, recalling his assurances that he was only trying to help her.

She sighed heavily. Too late now. What was done was done. She sat down and began writing her name in each of her books. Before she could open the second book, her mother called.

"I'm coming." Alice dropped the book and ran to her, resenting the intrusion. Her parents rarely summoned her unless they intended to use her to run errands.

Her mother was waiting. "Ah God," she said, "I didn't know the meeting at the Church would be that long. Did you return early?"

"Not quite," Alice said. "I went with my friends to buy something."

"I see," her mother said, obviously uninterested. "Take this money and get me some *panadol* tablets. I feel a headache comin' on."

"Yes, Ma." Alice took the money, but ran towards her room instead of going out.

"Alice, did you hear me say that I have a headache?" Her mother shouted at her.

Alice made a sharp turn towards the front door and went outside, replying. "I only wanted to shut my door, Ma."

Alice only learned later that something about her tone had made her mother suspicious. While Alice was gone, the woman went into her daughter's room and found the pile of new textbooks. And she found the one inscribed, "Alice Udor, Class 5A, 030484." The day's date was inscribed beside this.

When Alice returned, she found her mother lying on the living room couch, the shades drawn. Without saying a word, Alice gave her the painkillers, then rushed to her room. There she found the books she had left in a neat pile scattered all about. Her heart skipped and she felt so dizzy, she wished she could take those painkillers herself. She knew there would be trouble over this. And she felt badly that she had caused her mother any more anxiety.

Her father might have been the domineering head of their rocky family, but her mother was its anchor. She always advised and monitored Alice, making sure her daughter practised what was preached at Sunday school. Her mother was caring rather than harsh. Yet Alice always seemed to bring her grief. So, feeling guilty about how she had come by the books, Alice packed the books back in the carton and pushed it under the bed.

Later when her mother asked about the books, Alice begged for forgiveness. Her mother seemed sympathetic and even admitted that she had been annoyed by her husband's indifference to Alice's need for the books. But rubbing Alice's neck soothingly, she had warned her daughter to be careful with men.

"Alice, even if your father cannot help you, that does not mean you accept favours from other men," she said.

Alice kept this in mind when Dupe suggested they go to visit Kehinde three weeks later. As the date drew closer, Alice's anxiety mounted. She was sure he would shower her with gifts, but she also suspected that she might not come back home without returning a sexual favour. And Alice saw sex as a sign of being controlled and dominated, and she hated it.

She felt her fear becoming a reality when shortly after they arrived at Kehinde's flat, her friends left to buy ice cream. Nervously, Alice sat on the couch as Kehinde served her a glass of cold *Coke* and settled beside her. He sipped a beer and made small talk. Pleasant enough. When he finished his drink, he got up and went to the bedroom. Alice wondered if he expected her to follow him, but after a moment, he returned with a large shopping bag.

"Thank you, Mr. Lawal," she said shyly, as she saw the three beautiful dresses.

"Don't say that, Alice," he said. "You have forgotten I told you at the bookshop not to thank me because my intention is to help you."

"Ah sorry, thank you, Mr. Lawal." Alice did not know what else to say in her confusion.

Kehinde laughed heartily at her embarrassment before retrieving another can of beer.

As Alice examined the dresses and nodded in delight, he continued to drink. Finally, he belched quietly into his hand.

"I am happy that you are happy, Alice," he said. "I hope my continued help will bring us closer and closer together."

"Yes," Alice answered, smelling the beer on his breath.

"We are likely to be friends, Alice. Maybe serious friends. And in that case, I will beg that you waive the 'Mr' and simply call me, 'Kenny'."

This was all happening so quickly, and the more Kehinde drank, the closer he leaned into her.

"Eh, Mr. Lawal, but that shows no respect for you? You are very helpful to me, and I must give you full respect."

"That is all the more reason why you should do what I like. There is nothing more respectful than obliging someone his heart's desire."

"I will try to do that, Kenny," she said, now fully aware of his motives. And the next words he spoke made her wish she had refused his gifts and walked away from him at the beginning.

"I have heard about your intelligence," he said. "For a long time now, I know you have been at the head of your class. But another thing I admire is your beauty. Behind your faded clothes lies an angelic beauty that your new dresses are going to make clear to everybody. Your flashy friends don't compare to you. And you also have very good manners. For all these reasons, I must be frank with you, Alice. I love you."

Alice had known what was coming but still couldn't help a cry of surprise. "What?"

"I am serious, Alice. I love you." He had reached for her right hand and had started caressing it.

"But, but Mr. Lawal, you said you only meant to help me. Please, please." She tried to wrest her hand free.

"I know you are not a virgin. This will only make us better friends."

Alice sighed heavily, confused and worried. "No, please."

Kehinde ignored her. He moved swiftly to the front door and locked it.

"Oh, no, Mr. Lawal. My friends will come … no …"

"Your friends understand." Kehinde moved towards her, smiling broadly.

"Nooooo!" Alice kicked hard, and her shoe connected with his groin. He went to his knees in agony. She took the opportunity to push past him and unlocked the door. Before Kehinde could recover, she ran out.

The following day, her friends told her he had been treated by a doctor for injury to his groin. The news made Alice feel guilty, even though she had acted only to defend herself.

Then a week later, her father called her to his room. Her mother was out and they were alone in the house. She warily asked what he wanted, but she could not have anticipated the answer. He opened a bag and pulled out the exact same dresses she had refused from Kehinde. Alice tried to catch her breath.

"Take them, Alice. Kehinde is my friend. He is a good man,"

her father said. "But your mother should not know about this."

He mentioned nothing about Kehinde's intentions towards her, and Alice dared not ask.

Devastated, Alice took the shopping bag without a word and left. Over the years she had learnt that it was futile to argue with her father. And she hoped this would be the end of it.

But, of course, it wasn't. Almost every week from then, her father brought her gifts from Kehinde, leaving her more upset, confused and guilt-ridden. And this made her more vulnerable to the pressure from her friends who urged her to make up with Kehinde. She finally decided to go to see him. Not to give herself to the man, but to ask him about his relationship with her father. So, one Friday, she appeared at his doorstep.

Alice went inside reluctantly and asked her question. Kehinde obliged her.

"I was his student when he taught briefly before he joined the civil service," Kehinde said. "It is sad he fell on bad times, but he knows I really want to help you. You see, there are always crossed lines between a man's good intention and the attractiveness of a beautiful girl like you." He smiled.

The truth stared her in the face. Her father had allowed this man to court her in exchange for money. He had sold her. At that moment, she was determined to take her life back. Not by rejecting this man, but by accepting his gifts directly. And for that, she would take the step she had been refusing for weeks. Her father wanted to be a pimp, and so she would be a whore. It would serve her father right.

When Kehinde reached over and began fondling her neck that day, she swallowed her fear and gave in. When she left his bedroom that afternoon, she had become someone else. She had left the innocent Alice behind. And to her surprise, she enjoyed his attentions, thrilled by his gentility and sweetness. She had started out wanting only to spite the man who had raised her, then turned her into a whore. But she wound up enjoying it.

So it was that Alice began dating other attractive men who were as resourceful as Kehinde and subsequently became trapped in a new lifestyle.

And so it was that she had come to be with a certain dinner companion that night at La Scala when she met, by chance, Peter Abel.

Peter was the first truly nice man she had met, but to her great disappointment he did not want to share a bed with her. She lay there in the dim bedroom light, thinking about how to handle Abel until sleep swept her away.

CHAPTER NINE

An hour after Abel rose drowsily from the settee at six a.m., his guest still had not emerged. The summer sky was already bright and he could hear tawny-flanked prinias chirping happily in the trees that lined the road. As he drank his morning coffee, he remembered that Alice needed a dress.

Ikomma was already awake and prepared to begin work, but not to go shopping that early. Certainly not for the woman with his boss the night before.

Ikomma did not mention it to Abel, but he had recognised Alice as a prostitute who often accompanied men to the restaurant where Ikomma worked as a cook. She was certainly not the kind of wife he wished for Abel, but protocol between employer and employee required that he keep his counsel to himself. So, when Abel asked him to run to town and pick up an outfit for the girl, Ikomma did so without comment.

He returned an hour later and handed a modest grey flowery blouse and skirt to Abel, then turned unhappily for his own quarters.

"Not so fast, Ikomma," Abel called after him. "Please go to 126 Antioch Road in Yaba and call Mrs. Udor to come see her daughter. Tell the woman Alice had some minor trouble near the museum last night. I had to help her."

"Yes, Sir," Ikomma said, smiling. Abel knew his house help hadn't been happy about the girl's presence. He could only surmise this smile meant he was pleased she would be leaving soon.

"And Ikomma. Try to keep the story from Mr. Udor."

"Yes, Sir," Ikomma said again as he rushed to the car.

Shortly after Abel returned to the living room, Alice appeared in a bathrobe. Abel suspected the only other thing she wore was the same seductive smile she had on the night before.

"You had a good night?" Abel asked, as he quickly handed her the dress in an attempt to keep the moment from becoming any more awkward than it already was.

"Thank you. It is beautiful," she said, obviously disappointed to be rebuffed yet again. Abel felt he needed to get the girl dressed as quickly as possible. Her lithe young body strained at the robe, and he couldn't help but be tempted.

"I am sorry about the rush, but could you put the dress on so we can have breakfast? You wouldn't mind oats and bread, would you?"

"No, I wouldn't, but I would have loved to prepare it for you." Was this seduction or just good manners?

"You slept late." Abel shrugged his apologies.

"I could not get to sleep last night thinking about what a good man you are."

This girl just didn't give up. Abel waved her towards the bedroom. "Thank you, Alice. Now, if you could just get ready …"

"Sorry," she turned like an unwilling but obedient child and finally disappeared down the staircase that led to the guest room. Abel sighed, relieved, as he headed for the kitchen to prepare breakfast.

Once Abel served her, Alice chattered away happily about the size of the dining table for twelve and the oil painting of a Lagos scene on the wall. Abel finally interrupted to tell her about sending for her mother. At the news Alice fell silent and kept her eyes fixed on her plate. She answered Abel's questions in monosyllables. Abel was sorry he had ruined her morning, but felt relieved she was no longer flirting with him.

A half an hour later, she was still in this foul state when Ikomma returned with her mother.

"Mummy," she said as jumped up and hugged her mother to Abel's utter surprise.

In that split moment, her mood turned a complete 180-degrees. Abel had expected Alice to greet her mother as coolly as she was treating him, but there she was, smiling. On the other hand, her mother did not share her daughter's good humour. Limping slightly, she accepted the hug but seemed sad and anxious.

Abel watched them. Physically, Alice was every bit a replica of her mother. The few visible differences were signs of age: the wrinkled face, sagging skin around the neck and flecks of grey in her hair.

"Good morning, Mrs. Udor," Abel said. "I'm sorry to have called for you so early." Abel stood up to greet her.

"Good morning," she answered quietly.

"Please, sit down. I am Peter Abel." He gestured toward the three-sitter opposite him that Alice had been occupying.

"Thank you." The woman limped and threw her right hand around Alice's shoulders for support. When she eventually sat down, she winced in pain. The way she arched forward made Abel think her leg problems extended up into her back.

"Alice, would you serve us tea while we talk?"

Abel hoped the girl wouldn't balk at the request, but he wanted to show her mother that Alice was on her best behaviour. Alice, far from objecting, leaped up, eager to complete the chore.

"Yes, Mummy, you surely will have a cup of tea." Alice headed off to the kitchen.

The minute she left the room her mother's brave front broke, and she began to weep.

"You saved her from the streets," she said, sobbing, her voice strained.

"Yes. From a man she was with. I don't think she was a willing partner ..."

"I know what my daughter is, Mr. Abel."

Abel sat back. The woman, while apparently crushed by her daughter's behaviour, was nonetheless direct and brutally honest. He waited for her to continue.

"Alice is my only daughter, and I have tried to give her a good upbringing in spite of our grinding poverty," she managed to say. "I thought I had succeeded and she would marry a caring gentleman. Then, I began seeing strange gifts in our house ..."

"It will be all right, Madam." Abel found himself saying the same thing he had said to Lola. In both instances, he felt the need to help even when he had no immediate way of doing so.

"In Nigeria, when a child is bad, they say it is because the mother is bad. I came here, hoping against hope that she may have found the right place to be." She dried her face with one end of her cloth and looked up.

Even under the circumstances, Abel thought this sentiment was a bit over the top. Was she suggesting he take the girl in as his wife?

Abel glanced toward the kitchen. He wished Alice would hurry up with the tea. The last thing he wanted was to hear the mother offer up her child to him for one act of kindness. Abel called, "Alice, please, at least bring your Mum some water while you prepare the tea."

Alice entered with a tall glass of water, ice cubes tinkling. The two adults fell silent. Alice saw her mother was upset.

"Mummy, have you been crying?"

"It is no concern to you. Go on, Alice. Finish preparing the tea."

Alice bowed slightly and moved sullenly to the kitchen.

"She is so full of life and very intelligent," Abel said, trying to lift the mood.

"Indeed, that is why it is so painful," she had a long drink from the tall glass. "And why she needs the guidance of a good man."

Abel shifted uncomfortably in his seat. He hoped to short-circuit any thought of becoming a husband to this girl. Before he said anything, the woman saw he was ill at ease and guessed the reason.

"Please, Sir, I am only asking for help for my daughter. Nothing more."

Abel relaxed. His opinion of Mrs. Udor immediately improved. She was not another one of those parents who sell their children like merchandise. So he felt free to offer what help and advice he could.

"I still think something can be done to change her behaviour," he said. "I have had a word or two with her. She needs talking to by people she can trust ..."

"That is the problem, my brother. That is the problem. She is a beautiful girl as you can see, and many a man for whom she had respect betrayed her trust. They showed interest in something else."

Abel's eyes widened. It was almost funny. Mrs. Udor, far from trying to pimp Alice, seemed to be accusing him of taking unfair advantage of the girl. He realised she had been just as suspicious of his motives as he was of hers. He tried to allay her fears.

"I assure you, Mrs. Udor, nothing happened between your daughter and myself. Nor did I encourage such a thing."

The woman nodded, clearing her throat and sipping some more water.

"If you slept with her, you could not play the fatherly role you are now enjoying," she said. "But I am happy to hear it from you." She paused again before going on.

"The situation has been made worse by her girlfriends. Bad influences all of them. They have led her into this life."

Abel suspected Alice's girlfriends were not the worst of it.

"Alice does not seem to have much regard for her father," he paused and met her gaze. "She does not even want to talk about him."

The woman's eyes betrayed alarm, and she squeezed her hands together tightly. Yes, Abel had guessed correctly. But then she shook her head as if to dismiss the topic.

"At one time, they fought. But not anymore. Now they simply do not speak."

"Since when, if you don't mind my asking?" Abel was pressing her.

"My brother, the whole thing baffles me." She sat up and unclasped her hands. "You must be familiar with the father-daughter relationship. In this case, as an only daughter, she got so attached to him that they always dined together, and she would not sleep at night until she had seen him. Even poor as we are, he would buy her things we could not afford. He used to boast that he had the most beautiful daughter in the world."

"But that changed."

The woman nodded. "When she was eleven, I travelled to the village to see my own mother. When I returned, to my utter shock and surprise, I found them to be totally estranged. I did everything I could to discover from her what had happened. Nobody would talk. When I asked Alice, she would only say that her father was not providing her needs at school as other fathers were doing for their children. This explanation made no sense to me. In my confusion, I turned to the father for the reason, but it degenerated into one of our ugly arguments. My husband is a dictator. Arguing with him is pointless."

Abel again tried to size up this woman. She wanted the best for

Alice, this was obvious. Maybe she was too terrified of her husband to admit the truth. Any rational person would have suspected the father of some kind of deviant behaviour. But the wife seemed blind to the possibility. And perhaps this was the problem. This was the source of Alice's anger. She felt betrayed by her father who had abused her, and felt equally betrayed by a mother who failed to come to her rescue.

But Abel said none of this. He only nodded sympathetically.

"Madam, it is paramount now to keep Alice from going back to the streets. She was lucky this time. But next time, there might not be a good Samaritan on hand."

"And how can we do that? I have no way of controlling the girl."

"For starters, we need to get her a part-time job. Between that and school, she will have less time to find trouble."

"You would do that for us?"

"Yes. But what she needs most is support and love from you."

"She has both things, my brother. I have always wanted the very best for Alice." As she said this, Alice re-entered the room.

"Can I serve the tea and fried eggs now?"

"Yes," Abel said, standing. "Serve her in the dining room and sit with her while she eats. I'll get ready, and after that we go to Yaba."

Alice reacted to this suggestion angrily.

"I have said already that I am not going. But for Mum, that place would be miserable."

"It will be all right," Abel assured her.

"No, it will not. Why can't I stay with you?"

"Alice. Please ..." her mother pleaded, embarrassed.

"I love him."

Abel moved to the girl and placed a hand on her shoulder.

"Alice, I am touched you feel so. But that isn't how it can be between us."

Alice looked off, hurt.

"But I will not abandon you. Do you understand? I am going to help you. I promise. But for now you must return with your mother. Trust me. It will be all right." There it was. The phrase he kept repeating. Finally, Alice nodded, giving in to Abel's request.

"If you say it will be all right, I believe you," Alice said without much conviction and retreated to the kitchen.

Abel and her mother exchanged a glance. Neither spoke until Alice returned with a tray of breakfast. Abel left them eating together.

He was relieved to overhear them chatting happily. A couple of times, he heard Alice say, "He is a very good man," and this strengthened his resolve to help them.

After they had finished breakfast and Alice had helped clean up, something she insisted on doing, she and her mother bade him goodbye. As they were about to board the taxi, which would carry them home, Abel saw the pain in Alice's wet, red eyes. As he hugged her goodbye he whispered, "It will be all right."

This time, when Abel made that promise, he had a plan. He was going to see Alice's father himself and confront the man who had caused his family so much pain.

CHAPTER TEN

That Winston Udor was a dictator in his own household was obvious from what both Alice and her mother told Abel. This only made Abel more determined to confront the man. As a reporter, he followed a familiar routine before interviewing a difficult subject. He researched the man thoroughly, learning all he could from available sources.

Abel uncovered the history of a man fallen on hard times. He had nothing to show for his 68 years but a bald head, a face lined with furrows dug by poverty and a meagre pension, which paid him peanuts.

As a young schoolteacher fresh from Edo Catholic College, Udor had been stocky and athletic. He had a sense of style, dressing well and speaking eloquently, self-consciously using big words. However, jovial as he tried to be, he had a vicious hot temper, which four years of weekly homilies preached at his church could not cool. Volcanic and increasingly unpredictable, people often avoided him like a thorny ring.

During his college days, he loved and chased women. But once he graduated and became a primary school teacher, he was required to live an exemplary life. He worked in Ashi, a village, where eligible women could be counted on one's finger tips. There he had to try hard to hold his libido in check. And of course the stress of all this made it difficult to handle his boisterous pupils without exploding in fits of temper.

Not surprisingly, Udor soon lost favour with both administrators and parents whose children openly complained about him. He finally quit and went home to live with his father. Returning home allowed him to spend time with Mary Momo, the most obedient of his three girlfriends. One day he unexpectedly presented her the gift of a sky blue flowery dress and a black handbag. They signified his serious interest in her. He had decided

Mary would be his wife and sure enough, they were married three months later.

At 24, he was four years older than Mary. They had met when, on her way from a public water tap two years earlier, she had turned to look at Winston jogging nearby in white shorts and a white T-shirt. In the process, she tripped over a stone step and lost her balance. The bucket of water fell from her head, splashing water and mud on him. To her surprise, he rushed to her aid. The combination of his neatness and kindness attracted her to him and they became friends.

His mother was elated by the friendship of her only son to the tall fair-complexioned beauty, who was so quiet, obedient and respectful.

Soon after the marriage, Winston proceeded to the University of Ibadan to read history. He went from there to the civil service, rather than the classroom, to which he had proven to be singularly unsuited.

In the civil service, he rose to become a senior officer in Immigration in Lagos until his retirement. Even here, Abel's personality held him back. A supervisor once told him that but for his temper, he would have risen to the top echelons of government.

Faced with a limited future, Winston took out his frustrations on his family. Mary often was the victim of misplaced aggression. Mary told friends she was tempted to flee, but with three children, she thought it wiser to stay to protect them and to continue to pray that Providence change her domineering husband.

Alice's birth brought some relief because Winston became obsessed with his beautiful daughter. And true to the Oedipal model, she became equally attached to him. So much so, that outside of school hours, father and daughter were inseparable.

Over the years, Mary watched her only daughter blossom into a beautiful and intelligent young woman, loved by all. But then the once-warm father-daughter relationship came to an abrupt end. It happened three years after her husband's retirement and their fall into poverty.

To the family's complete surprise, Alice suddenly developed a fear and deep hatred for her father. If Mary pressed Alice to explain

77

her behaviour, the girl would tremble uncontrollably and break down sobbing.

Mary saw a glimmer of hope some months later when Alice grew close to a few girls her own age who attended the same church. Mary took it as a sign her fervent prayers for divine intervention had been answered.

Abel uncovered all of these details, but they did not tell him what he most wanted to know: why such a change had occurred? His sources exhausted, Abel knew the only way to uncover the rest of the sad story was to meet Alice's father, Winston Udor.

He chose a Sunday morning, when he was sure the rest of the family would be in church. Abel rose early and drove to Yaba. The streets were free and quiet and the mild breeze so soothing that he shut off the car's air conditioner and rolled down the windows. The air smelled good as he whistled his favourite song, Bob Marley's *Natural Mystics,* bobbing his head to the right and left in tune with the rhythm.

He understood the song to mean that there was a lot more happening in the spiritual realm than most people could ever appreciate. Abel wondered if understanding that realm would help him deal with this one. Despite the upbeat mood brought on by the beautiful morning, Abel was anxious about meeting Alice's father. The man's temper and tyrannical nature had taken on, for Abel, a kind of mythic quality. He hoped the reality of the man would be less intimidating than his reputation.

No. 126 Antioch Road in Yaba turned out to be a weather-beaten two-flat building. The whole street was so quiet it appeared as if all the residents had departed in favour of the churches which beckoned one and all every Sunday.

As Abel sat in his car, he thought perhaps Winston would not be at home after all. He felt a mix of disappointment and relief. It was then he heard a baritone voice humming a song he could not place. The voice was coming from Winston's flat. Had it not been such a nice day, Abel's window would have remained up and he never would have heard the man. But circumstances seemed to be driving him towards a meeting with Winston Udor after all.

Abel left the car and walked up the short cracked cement

pathway which led to an old, dirty wooden door. Finding no doorbell, he knocked.

"Who is that?" the voice boomed.

The door creaked open before Abel could answer. His host looked up enquiringly, and coughed into his right hand. He wore brown pyjamas and his feet were bare on the cement floor.

"Sorry to disturb your meditation, Mr. Udor. I am Lazarus Adio." Abel, as usual, had prepared a new identity for this interview, one meant to gain the confidence and trust of his subject. Peter Abel's name was too widely known as a journalist. And for all he knew, Mr. Udor had learned of his encounter with Alice and Mary.

Winston looked past him at Abel's expensive car and, apparently sensing he was a man of means and therefore might do him some good, invited Abel inside.

Abel followed the lean elderly man with a shiny bald head into a house rife with signs of poverty. The living room had a greasy four-piece settee to the left of the door, and to the right, a large, old, dented Sony television. As Abel sat on one of the settees, his eyes caught the wooden plaque hanging on the wall above the television. "The timidity of the Omnipotent is the commencement of sagacity."

Winston's famous love of big words, Abel thought and swallowed, unable to hide the smile that broke impulsively around his lips.

"Oh, that?" his host said, seeing Abel reading the plaque. He coughed into his hand again, a disconcerting repulsive habit. "It simply means the fear of God is the beginning of wisdom." He grinned. "It is a reminder that there is a living God, even though some of us don't attend church."

Abel thought there was something wrong here in the translation of the words on the plaque. "The timidity of the Omnipotent ..." would mean God is timid. But he didn't want to be disturbed by his thoughts. "My personal experience has proven that beyond doubt, Sir." Abel took his eyes off the plaque and looked directly at his host.

"So, what can I do for you, young man?" he asked and sipped water from a big jug beside him. He offered none to his guest.

"I have come about Alice, Sir."

"You want to marry my Princess?" Winston put the jug down in excitement. Abel wondered at his immediate offer of the girl.

Nothing subtle about the old codger. Abel thought all he had to do was name a modest price and the girl would be his. No different than shopping for a new piece of furniture. "Alice is not here at present. My wife has taken all the children to church."

Time to strike, Abel thought. "We attend the same church, even though I am not a regular there. I am not even sure that she knows me."

"No matter." Winston didn't seem the least bit disappointed at this news. Clearly, having actually met Alice was no requirement for a prospective husband.

"In any event, I have not come to barter for her hand." Abel couldn't help but reveal some of the contempt he felt.

"Then, what do you want with her?" It was as if sex or marriage were the only options. Again, Abel had to keep his cool.

"Your daughter was once admired as a beautiful and decent girl, but she seems to be turning to the streets now, and I thought that should be controlled from home in order not to repel prospective suitors."

"Then you are indeed a prospective suitor." Winston stated bluntly and locked his red eyes on Abel's face.

The man has a one-track mind, Abel thought. But he had come here to play a role and it was obvious what role would get him the most information.

"Yes," Abel lied. "I am a businessman based in Festac Town, who needs to settle down ..."

"Just in time, young man. Alacrity in life is always a winner. Her mother will be happy."

This was news to Abel. Mary didn't seem in any hurry to marry her precious daughter off. "Why is that?" He asked with more genuine curiosity than Winston could have known.

"Because she is unhappy with certain men who have showered our daughter with gifts and promised to take her overseas for employment."

Abel was speechless. Here it was. The trafficking he had been seeking.

"And why would you want your daughter taken from the country?"

The old man laughed until he coughed.

"You are a naïve young fellow. My God. If Alice were taken abroad to work, it would ensure our sustainability, don't you see?" He coughed again, rather deeply. "That car is yours, am I right?"

Abel could see where this was headed. The man was so transparent.

"Right, Sir," Abel said to the excitement of his host, who drank some more water. "My only problem, Sir ..."

"What problem?" Winston cut in. He sensed a sale and did not want anything interfering.

Abel took a breath as if bringing up a delicate subject, but one he wished to resolve.

"I am told you have a strained relationship with Alice. It is likely to cause us problems in future. A couple should maintain a cordial relationship with their in-laws ..."

Winston got up, agitated, and paced about acting every part the unfairly wounded man.

"That is an unfounded rumour. A blatant lie, calculated at discrediting me and bringing my family to public disrepute." He coughed yet again, and Abel wondered if he might be seriously ill. Winston continued after the brief interruption. "I will show you ample evidence of love."

Then, he stormed out of the room. Abel heard him crashing about somewhere towards the back of the house.

Winston soon emerged with an old notebook and sat down, breathing heavily.

"Look at this if you doubt me. I loved my Princess so much that I kept notes of her physical and emotional development. Please read it aloud." He handed the open notebook to Abel.

Abel hid his excitement by clearing his throat. He peered down at the worn pages. Although slightly faded, the handwriting was beautiful and legible. He read aloud: *My beautiful Alice walked at twelve months. She started babbling at eight months and she spoke her first word at nine and a half months. She displayed emotions like affection, anger and jealousy before one year. At fifteen months, she showed considerable curiosity. Between then and two and half years, she wanted her will done. She hated restraint and fought it with aggression.*

As Alice got close to four years, I saw my daughter filled with unconscious impulses of curiosity about the genitals."

Abel paused, thrown by this unexpected reference. The man was either a monster or completely insane. Both wouldn't be out of the question. Abel took a breath and continued.

"They had become a source of displeasure to her. That was not all. I had become sexually attracted to her. She demanded full and unshared attention from me. She often asked me to dress and undress her, take her to the toilet, bathe her, put her to bed, and even tickle her.

"That was, perhaps, the Oedipus complex at work. This complex was named after the Greek figure Oedipus, who unknowingly killed his father and married his mother.

"It was natural for children at that age to display unrestrained love and affection for the parent of the opposite sex. I learnt from child psychology books that if her love for me was not properly resolved, it might cause personality defects in her life. She could later become neurotic in her attitude towards men. She might even be overtly fearful that no man would love her."

Abel stopped reading and looked up.

"What is it? Why have you stopped?"

"If what you write here is true, then something must have happened for your relationship to turn sour."

"Nothing I did, I can assure you!" Winston was defensive. Abel waved away the possibility.

"No, of course not. I suspect bad peer influence." Abel continued to probe. He wanted to give the man enough rope to hang himself.

"Maybe." Winston took some more water. "But I believe its source is her mother's religious fanaticism. I love my Princess so much that I did everything to protect her, even against the powers of earthly principalities."

Abel had no idea what the demented man was ranting about, but he encouraged him to go on.

"What do you mean, Sir?"

"I once took her to a popular spiritualist in Ajegunle to seek protection for her."

"Protection from what?"

"I have already said. From earthly principalities. But she hated this spiritualist. And she has kept away from me since then."

"How old was she when you took her?"

"Eleven."

He shifted away from Abel, his skull suddenly reflecting light from the dim bulb overhead. It gave him a ghoulish appearance. In the eerie half-light, the narrow face and discoloured whites of the eyes transformed the old man into a palpably demonic presence. And it shocked Abel out of the role he was playing. He went on the attack.

"Think what you are saying! Your loving daughter has hated you for four long years simply for taking her to see this man. It is impossible."

Winston became angry, a sure sign that he was hiding something.

"You doubt me? Who can explain these young girls? What they will take offence at?"

"I am trying to get at the truth. And so far, I am not hearing it. What did you do to her?"

The old man snatched up a walking stick which had been leaning against the settee. His famous temper was very much in evidence.

"You are no suitor! Get out! Get out or I will smash your head in!"

He took a step toward Abel who held up his hand as he retreated toward the low doorway.

"I'm going. But we aren't finished."

Abel ducked quickly out of the flat, the old man following, stick still raised. He stood outside his ramshackle home amid the weeds and cracked cement like a mangy dog guarding some rotten, maggot-infested scrap of meat.

As Abel drove off, he glanced at Winston in the rear view mirror. He had turned away and was greeting a well-dressed, tall, dark-skinned young man. Abel watched as Winston pointed emphatically toward his retreating vehicle with the walking stick.

A chill went down Abel's spine. Something about the two men standing together made him afraid, not for himself, but for Alice.

83

And he had no idea why. But he was certain she was in danger. And he was certain his meeting with this deranged miscreant had made her situation even more perilous. Abel had to move quickly. To prevent what, he did not know. He only knew that time was running out.

CHAPTER ELEVEN

Safely away from Yaba on the Third Mainland Bridge, Abel breathed more easily. The encounter with Winston had shaken him. And he was not easily thrown off balance. But he would not let anything deter him from discovering what Winston did with Alice in Ajegunle and what part this spiritualist played in the tragedy.

Abel had no use for such people, but he knew many Lagosians who faithfully attended church on Sundays, and then secretly patronised *jujumen* (practitioners of voodoo).

Stories of fathers who took their daughters to *jujumen* for various reasons were common. As Abel drove, he pulled out his cell phone and accessed the stored numbers. He scrolled through them until he found the number for the religious editor of *The Zodiac*. Once he had him on the line, Abel asked for the names of popular spiritualists in Ajegunle.

The editor told him the best known was Inila, who lived and worked two blocks west of the *Coke* depot on Sambia Street. Abel thanked the editor for taking his call on a Sunday and disconnected. Before he could put the phone down, it rang. A glance at the readout told him it was Ikomma.

"Are you okay, boy?"

"*Oga*, Mrs. Picketts called. She sounded unhappy."

"Yes, I understand. I will see her soon," he promised before disconnecting.

But Lola was now on his mind. He remembered the last time he had seen her, the day of Tunde's murder, and his promise, "It will be all right." He regretted that although Tunde's killers had been arrested and *The Zodiac* was giving her personal support, he had not been to see her since that unhappy day. He was tempted to make a detour to her house, but the run-in with Winston made that impossible. He had to take care of Alice first. There would be time for Lola later.

And he was doing all this for his murdered friend, Tunde. He was going to finish investigating the story Tunde had begun.

The spiritualist lived in a lively downscale part of town, bustling with activity, even on a Sunday. Everywhere, young men in casuals walked the streets, smoking, drinking and joking with friends. Many danced to music blaring from the large, croaky speakers planted in the doorways of music shops.

To Abel's surprise, his expensive Peugeot 406 did not spark any undue attention as he pulled to a stop in front of Inila's apartment building. Perhaps their indifference hinted that they had seen many upscale cars, flashier than his, park here. Inila's clientele had money.

The building, painted white, was the familiar Lagos slum architecture. It consisted of a long one-storey building with single rooms opposite each other. The rooms were lined along a corridor that led to common kitchen and toilet facilities. *That is the face-me-face-you style*, Abel thought, remembering his early days in Lagos when he lived in one. People had to queue up early in the morning to use the toilet and bathrooms. Unlike the building he once lived in, where people kept all manner of things in the corridor, this one was neat. The two rooms nearest the road had been converted into retail stores, selling food and household goods, convenient for the residents.

In one of these shops, Abel found a fat woman sitting on a stool. Nearby a man in his sixties, dressed in a white robe, rocking back and forth in a leather chair. Abel noted with some amusement that they did not react to the presence of a sophisticated stranger. *An interesting show of confidence*, Abel thought as he stepped into the crowded shop.

"Can I help you?" the woman asked.

"Good afternoon, I came to consult Mr. Inila."

Abel looked at the old man who watched him as he kept rocking.

"You have not been here before," she announced, seemingly proud of the observation.

"No," Abel admitted, keeping his eyes on the elderly man in a white robe.

"No wonder you looked lost," the woman laughed. "But

whatever is your problem, my husband will make you happy again."
She gestured to the man in the rocker.

Abel nodded his greeting to Inila who made a gesture of welcome with his hands.

"Okay. Let's go inside." Inila rose slowly to his feet and led the way through a door that connected the shop to the dimly lit corridor.

Two rooms away from the shop, Inila peeled a thick red curtain aside and opened the door.

"Please remove your shoes," he said to Abel and then went in.

Abel was wearing sandals. He bent over quickly, removed them, then entered.

The small room, half the size of the shop, was brightly lit, almost garish. Fluorescent lighting didn't match Abel's image of the spiritualist experience. Maybe this was the modern way. Inila probably took credit cards too.

Animal skins covered the couches. This might have been for effect, or it might have been because the couches were old and worn and needed the help. In any event, his host slumped onto the one near a partitioned corner. Abel followed suit, settling onto the other.

Inila's grin had transformed into a businesslike expression. His eyes had narrowed and frown lines etched the corners of his mouth. His thick head of black hair was flecked with specs of grey, his fair complexion sported freckles.

"Tell me your name."

"Akani."

"So, what is your problem, young man?" He spoke quickly, licking his lips.

"I am a businessman from Ikorodu …"

"Yes, many businessmen and even policemen come here for spiritual protection," Inila said proudly, interrupting Abel. "Robbers in Lagos have become very daring, so people come here for charms against gunshots and machete cuts. We even help people travelling overseas."

Abel found that interesting, but he was careful not to overreact.

"Women?" he asked.

"Yes mostly women, so they are not caught. But I take delight in protection against robbers. Lagos is dangerous," he said and looked up at Abel.

"Yes," Abel agreed, following Inila's lead. "It is a dangerous world, and you are correct. I need protection. I only hope you have something to help me."

Inila beat his chest and pointed to the partitioned corner.

"There is nothing you cannot find in this corner. Eda, the God of my ancestors, passed them on to me." He moved to peel the partition slightly and whispered some incantations on a small cowries-studded mound.

Then he turned back to Abel. "You will make some deposit of money for me to prepare the charm and you come for it same time next week. I will spend three days in the evil forest to prepare it."

That didn't take long, Abel thought. *After two sentences he's asking for money. The guy might be a spiritualist, but he knows what makes the real world go round.*

"Don't you need to know more about my problem?" Abel couldn't help needle the man a little.

"Not at all. I deal in categories not specifics." This sounded like complete nonsense to Abel, but he wasn't here to expose spiritualists. So he reached for his wallet.

"How much, Sir?" Abel asked with feigned interest. He choked back an impulse to laugh out loud at the performance.

"Only twenty thousand naira." He saw Abel's eyes widen.

"I suspect that you had no idea of the cost. But next week, you will have to bring an additional hundred thousand naira to collect the charm."

Abel shook his head.

"That's a lot of money."

"On the contrary. For magic, it is a bargain."

"How would I know that? What's the going rate for magic?"

The man watched him a bit, then nodded.

"You must trust me."

Abel gave him a wry look and Inila continued.

"You see, Eda forbids us from overcharging, otherwise we get punished with some strange diseases. I am sure you have seen some other *jujumen* who have gone mad? That is the reason. Overcharging their clients."

Well, it was original. Abel nodded as if Inila had just made a cogent argument for trust and began counting out his money. As he went to hand the cash to his "spiritual guide," he was shocked to see his host's eyes suddenly turn vampire red. A trick of lighting? Or was it something else? Whatever the cause it was a pretty convincing sales tool. Abel handed him the cash, which Inila put behind the partition.

"So, we see you next week," he said and stretched his back.

"There *is* something else," Abel said.

"I am not surprised, young man. Many people who come here have multiple cases. Our elders say one reason does not take a man out of his house." He smiled.

Abel did not. He looked him in the eyes.

"Sir, some years ago, a retiree from Yaba named Winston Udor brought his daughter here to see you, but soon after, and since then, the daughter has hated him. I know this was years ago and you may not remember right away …"

The spiritualist held up his hand.

"I remember him."

Abel was surprised, but continued, eager to make his point.

"I was wondering how a powerful man like you could make a girl hate her father."

The frown lines on the man's face deepened in anger.

"I remember him because he was a fool! He came to me as others do to get rich. The rituals are painful, but simple. Among the lot, he chose the one which involved sexual intercourse with his daughter."

As Abel had suspected, Winston had raped Alice. This was the source of her fear and hatred. But if this spiritualist suggested such a thing he also had something to answer for.

"I would hardly call violating one's own daughter 'simple,'" Abel said, anger rising in him.

"I know it is not simple, and that was why I warned him to do it only once."

"It only takes one time to scar someone for life!"

"Had he followed my instructions, the girl would never have

even known."

"And how was that possible?"

"I gave him some charms to put his daughter into a deep sleep. But instead of only one discrete encounter, he repeated the act. Many times. Ceremony and magic were overcome by his lust. The *juju* did not work, and he has remained poor. This is something I have done for many politicians, but that man was stupid." He fumed.

"I see," Abel said, nodding.

"Then you understand what I advised was not harmful."

"I can see you thought no harm would come to the girl," Abel lied. He didn't want to alienate this source as he had Winston, so he added, "Business fortunes in Lagos are not stable, so when I face a downturn, perhaps I will return to you."

The spiritualist nodded, satisfied he had not lost a client.

But Abel could not help himself, and just before exiting, he turned and said, "No matter how desperate my circumstances, I would never use the option Winston Udor chose." He left without further ceremony.

Driving home, Abel tried to put the pieces together. The sexual abuse undoubtedly made Alice hate her father. And her situation was made worse because she held the secret. Nobody could share the burden, relieve her of the guilt she felt, or offer her counselling. *Winston may have threatened her*, Abel thought. He wondered if that was why she ultimately turned to the streets.

When she couldn't get love from her father, the love any child would crave, she tried to get it on the streets, from strange men who offered her gifts. But that didn't satisfy her need. It only made her feel worse.

Abel remembered how cheerful she became at his house and how her beauty had blossomed in front of his very eyes. She had at last found a man who treated her with respect and real love. It had transformed her, at least for a moment.

Then he remembered the promise he had made to her – *it will be all right*. He wanted her to have that feeling of happiness always.

As Abel pondered how best to help the girl, a small red Honda in front of him made an abrupt stop. He was forced to swerve dangerously to avoid a collision. He saw the driver make an apologetic gesture.

Abel was so distracted, he didn't notice when a black SUV appeared on his rear bumper. It was dangerously close. The driver honked his horn continuously. Annoyed but unwilling to make an incident of this, Abel slowed down and moved to the right lane, waiting for the speeding SUV to pass.

Instead, it slowed down behind him. Annoyed, Abel was about to brake and confront this idiot, when his rear window shattered, a bullet brushing his right ear before making a pin-sized hole in the windscreen.

Abel looked down to see his fingers were stained with blood. He reached up and discovered his burning earlobe was the source. A vision of Tunde's severed ears flashed through his head when more shots rang out, flattening his rear tyres. Abel's car ground to a halt on a bridge, which crossed a peaceful lagoon. It was surreal. Abel wondered how the beautiful aquamarine water below and the idyllic cloudless sky above could possibly exist in the same world with gunshots and blood. Vehicles in the opposite lane of traffic whirled past unaware of the attack, adding to the unreality of the moment.

Time slowed down for Abel and everything happened as in a dream. The attacking SUV slid past his car and parked about ten metres in front of him, blocking any possible escape. Abel regarded it through the cracked windscreen. He finally recovered his wits and reached for a revolver hidden under the seat.

Abel flung open the driver's side door, leaving it open, hoping his attackers would think he was hiding behind it. Instead, he slid under the car.

From this vantage point, he could see the driver of the offending SUV, but could not make out his features. There were two men with him. Clutching knives that glinted in the sunlight, they rushed toward Abel's car.

Abel took aim and shot at the legs of the one closest to him.

"Yei!" he heard an agonising scream and a heavy thud on the hot road.

"Boss, the gun," the other man screamed. The driver jumped down from the SUV waving a gun.

From his vantage point under the car, Abel could only see him from the chest down. He watched as the attacker raised his gun and fired repeatedly into the driver's side door of Abel's car.

Abel returned fire, emptying his revolver into the man's knees. As the assailant fell, blood, flesh and bones splattered on the road.

That still left one attacker, and Abel's weapon was empty. But the last man standing must not have realised it because he ran back to the SUV, jumped inside and slammed the door.

As Abel crawled out from under his vehicle, a second SUV arrived, screeching to a halt next to its compatriot. Someone in the passenger seat opened fire. Abel ducked away, circled back around the rear of his car, and leapt off the bridge into the lagoon below.

He remained underwater until he reached one of the bridge's pillars, cautiously poking his head out of the water to take a badly needed breath. He heard voices above and suddenly, gunshots erupted and the water all around him exploded. Abel dove down again.

He swam farther under the bridge where he would not be exposed. Then he surfaced and waited, barely breathing. Would the men come down after him?

Abel prayed for the sound of police sirens. Surely someone must have called them by now. The entire Lagos commuter population couldn't be blind to a gun battle raging right in front of them!

At last he heard the two SUVs roar off.

Abel held on to a pillar of the bridge, wondering what to do, then he heard sirens. The police had finally arrived. They would find his car riddled with bullets, and contact Chief Benson. Abel didn't want his boss to worry, but he was too exhausted to deal with the police at the moment. There would be endless questions and formalities. He waited there until he saw a fisherman in a canoe, rowing past. He shouted for help. Out of the lagoon later on, he found a café where he called Chief Benson.

Twenty minutes later, an unmarked car arrived and whisked him off to Dr. Jos Atim's clinic, a euphemism for a five-room private hospital located in a guesthouse owned by Chief Benson. There the doctor cared mainly for the Chief, but he also looked after *The Zodiac's* employees.

As Abel climbed up on an exam table and lay down, the doctor began dressing his wounded ear. The last things Abel remembered were the bright light, the smell of antiseptic and Chief Benson's face appearing overhead peering down at him. Abel nodded his hello, then passed out.

CHAPTER TWELVE

When Abel woke up two hours later, he tried to get out of bed. He had work to do. The attack meant he was getting close to something and that Alice might be in jeopardy.

But just as his left foot hit the floor, Dr. Atim entered and ordered him back to bed. One of the conditions the physician had imposed in exchange for working on demand at the private clinic was that his medical decisions would take precedence over newsroom deadlines. Abel obeyed and collapsed back into bed.

The next morning, Fakorede arrived to take a statement. He gently chided Abel for running from the scene of the shoot-out. Abel explained what happened, but Fakorede noted his revolver wasn't registered. However, because of Chief Benson's intervention, they were not going to press charges.

Abel nearly exploded. "Press charges! The bastards tried to kill me!"

Fakorede laughed and slapped the table, amused at Abel's outrage. He told Abel to calm down, that witness statements corroborated his story.

Annoyed, Abel asked about his attackers. Fakorede said they had tracked down one SUV from a witness description and partial licence plate. They had two of Abel's victims, both suffering multiple gunshot wounds and broken limbs, under police guard at the Ikeja General Hospital. But they were refusing to cooperate or name any accomplices. But there was another suspect.

When Abel asked who this suspect was, Fakorede said the man's name was Sanko. Abel immediately recognised him as the man from whom he had rescued Alice. The policeman saw from Abel's expression that the name meant something to him. Abel explained how he had saved Alice and what she had told him about Sanko.

As they talked, a stream of questions flooded Abel's mind: *What did Sanko have to do with Winston? Did he trail him to Inila? Did*

Inila call Winston? And what did all this have to do with Alice?

He needed to speak with the girl immediately, so he answered the rest of Fakorede's questions as succinctly as he could and saw the policeman off. Then he summoned Dr. Atim and informed him he'd been held captive long enough. The doctor, seeing there was no convincing Abel otherwise, prescribed some antibiotics and gave him permission to leave.

Once home, Abel retreated to his study to review recent wire service stories. As he sat down and began to read, a very agitated Ikomma rushed in.

"Oga, Alice's mother is here to see you."

Abel immediately got to his feet. "Bring her in."

But before Ikomma made it to the door, Mary burst in, breathless, tears streaming down her face.

"Alice is gone! Alice is gone!" She screamed and slumped on the rug, pulling at her hair.

Abel moved quickly to her side. "Please calm down," he said. He pulled her up onto the nearest settee. As he watched her, Abel was wracked with guilt, immediately fearing his investigation had somehow triggered this turn of events. He asked Mary to tell him what she knew, but hard as he tried, he couldn't get a coherent word out of the distraught woman. Finally, in an attempt to shock Mary out of her hysteria, he pointed to his bandaged ear.

"Madam, please look at my ear," he said and bent down to get the ear closer to her. Mary immediately stopped crying and looked up at him, catching her breath for the first time.

"Oh, Lord, what happened to you?"

"Gun shot. Some people tried to kill me when I was looking into why Alice changed from a sweet girl to one who relished street life." He sat down opposite her.

"Please tell me, when did this happen?" she said.

"Yesterday."

"I am very sorry for you, Mr. Abel. But please promise me this will not stop you from looking for her." She sobbed again. Abel figured each of them was playing a role to manipulate the other. But he had to admit, her pain trumped his.

"She is my only daughter," the woman continued. "I love her,

95

and she liked you, always talking about you as the only man who understood her." She wiped tears with the back of her trembling hand.

Abel couldn't help but be touched, and he felt tears welling in his own eyes.

"Have no fear, Madam. I am going to help you." He was gratified to see her calm down. "Kindly tell me what happened, everything you can remember. Leave nothing out."

Before beginning, she wiped her face with the palm of her hand.

"Alice went out Saturday night but did not return home. It's happened before, but she always returned the following day, saying she was with friends. This morning, when she was still missing, I raised an alarm with her father. He said he heard she had travelled."

"Travelled?" Abel felt something in the pit of his stomach. *Oh, God,* he thought. *No.*

"Did you ask him what he meant?"

"Yes, for once, I was not afraid of his abuse. I demanded he tell me where she was. He knew the answer. I could tell. For a long time he did not say anything. Then he said, 'Don't you want your daughter to make money like other girls who are acquiring property all over the place?' He would tell me no more. I broke down at that point, Mr. Abel. I have not stopped crying since."

"How does your husband know she travelled?"

"He would not tell me. He terrorises us so it is difficult to press him too hard without setting the house ablaze."

Abel nodded for the beauty of that expression and not the fact, which he knew so well already.

"I asked him one more time before I came here. He said, 'You are crying now, but just wait until your daughter begins to send us money'. He is such a fool. If men had wombs to carry their child for nine months they would understand what our children mean to us. Alice is my only daughter." She began to weep again.

"So he gave you no hint where Alice might be?" He cut in to redirect the emotional outpouring.

"No. He only said Alice will continue her education and get a good job."

"But Madam, Alice was never happy in your home because of

96

her father. Do you think perhaps she was so unhappy that she left on her own?"

"Why do you say that?" she asked and straightened up.

"It is obvious that Alice has been abused by your husband for years. If he abuses one, he probably abuses the other. Has he beaten you, Madam? Forced himself on you sexually? Marital rape is possible." He paused for her reaction. She looked down and, ashamed, nodded.

"He began raping Alice when she was eleven, didn't he?" Abel decided to press her.

She took in a deep breath, her eyes rolling back as if she was going to faint and let out a loud cry. "I suspected it. Oh, Lord, I suspected it, but she would not tell me. Maybe he frightened her with some superstition, or she thought if I challenged him he would beat me up." She stopped and swallowed. Abel reached across and laid his hand gently on hers.

"I am sorry, Madam, but we cannot rewrite all that."

She looked at him, suddenly angry.

"Perhaps it is time to act."

"No, don't confront him with this. If I am reading the situation correctly, your life could be in danger. And Alice will want her mother there when she returns."

Mary managed a weak smile at the thought.

"You are correct," her voice firmed up. "Alice asked me not long ago why I had not married a man like you. I am old and unattractive now, but how I wished Alice had the opportunity to be your wife ..."

Abel thought again of his young sister who had died so many years before. She would have been like Alice as a teenager. Beautiful, bright, full of life and energy.

Alice was attractive, but he was middle-aged. What on earth could he offer a girl so young? He was a father figure, not a husband. But in her anxiety and grief, Alice's mother had confused the two. She wanted a man in her daughter's life who would be kind. He was prepared to be that man. But not as Alice's husband. The minute they had sex, Abel would go from being her saviour to being her master.

"Alice still has the opportunity to have a good life and find someone who will treat her well," he said, hoping to diffuse the woman's sudden burst of passion. Abel wanted to get the discussion back on a useful track.

"Could Alice have moved in with one of the men who has been coming to see your husband lately?"

She shook her head. "My husband would have told me if that were the case. And he would be waving around a great fistful of money." She smiled ruefully at Abel. "Winston would never give Alice up without demanding a large payment. And my husband's ego would force him to show off his sudden good fortune."

"Could she have travelled with any of her female friends?"

"I asked them, of course, but they claim to know nothing. And they cared not a whit when they saw my tears. These girls know I disapprove of them and they hate me. If my poor girl was dead they would not tell me!"

The hysteria which she had controlled suddenly overcame her again and she collapsed into a heap at his feet.

Moved, Abel pulled her up.

"I will hunt for her as if she were my own child," he promised. And in his heart he swore that he would never give up until Alice was safely back and the people responsible for her disappearance either dead or in jail.

CHAPTER THIRTEEN

After Ikomma left to drive Mary home, Abel retired to his study to plan a course of action. This was a different kind of assignment for him. In the past, he would have painted a compelling picture of the odious practice of trafficking in women by telling the story of one sad victim. Then, public outrage would force politicians and police to crack down on the criminals. But this time, it was personal. Abel not only had to find one missing girl, he was determined to expose the barons and masterminds. He sketched his plans on paper.

Ikomma's return interrupted his planning. His servant entered the study, a picture of concern, looking as if he had lost something precious.

"Is Mary all right?"

"She is fine, Oga."

"Then why the worried look?"

Ikomma took a breath before speaking. "Oga, I hope you are not marrying that girl, Alice."

Abel laughed and shook his head.

"Why do you say that?"

"Em," he looked away. "Good men deserve good things, Sir."

"You know she is not good? Tell me about her."

Abel had no intention of marrying the girl, but he was curious to learn what Ikomma knew. If he'd been holding something back now was the time to hear it.

"Alice and her friend they call Dupe have been hopping from one man to another for money. I used to see them regularly in the restaurant where I worked until I joined you. I know them very well, and the night I saw her here I was alarmed. No, she is not good." He shook his head.

Abel felt a twinge of disappointment. He already knew of her activities. He just didn't know they went so far back. However, the name Dupe was new to him.

"Okay, but she's disappeared, Ikomma. Do you know where I can find this Dupe?"

"Em," Ikomma fell into silence again. Then he said slowly, "She prostitutes from one street corner to another, but you are most likely to find her on Fridays on Sanusi Fafunwa Street, but Oga," he stopped, rubbing his ear in anxiety.

"What is it, Ikomma?" Abel asked sternly.

"Oga, you have not said you won't marry her."

"Ikomma, I think you misunderstand my interest in the girl. You see, some people are not lucky with their parents and, frankly, it messes them up. They aren't able to fulfil their potential." Ikomma nodded attentively.

"Alice is only fifteen. She's still a child, really. But she's taken to the streets. She's intelligent and still could be turned around. That is what her mother wants, that is what I want. For now, the primary concern is to find her. We will look for Dupe tomorrow night."

"Then you are not going to marry her?"

"No, Ikomma. I am not going to marry her. Now, let's have lunch."

Ikomma sprang to his feet and headed to the kitchen, a happy man.

With more than 24 hours before he could talk to Dupe, Abel decided to follow the few other leads he had. He hopped into the new SUV his publisher had given him, and drove to the Central Christian Church on the Tagry Road.

There he found Junior Pastor Joshua leading a Bible study class of some 20 worshippers. Joshua looked radiant in a white robe. He nodded slightly when he spotted Abel. After a few minutes, he dismissed the class and joined Abel near the back of the church.

"We didn't see the story, Mr. News Breaker," he said shaking Abel's hand and smiling as if sharing some private joke.

Abel had rightly anticipated the question, but Joshua's warmth pleasantly surprised him.

"I told you your Pastor would be released, didn't I?" Abel said. "So I didn't have to do the story after all."

"We are all grateful."

You should all be in jail, Abel thought but kept the sentiment to himself.

"So what can we do for you this time?" the young supplicant asked.

Abel drew closer to him. "I need to see the Pastor."

"Ah, he is not around."

"Travelled?"

"No. In retreat. He has been humiliated."

"How? You mean by that dust up with the police?"

"Yes. There is nothing more humiliating than to have a policeman preach to a Pastor. He and others, including the colleague of mine you saw here the other day, are on the mountain-top praying for forgiveness."

"What do you mean? Forgiveness for what?" Abel asked.

"For a whole hour, the police commissioner was telling us how we disappointed God by supporting these men who take girls overseas into prostitution. He came here and addressed the congregation."

Well at least these people can be shamed into acting like Christians, Abel thought. Frankly, he was surprised. But wonders never cease.

The supplicant reduced his voice to a whisper: "We didn't know the girls were subjected to inhuman treatment, and it is more annoying that the traffickers make so much money only to give us peanuts."

Abel looked at him wondering if he'd heard correctly. If the traffickers had given them a decent cut of the profits would that have made it all right? Abel didn't ask the question. It seemed pointless. So he barrelled ahead with his mission.

"I'm looking for a girl who may have been taken abroad by these men. She disappeared over the weekend."

"You don't understand, Mr. News Breaker," Joshua said impatiently. "We have stopped all that nonsense now."

"Did you give the police any names? I mean names of people who were trying to get visas for these girls."

"Sorry, we met with those men in confidence."

"And the police let you get away with that answer?" Abel was angry. What was wrong with the police? Now they were granting criminals privacy privileges?

"We met with these men under the guise of prayer."

"You met with these men under the guise of commerce. It was a business transaction. There's nothing holy about it."

"Nonetheless, privilege holds. The police even had to agree. But I can assure you," he added hastily, "we learnt that all of these men have fled the country."

Junior Pastor Joshua placed his hands together in front of him in a prayerful attitude and bowed slightly. "I must go pray now," he said, then turned and exited. Abel doubted God wanted to hear from Pastor Joshua or anyone else connected with the Central Christian Church.

Fakorede confirmed Joshua's story when Abel called him on his way home. He admitted it was aggravating letting these religious hypocrites off the hook, but they had no choice. Abel thanked him with as much sarcasm as he could put into his voice and hung up.

As Abel drove into Ikoyi, he remembered Lola had wanted to see him. He decided he really should visit the poor woman, and so drove to her apartment.

There were 10 three-bedroom chalets in the leafy compound dotted with fruit bearing trees. The evening air was cool and Abel had rolled down the driver-side window. He smelled orange blossoms.

Five plain-clothes policemen on guard greeted him at the gate of the complex owned by Chief Benson. He waved to them and drove to chalet Number Nine in the section called "Orange" after the variety of tree, which surrounded it.

Lola and her sister Bimpe, whom she had begun to call "My Woman Friday," were in the living room watching a home video on a giant flat screen when their security man ushered Abel into the tastefully furnished flat.

"Welcome, Sir," Bimpe knelt down politely to greet him.

"Hello, Bimpe. Good to see you," he said, pulling her up to hug her.

"Hello, Stranger," Lola teased him.

"Lola, you look good. That is a quick recovery, I must say. You are a strong woman."

"God did it, Abel. And of course thanks to Chief Benson." She rose up lazily from the rug and sat on one of the settees. She wore jeans and a loose shirt. Her hair was intricately plaited into what is called the Bob Marley style, which gave her a girlish look.

"Would it be any trouble to ask for some water?" Abel said. Bimpe jumped up.

"Of course not. We could offer you something stronger if you like. Rum?"

"Water will be fine."

Abel turned to Lola as Bimpe went off towards the kitchen.

"Please, forgive me for not coming sooner. I have been working underground."

"I know," she said looking at his bandaged ear. "I heard about the attack."

"Chief Benson told you?"

"Yes. There were already rumours. It was best he told me." She smiled. "There is nothing I ask for he doesn't give me, and I know it is all because of you." Her voice started to quiver. "Thank you, Abel for …"

Bimpe came in to serve the water and, seeing them deep in conversation, returned to the kitchen.

"No thanks needed, Lola. I take promises seriously." There was an awkward moment between them. "I hear you are going to the UK."

"Yes. Thanks for that, too. I know you suggested it to Chief Benson. And my bank has agreed to give me a long vacation." Their gazes met.

The tears he saw in her eyes made him look away. "You need to get away for a total recovery and to sort your life out," he said.

"You are not abandoning me, Abel?" She broke down then, sobbing.

Abel moved to her. "You have to be strong, Lola. Tell me you will."

She nodded and dried her tears.

"Good. You have many things going for you. An employer who stands by his people. Me, who has an obligation to Tunde's memory. And above all, you have God. Now cheer up and see me off."

103

"Yes, Sir," she said mockingly and stood up.

Abel smiled, spreading his arms for a hug. She smiled back and fell into the open arms.

"It will be all right. Lola, I don't know how, but I know," he whispered.

"I believe that, Abel. Keep in touch?"

"I will." He broke the embrace. He took her hand. "Walk me to the car."

Still holding hands, not as lovers but almost as children lost in the woods, they made their way to the car.

As Abel drove off, leaving her standing on the driveway, he thought of the many times he had said goodnight to her and Tunde after a friendly meal. She assumed that same familiar attitude, hands akimbo, smiling as he left. Only now, she would return to the flat alone.

CHAPTER FOURTEEN

Eight o'clock the following evening, Abel prepared to meet Dupe. He stood before the full-length mirror, admiring his boyish looks. He was dressed in a striped yellow shirt, which he had tucked into his black trousers. He smiled at the image and muttered, "Cool, man."

But clothes and style only took you so far. Abel reminded himself that his real strength lay in his charm and intelligence.

Ikomma had done some early reconnaissance, confirming Dupe's location. And he confirmed she would be working her usual street corner that night.

As Abel polished his black leather shoes, he remembered his early days in journalism, when he celebrated every big story with booze and all manner of women. He had enjoyed himself, but felt a vague sense of guilt. Knowing the tragedy which brought these girls to that particular lifestyle now made him ashamed. He wondered if this crusade was partly driven by the guilt over his past indiscretions.

Abel was ready by eight-thirty. Just as he started out the door, a sudden flash of lightening cut through the night sky, lighting up his living room. It was followed by a loud thunderclap. Abel rushed to the window and looked outside. The rain clouds, invisible in the darkness, threatened the meeting he hoped would provide him a lead. A sudden storm with the inevitably flooded streets could drive the girl indoors. Dupe might simply write the night off and go home. Hookers and rain didn't mix when their office was a street corner.

Despite another flash of lightening and its attendant thunderclap, Abel resolved to try, anyway. He didn't want to waste more time, and meeting her as a potential customer was much better than a direct approach. He grabbed an umbrella and dashed to his SUV.

Once safely inside, Abel put an old Miles Davis CD into the

changer. *Sketches of Spain*. It was one of Abel's favourite albums. The master was smooth and cool. His music spoke pure confidence as he improvised his way through each piece. Abel felt himself relax, but not because of the music. It was the performance. Abel thought he had a lot in common with a jazz musician; making his moves up on the fly, cool under pressure, always in control. Abel smiled and tapped the steering wheel as the SUV hurtled down the wet road.

Abel's concerns about the weather evaporated when the rain departed as quickly as it had arrived. His SUV moved easily through traffic. Cars all around him cruised down the main thoroughfares, their passengers in search of Lagos nightlife. But he was on a different mission.

As Abel veered off Adeola Odeku onto Sanusi Fafunwa Street, he saw several girls working the corners. But he didn't see the girl Ikomma had described. Then as he made his third trip around the block, he saw her emerging from a small shop, coffee cup in hand. He could not mistake the dark plump lady in a tight fitting black blouse over a red mini skirt which struggled to contain her enormous bum.

She flashed a smile as Abel pulled to a stop next to her.

"Are you at work?" Abel asked, the Miles Davis CD still playing.

"Wouldn't be standing in the cold for nothing, dear."

She wasn't very old in years, but experience had given her the air of a decrepit piece of architecture, crumbling under some enormous burden, fit no longer for habitation, existing only because nobody had bothered to tear it down. A ruined wasted life.

Abel blinked. It was hard to believe that the woman who smiled at him without joy or warmth had not so long ago been a happy, innocent child. He forced a smile.

"Okay, hop in. You are my girl tonight." He opened the passenger side door.

She walked coquettishly to the other side of his SUV, tossed away her coffee cup and lowered her heavy frame into the seat. Her perfume, which Abel could not place, was sensuous but applied so heavily it almost made him sneeze.

"Thanks. I love being warm."

"I'm Peter. And you're most welcome."

Abel held out his hand. Dupe saw the gesture and broke into a laugh.

"A gentleman. I am Dupe, and you've made a good choice." She grinned.

"What u gat?" He blurted out. Abel had no idea if this was proper procedure, but he figured she'd let him know if he went astray.

"I'm an expert in blow-jobs and, honey, I will blow your head off."

"Sounds good to me." He started the car.

"So where we going?" she asked.

"If you have a good place, I like away matches," he said.

"Fine," she said. "But you pay more."

It struck Abel that his meeting with the spiritualist hadn't been much different. It didn't take either one very long to ask for money.

"How much will this cost?" He tapped her on the thighs.

"Usual rate 30K, but my place, additional 20K."

"Like a rent tax."

The girl laughed.

"Yeah. A rent tax." She turned serious. "And no warm-ups in the car. Know what I mean? You keep your eyes on the road. I got hot legs and don't want 'em getting broken up a in crash."

"Fair enough. So, where do you live?"

"Muri Street in Surulere."

They rode in silence for most of the trip. The girl looked blankly out the window speaking only to give him directions. The faux charm she'd displayed a few minutes before had completely disappeared. She wasn't being paid for this part of the night, and she had withdrawn into her own world. Abel was shaken by the encounter and nothing had even happened yet. He turned up the CD, trying to learn something about being cool from the master. The girl didn't seem to notice the music.

Surulere was notorious for traffic jams day and night. It was full of hot spots, and the streets were crowded with casually dressed young men and women out for a good time. They passed fast food joints and kebab spots and bars that blared live music. They turned a corner where skimpily dressed ladies waited for clients. Dupe grunted.

"I'm better, honey," was all she said. There was no rancour in the comment. It was simply an objective assessment of the competition. The girl viewed the world with a complete detachment, everything a matter of procedure. Nothing touched her. As Abel glanced at Dupe, he worried there might be no way to reach such a creature.

Muri Street, some 30 minutes from the ever-busy Adeniran Ogunsanya Street, was a residential area and therefore quiet this time of night. The street itself was bare, dusty and bumpy – more suitable for commercial motorbikes than cars. Like a stream, the bikes meandered around the bad patches, sometimes at top speed, which suggested the drivers were familiar with the terrain.

10 Muri Street was a series of six flats, but only the three on the ground floor had been completed. Piles of sand and cinder blocks took up most of the space in the fenced compound. Abel manoeuvred his SUV through the yard and found an empty spot in front of Dupe's place.

Dupe started to open the SUV door, but stopped abruptly, turning towards her customer.

"I hope you are not staying overnight. My flatmate comes home in three hours." She looked at her slim *Citizen* wrist watch. No romance in this encounter. Sex regulated by money and performed in specific increments of time.

"Not to worry, Dupe," Abel said exiting the SUV. Cool, soothing air hit his face, making him take a deep breath. Despite her excessive weight, Dupe walked at a brisk pace. She led him up the steps and to the front door, smiling at him as she unlocked it. They entered without speaking.

The living room, with three brown sofas arranged around a glass centre table, still smelled of fresh paint.

"Relax. Take a seat."

Abel slumped into the sofa nearest the front door and crossed his legs, trying to appear casual. "I guess we should have stopped somewhere for a drink or two …"

"Yeah, except that you have been behaving like a guy who's sex starved. Is your wife lazy?"

"You have anything to drink?" Abel ignored her question.

"Yeah." She waddled to the giant double-door fridge beside a dining table. "And what would you have?"

"Cans of stout. Just keep them coming."

"Never seen a handsome man so starved." She giggled as she brought two cans and sat on the sofa next to Abel.

He eyed the blue-coloured draperies. "I like those," he said, trying to sound casual. Instead, he sounded lame. Abel winced inwardly at the inane comment. Miles would be ashamed of him. The remark was not cool and not in control.

"Yeah, we're trying to make this place as comfortable as possible, you know? But it's gonna be gradual."

Abel was relieved she hadn't commented on his awkward attempt to make conversation. She was probably used to men like him. Or she might be dense. Or she might not care what he was feeling. Money and sex. That was the extent of her interest in him. No, that wasn't right. Money was the extent of her interest. Sex was simply a means to an end.

She broke the lids of both cans and gave one to Abel. "Cheers."

"Cheers," Abel said. He grinned, feeling dumber by the minute.

After a few seconds, Dupe stood up.

"Okay, let's move to my bedroom."

Abel guessed that meant the cocktail hour was over. She held out her hand. He thought she was offering to lead him to the bedroom, a gesture of intimacy. But then she spoke.

"Cash in advance." Nice, cosy touch.

Abel had packaged his money carefully for this assignment. He drew a blue envelope from his left pocket and handed it to her. "Fifty K, but you have the opportunity to earn more."

She ran a finger around her nipple, which was visible through the tight blouse. Apparently, she was back on display.

"Just be sure you have some breath left to call 911 when I finish with you," she teased as she counted the money. "Wait here a sec."

She trotted to an adjoining room. Abel could hear her kicking off her shoes, unzipping the skirt and removing other clothing. She returned, stripped down to her underpants.

Cupping her voluptuous breasts in her hands she grinned at him naughtily. Her white lace panties were so small, they barely covered the bushy pubic area.

"You look dashing," Abel said. He locked his eyes on her pubic region and caressed the can in his right hand.

Abel was doing his best to get into the part, but it was difficult for him to generate even feigned interest in this sad, overweight girl. Dupe sensed a problem.

She walked over impatiently. "Don't tell me you are the slow-to-start type." She sank to her knees, her enormous breasts spread on his thighs as she stroked the groin area of his trousers.

Abel knew he only had so much time with the girl, so he put a hand on her arm. "Dupe, please get up and let's talk a minute."

Abel moved to the sofa as Dupe followed, obviously puzzled.

"There's a time limit here don't forget," she said. She lumbered onto the sofa opposite him. This wasn't part of the routine, and it clearly wasn't sitting well. Abel guessed he was breaking a lot of unspoken rules.

"Dupe, it is difficult for a man to resist you, but we have to talk first."

Dupe reached across and put her hand on his erectionless crotch.

"You're doing a pretty good job of resisting. Limp as a punctured balloon. You're not one of those guys who only gets off if someone talks dirty are you? 'Cause I use my tongue better for other things."

Abel couldn't stall much longer, so he decided to lay his cards on the table and hope he wouldn't scare Dupe off.

"No. But I'm not here for a blow job."

Dupe suddenly looked concerned. "Shit, you're not a cop are you?"

"No. I'm here about Alice, your friend ..."

"Heeeeei!" She leapt up, fuming. "Alice, Alice all the time, all the men, what has she got that I don't have?" She turned to display her breasts and buttocks. Abel noticed that her big tummy distorted the curves she was trying to showcase.

"Calm down," Abel pleaded with her. It was the first time she'd displayed any honest emotion, and it wasn't a pleasant sight.

But she was still in a rage. "Everybody is talking Alice, Alice because they say she has firm breasts and when she climaxes, it is like an earthquake has hit the bed. Is that what you are looking for?"

Abel held up another envelope of money, which immediately soothed Dupe's bruised ego. She reached for it. Abel held it back.

"You want this, I need information."

"What kind?"

"Alice disappeared, and her mother is desperate to see her. I promised her I'd find the girl."

Dupe looked off, nervous.

"She went out of the country. Her father knows that. He sold her."

Abel's worst fears were confirmed.

"Who took her?"

"Man named Kenny. I introduced Alice to him one day. He started sending her gifts and buying her things."

"Kenny was a regular donor?"

"Yes, to Alice's father."

"This was a payoff so he could take Alice out of the country?"

"Yes. Of course, the asshole was supposed to take all of us. We were happy thinking of going and earning money. But in the end, the bastard took only Alice out because she has an aura men can't resist."

"And you all knew you were going into prostitution?"

"He said we'd have a better life. What? You think Alice didn't know? She knew, and she was all for it."

"She wanted to go back to school." Abel regretted his words the minute he said them. He didn't want to sound defensive.

"That's what her mother said?"

"That's what Alice said. To me."

"You sleep with her? That what this is? Looking for your long lost love?"

"No. But she spent the night at my house. I got to know her a little."

Dupe laughed. "You're rich, right? Live in a nice place? Nice part of Lagos? Alice tells you she loves you. Wants to marry you. And you believe her? She wants what we all do, Mister. She lied."

Abel watched Dupe. This bitter girl who clearly hated Alice couldn't imagine anyone wanting to better their lives. Everything was a con. It's how she experienced the world. But there was no point in debating this. Not with Dupe. Now it was a matter of getting anything he could from her.

"This Kenny. He took her?"

"Yes."

Abel looked around the room. There was a series of pictures in frames on a side table. Alice was in one of them, along with Dupe and several other older businessmen.

He got up and went to the photo. "Is this Kenny here with Alice?" He believed that if it wasn't Kenny, Dupe would show him his correct photograph. The trick worked.

"No, that is not him," She stood up and pointed to another picture with herself and some men.

"That's Kenny with me."

Abel studied the picture. Kenny was tall and smiled broadly into the camera, a glass of beer in hand.

The second man in the photo caught Abel's eye. He looked familiar. Then he realised who it was. Sanko. His attacker. Sanko and Kenny. Probably business partners in trafficking. But who was behind them?

Abel turned to Dupe who had disappeared into the other room while he pondered the photos.

"What's Kenny's real name?" He called to her.

She returned from the bedroom now wrapped in a robe.

"Kehinde Lawal."

Abel made a mental note of the name as he took the photo out of its frame.

"I need this, Dupe."

She frowned, and Abel saw doubt begin to creep into her mind. He knew she regretted talking to him. As a reporter he had seen the expression before.

"I don't think so ..."

"Nobody will know where I got it, Dupe. Don't worry."

"These are bad people, Sir. If they thought I was telling you things, it would be bad for me."

"I know how to keep confidences. And protect sources," he promised.

She shook her head, her eyes shutting in regret about what she had divulged already.

"Where did he take Alice?"

"I don't know. The last time he called me, they were only in transit. Please you must go."

Abel nodded. "I may need to talk to you again." As he said this, he gave her the last envelope of money.

But he never got a chance to talk to her again.

Two days later, Dupe was murdered as she stood on the street corner waiting for a customer. She was shot seven times. There were no witnesses. Or none who would come forward. Abel's one solid link to the man who had taken Alice out of the country had been silenced.

CHAPTER FIFTEEN

Abel read about Dupe's murder in a Saturday evening paper, *PM NEWS*. Ikomma had just served him his after dinner coffee, which sat untouched now. It would remain untouched.

Abel felt as if he'd been punched in the gut. All his energy evaporated, and he sat motionless thinking of the pathetic girl whose death he was sure he had caused. Why else would anyone bother to kill her? She knew too much. She talked too much. And Abel, knowing both, had led her right down the path.

He had used the girl no less than the men who paid for her time. Except they had only taken her innocence. Abel had taken everything she had.

Dupe's death reminded him that what he did for a living had consequences. Just as they had consequences for his executed friend, Tunde. And her death was a stark reminder that his current assignment wasn't just another story. People were dying. This was the most important thing he had ever done. Certainly the most personal. His debts were mounting. He owed Tunde. He owed Lola. He owed Alice. And now he owed Dupe.

Abel decided he needed to talk to Sergeant Fakorede about the murder. He was the only cop who wouldn't pose behind some official statement, stonewalling.

The clock on his computer's toolbar read 7 p.m. It was Saturday night, but Abel hoped Sergeant Fakorede would still be at work. Since his promotion, Fakorede had become more dedicated to duty and worked longer hours. Abel picked up the phone and dialled. Much to his relief, the Sergeant answered on the third ring.

"Fak," he said unable to keep the sadness from his voice.

"Hei, you sound like you've been hit by a crane," Fakorede answered. "What are you up to?"

Abel dispensed with any pleasantries. "What have you got on the murder of that prostitute last night in the Surulere area?"

"Nothing more than we gave the press. Shot while standing on duty. Random killing. Drive-bys happen all the time down there."

"You're not even looking into it?" Abel said. His facial muscles tightened in anguish. It occurred to him for the first time that either Dupe's room was bugged or he was being watched. Whoever these people were, they were serious.

"What do you care, anyway?" Fakorede asked, a little put out.

"I spoke with the lady three days ago as part of ..."

"Wow, wow," Fakorede interrupted, laughing. "Now, this is getting ridiculous, Abel. You mean you also dip your stuff in there. Ever hear of AIDS? Don't let some condom theory deceive you. The thing is real, my friend!"

"Listen, Fak, she was part of my investigation into that trafficking syndicate," Abel said slowly and pouted his mouth. "The paper reported she was hit seven times. All in the head. Now, the guy who did that must have been an expert, not some monkey hunter. You guys had better check that out."

"Maybe I should tell the Police Commissioner you want to join the police force. Oh, wait. We don't take old guys."

"Funny."

"Seriously, we'll check that angle. But the odds of finding the shooter are pretty slim. A gunman in the dark that nobody saw — you tell me the odds."

"But you'll look?"

"Yeah. What did the girl know that got her killed?"

"She was seen with me. And she told me she thought a businessman named Kehinde Lawal took Alice Udor out of the country."

"Which means Kehinde Lawal isn't around to ask. And was out of the country when the girl was murdered, anyway."

"A syndicate's behind this. They had the girl killed. They're the same people who killed Tunde."

"And of course you have proof of this."

"I feel it in my gut, Fak."

"Strong evidence, my friend. I can hardly wait to tell the Police Commissioner to issue arrest warrants based on your gut." Abel didn't take the bait. He wasn't in a mood for Fakorede's jibes. The policeman must have sensed his anger.

"I'll check into this, all right?"

"Thanks," Abel said and clicked off.

Abel pondered his next move as he plodded to the kitchen to warm his coffee. He couldn't sit and wait for Fakorede to make his inquiries. They might not lead anywhere anyway. The policeman was right. Finding the shooter was unlikely.

Abel took his fresh brew and sat down in front of the computer and poked around on the Internet, reading papers from around the world. What was he looking for? Signs of this slave trade. Murdered girls. Prostitution rings that had been busted. Anything that would point him in a direction.

Tired, he finally gave up and played a few hands of a complex computer solitaire game. It cleared his mind and relaxed him, except when he lost. But he rarely did. He won eighty-six percent of the time. It was a source of great pride, which he shared with nobody. His secret talent.

As Abel shut down the computer, he decided his best lead was Alice's mother, Mary. He must see her tomorrow, first thing.

The streets of Yaba were quiet this Sunday morning, as they had been the Sunday Abel visited Mary's husband, Winston. In sharp contrast to the streets, the First Baptist Church presented Abel with a sea of people beautifully clad in their Sunday best. He fitted right in, sporting a coffee-collared suit, cream shirt and matching tie. Abel was swept along as the worshippers moved inside the church.

Abel hoped Mary would be attending this second late-morning service. He was guessing she'd be here since this was the service she attended while he was sparring with her degenerate husband. And people are creatures of habit. That much Abel had learned in his years as an investigative journalist.

Thinking that only Lady Luck would let him run into Mary in such a large throng, he made his way to a pew at the back of the church, scanning the crowd as he went. From here, Abel hoped to spot Mary. There were two doors that allowed access to the church, and Abel tried to watch both. But this was no mean feat, given that the church seated more than 500 worshippers.

By the time the processional hymn was announced, Mary still

had not arrived, or if she had, he had missed her. He joined the rest of the congregation, standing up as choristers and ministers streamed in from the rear singing, "Stand up, stand up for Jesus." It was one of his favourite hymns at school, so Abel joined in. He liked the check-blue robes of the choristers as he did the dark suits of the ministers. During the five minutes it took for all of them to make their way down the aisle to the altar, Abel watched, wondering if Mary might be among them. But she wasn't.

To his surprise, the act of singing this hymn brought him a feeling of peaceful calm. The first time he had taken an easy breath since he'd read about Dupe's murder the night before. He began to enjoy the service and found himself worshipping with the congregation as if he came every week. In truth, he hadn't been to church in 10 years, since he attended the funeral service of the Publisher's mother. He didn't even worship after his wife died. He was in no mood to converse with God over that little mishap.

After the pastor's opening, the church band led the congregation in praise, singing. Abel sang along heartily, and when others around him spontaneously began to dance, he joined them, losing himself in the physical joy of pure movement devoid of thought.

After some 10 minutes of singing and dancing, a call came for the congregation to shake hands with as many people as possible, singing, "Welcome in Jesus Name" all the while. The call reminded Abel he had a job to do. He had to find Mary. So, he danced and moved as far as he could, pumping hands, looking for the woman.

When he reached the third row from the front, a familiar hand took his. "Oh, you are a Christian?" Mary whispered, forcing a smile on her rather frail face. Even in the shiny blue native dress with matching high head tie, she looked sickly and worried.

"I attend church from time to time, but I am here to see you after the service," Abel whispered back and moved on to the next row. Mary watched him, looking surprised. He smiled at her, trying to put her at ease.

After another round of prayers, the pastor announced thanksgiving envelopes from people who had reason to be grateful to the Lord. These envelopes contained money, donated to the church for charitable uses.

The pastor paused before raising the last envelope. Its bulk caught the congregation's attention. This envelope contained more money than any of the others.

The pastor nodded his head in satisfaction and said, "This is from an anonymous mother who is donating a goodly sum of money, sent by her daughter, who is overseas. In this note attached to the envelope, the concerned mother says her only daughter has been tricked into leaving the country, possibly into prostitution."

He paused and the congregation gasped audibly, the women clucking their sympathy, the men muttering about the crime. The pastor continued.

"This mother wants her daughter back to live a decent life, marry and bear children. The woman who gives this is a poor woman who says she would rather remain in poverty than to have sinful money. She wants us to pray for her daughter to return as soon as possible. Jesus is Lord!"

He nodded his head and sighed as the congregation rose to a thunderous sustained applause.

Abel saw tears in the pastor's eyes as he raised his head and turned to move from the glass pulpit. He cleared his throat noisily and asked the church to pray for the donor for her exemplary behaviour in a country where too many people worship money. Abel heard many in the congregation sob as they prayed for the woman. Abel knew this anonymous mother had to be Mary.

After the service, Abel followed Mary outside.

"You did that? You can hear everybody talking about it," Abel said as he drew level with her in the milling crowd.

"And I feel very relieved," she said, the pain in her eyes ameliorated slightly by a rueful smile. "My husband said it was my share of the money Alice sent to the family." She spoke in a whisper and moved away from the stream of the congregation.

Abel followed in silence into the shade of a mango tree in front of the pastor's residence.

"You are a virtuous woman, Madam. There will be cheers in heaven for what you have done."

Mary didn't seem to care, either about Abel's open admiration or about the purported heavenly reward awaiting her. Instead, she looked at Abel and said simply and directly, "You will find her for me?"

"Yes, I have promised that. But where was the money sent from?"

"My husband wouldn't tell me. He just said she and her guardians are on their way overseas. I'm assuming maybe Mali or somewhere similar. I just want to see her."

"I am sure you will be united again. Yes, Ma."

"Thanks. It looks hopeless now, but I believe God will watch over her. And I want to believe you will bring her back. You are God's instrument."

Being thought of as God's instrument was a heavy mantle to wear, but Abel let it go.

"I will go after Alice this week, but please tell no-one, not even your kids," he said.

At this, Mary looked concerned. "There is danger?"

Abel smiled at her, again attempting to put her at ease. She didn't need to know everything he knew. She was suffering enough already.

"I do not trust your husband, dear lady." Abel reached into his pocket and withdrew his wallet. He offered her all the money he had there.

"This is money from a decent source in place of what you have given God," he said. "I will try to provide more later."

She slipped the money into her old black bag. Emotion caught words in her throat. "I will pray for you," she said.

Abel watched her walk through the church gate and out of the yard. He wished he could publish a story about Mary's selfless act in *The Zodiac* the following day. But of course that was out of the question. It might enrage Winston and worse, it might draw the syndicate's attention. And this syndicate did not hesitate to silence anyone who threw light on their illegal business. He would not martyr the woman.

Back in his car, he called Chief Benson. "I know it is Sunday, Sir, but can I see you now?"

"Sure, Abel boy. I'm in the office," Benson responded. That he was in his office on a Sunday did not surprise Abel. The man

119

worked seven days a week. The paper was his life. And as much as Abel often wished his boss would slow down and attend to his health, today he was grateful for Benson's workaholic nature.

"Good afternoon, Sir." Abel greeted Chief Benson with a slight bow, which did not stop his boss from roaring with laughter at his appearance. Abel realised he had not changed since attending church services and must appear overdressed for such a casual visit.

"What are you doing, dressed like this on a Sunday?" Benson asked amid more laughter and a dry cough. "Now come in and shut the door," his boss said without waiting for an answer. He ambled towards the set of black leather settees in the far corner of the office where he hosted visitors.

"Boss, you have always wished me to dress like a gentleman," Abel reminded him as he turned the key to lock the door.

"But you seldom did, Abel. Now would you tell me what is going on?" Benson said as he slumped onto the long sofa moving aside an open copy of *Today's Publisher*. Abel noted that Benson was always reading something, always thinking about the business, looking for ways to stay ahead of the competition.

"Boss, watch your ribs, but I went to church to ..."

"You what? Holy Moses!" Chief Benson threw his head back laughing heartily.

"Boss, yes, I went to church after many years and I am happy to say I left with an urge to reconnect with God."

Benson watched his friend and employee. He knew this wasn't all there was to the story.

"But why did you go in the first place?" he asked.

"To meet the missing girl's mother, Mary Udor," Abel said.

"Aha, I was wondering whether you weren't the Abel I knew." He sighed and sat up straighter. "Now, have they found the girl?"

"Not as yet, Chief. She or her masters have started sending money home to her parents..."

"She is gone!" Chief Benson cut in, dismayed at the realisation that Alice was already abroad.

"They may still be in transit. But I figure they sent the money to calm her parents. Look, the important thing, Chief, is that this anguished mother, Mary Udor, donated her share of that money to the church and asked for prayers for her only daughter to return home."

"What!"

"Yes, Chief, I wouldn't have believed it if I was not there to witness it. In a church the only time they clap is for an offering to God. For a good two minutes the congregation stood clapping for this woman."

"Wonderful!" Chief Benson reached for a half-drunk glass of soda at his feet.

"Unfortunately, she did it anonymously or it would have been a good story for tomorrow."

"You fear if we expose her name she will be in danger?"

"Tunde is dead. And the prostitute I spoke with is also dead. What do you think?"

Chief Benson nodded in agreement.

"What about an editorial to commend this rare action? We wouldn't name her, but it would give the church some good publicity. Who knows? Maybe your church-going has paid off somehow."

"Paid off for the church and for me, Boss. I felt the touch of God, the only one who can forgive all sins and offer one a clean slate for a fresh start ..."

"Okay, enough. Sit down, preacher man." Benson waved Abel onto the two-seater to his left. "You will write the editorial today."

"Yes, I will. But really, I came to tell you I will leave on Wednesday in search of Alice. I want to bring her home to tell her story."

He looked at Benson for approval, but for once, he saw his boss avert his eyes. In the long silence that followed Abel was not certain about getting an affirmative answer.

Benson took a sip of his soda, thinking. When he finally spoke, it was slowly, and he still avoided Abel's eyes.

"Peter Abel, I have been giving this whole subject some serious thought. So long as your country refuses to offer jobs to these poor people, nothing will stop them from going. Remember, they repatriate planeloads of them from time to time, but it does not stop others from going in their places. And bringing Alice home will not stop the trade." He engaged Abel's eyes briefly, perhaps expecting his employee to object, but instead Abel chose to hear out his boss. He remained silent so Benson continued.

"We have enough information to mount an effective campaign in *The Zodiac*. I would rather you not go on a wild-goose chase. Besides, if you find the girl, does she even want to leave this syndicate? And even if she wanted to return home, could you get her away from them?"

He stopped to have another sip of soda, as if the argument had exhausted him. When Abel didn't respond immediately, Benson prompted him.

"Don't just sit there staring at me," he said. "I know you have something to say. Go ahead."

Abel stood up and began to pace. It helped him organise his thoughts.

"Chief, I could write about the thousands of women trafficked abroad, but it would only be a string of statistics. Just numbers. But if I can report the experience of one victim and her family, it might leave a strong emotional impression. It would shrink the big picture down to a single human story. Our readers could relate to these people. If my experience in the church today is worth an editorial, then believe me, we will have an award-winning story reporting about Alice. She could become a poster child for the abused. With the public aroused, we might bring down the entire syndicate. The government would have no choice but to act more decisively. Already, there are some organisations and even a government agency trying to check this slave trade, but I guess they need more support. Fighting syndicates is a war!"

Benson watched Abel, and Abel saw the admiration in his face. He knew Benson liked his passion, thought it made him a great reporter. Abel felt confident that if the girl could be saved, he was the only one who could do it.

Before Benson could speak, Abel cleared his throat politely and continued "And Chief, remember that I once had an adorable sister like Alice. Her death devastated me."

Benson reacted as if he hadn't considered this angle, but the minute Abel mentioned the trauma of losing his sister, he nodded.

"I understand. You must find Alice in memory of your own lost sister."

Abel buried his head in his palms.

Almost moved to tears, Chief Benson got up and put a hand on his friend's shoulder. "Okay, Abel, you have made a compelling case." He then went to his desk.

When he returned moments later, he handed Abel a company credit card. Abel took it and the two men hugged.

"You can still do the editorial?" Benson asked as they separated.

"This afternoon." Abel stopped and thought a moment. "I don't know why I can't get over my sister's death. It's been years. I was a child when she died." His voice shook with emotion.

"I don't know, Peter. I wouldn't expect you to get over it. But a piece of advice. Embark on this assignment as a reporter, not as some vengeance-seeking Rambo. Keep your wits sharp." With that, Benson offered him his big warm hand.

"You never forget the rules of the game, Boss." Abel took his hand with a satisfied smile. He was back on the trail.

CHAPTER SIXTEEN

Abel spent a sleepless night confirming the routes favoured by traffickers who moved girls surreptitiously out of Nigeria. He already had narrowed his search to two: Mali, which Mary had suggested, and the Canary Islands.

Figures he had from Spanish sources showed that human trafficking through the Canary Islands was favoured by many. But there were other routes almost as popular via the Sahara Desert and Gibraltar Straits. He had ruled out the Benin Republic – Libya – Malta route because of the reported hostility of Libyan authorities to immigrants from West Africa.

The thought of Alice being taken by boat out of Nigeria was terrifying. On the Canary Islands route alone, a total of 14 boats ferrying illegal immigrants sank in 2004; 80 corpses were retrieved and 339 people were rescued. Many others simply disappeared.

Any choice Abel made was a weak one, largely dependent on luck. But Abel often had been lucky. He remembered the old saying, "Luck is the residue of good design." Plan smartly and good things will happen. That had always worked for him. He prayed it would work now.

Abel pondered starting his search in the Canaries. While he had always been captivated by the allure of the island group's eternal springtime, choice hotels and water games, he also felt this was the most logical route from Nigeria. It was possible Alice was still in the Canaries. In a short span of time, she had earned enough to send money home. It was possible she had been put to work. If so, Abel had time to catch up. He booked his flight that afternoon and boarded a plane the next morning.

Abel arrived at Tenerife Reina Sofia airport on a British Airways flight via London two days after the emotional encounter with his boss. He took a taxi straight to the four-star Vulcano Hotel, which he found delightful. Arranged around two swimming pools, the structure was nestled in sub-tropical gardens.

The hotel was a mere 300 metres from the beach in southern Tenerife's most popular tourist destination, Playas de Las Américas. The Vulcano's modern, cream décor with dark wood furniture and warm fabrics was to his taste. The lobby was large and the receptionists in similarly collared cream uniforms were exceptionally warm. The pretty young woman smiled as she handed him his room key.

"We will do everything to make you comfortable, Mr. Abel," she said.

An efficient bellboy led Abel to his double-bed air-conditioned room, which had a furnished balcony overlooking one of the swimming pools. A large central fountain filled the air with the continuous sound of rushing water. It had no doubt been placed there to make the guests feel they were in the presence of a jungle waterfall. And when Abel closed his eyes, he could almost picture the serene setting. If only he were here for pleasure. If only this idyllic island did not harbour such dark practices.

Soon after the bellboy departed, Abel took a quick shower and retired to the rocking chair on the balcony. He found one local newspaper among the three complementary papers provided by the hotel. Its headline struck him immediately: "Another 13 Die at Sea."

He read the story with interest: *13 people died after a makeshift boat carrying 23 passengers ran into difficulties off Spain's Canary Islands, according to the rescue services. Rescuers said five more passengers were in critical condition, having drifted at sea for more than a week without food and only meagre supplies of fresh water. Apparently, the victims were all illegals attempting to reach the Canary Islands. The boat was intercepted by a naval vessel some 150 miles off the island of Hierro, the most south-westerly of the island chain in the North Atlantic.*

The story only confirmed what Abel's research had told him. The Canary Islands was a crossroads for traffickers and other illegals. And many who tried to find their way here did not make it. Abel felt he had made the right choice in beginning his search here. To this end, he decided to familiarise himself with as much of the area as possible before talking to people.

He strolled outside to consider a plan. The evening was cool and mildly windy. As he walked the grounds, people in casual holiday clothes streamed past giggling and chatting excitedly. Attractive young ladies clung romantically to men who might have been paying for the company. It reminded him of what he read before his trip. There were nearly 30,000 British prostitutes in Tenerife. They were known locally as Diana Prostitutes, and they financed their vacation fun by sleeping with men for money. A website he had visited described this as typical British behaviour. He had no idea what that meant, but since the website was established by someone with a French name, he suspected cultural bias. The British and the French had been trading abuse over the ages.

As he walked the grounds, Abel took a closer look at the outdoor swimming pools, which were overlooked by sun terraces, complete with loungers and parasols. Curvaceous women in swimsuits always attracted his attention, but this evening there weren't many of them in the pools, much to his disappointment. He was tempted to swim, but he promptly killed the notion with a mental reprimand. This wasn't a pleasure trip.

He walked on, hands in the pockets of his roomy black slacks, to the beach some three hundred metres away. Few people remained on the beach. He found a quiet area behind an outcropping of rocks, an isolated spot where he could do some breathing exercises. He had to come up with a plan for finding Alice, and breathing exercises always helped him focus.

After 30 minutes of this, he returned to his room and took a seat on the balcony to refine his plans. He became thoroughly engrossed, and didn't want to interrupt his thinking to go to the restaurant for dinner. Instead, he called room service and ordered rabbit with some local sauces and potatoes. His choice was out of adventure, rather than taste. He'd never had rabbit before, but he enjoyed the meal.

A lady with a toothy smile came by to collect the plates after dinner. As Abel watched her she turned to him: "Mr. Abel, I hope this is not how you want to spend your time on the island of fun. You came to rest or something?"

"Not really. I am just taking some rest before plunging into the fun. But why do you ask?" Abel looked at her more closely. She was a half-caste with a mix of African and Caucasian features. Her long nose sat well on her long face. Her hair was worn in African-style cornrows. Also African was her heavy bum. Abel noticed her large breasts for the first time, as she stood straight up, tray in hand.

"I have to go now, but when you want to be shown around, look for me. I'm Susan," she said almost in a whisper.

"I will, Susan, but I know you ladies are barred from consorting with hotel guests," he said.

"Yes, but the rule applies only in the hotel," she said, as if prepared for his objection. She left, walking provocatively out of his door. Just before disappearing, she turned and flashed him an enchanting smile.

"I will remember the offer," Abel said without thinking.

She nodded and disappeared.

Abel shook his head, getting back to the work at hand. Too many distractions! "I don't need some female guide," he muttered and poured himself a cup of coffee.

Abel had decided he needed to get a feel of the country. One of the tourist pamphlets in his room had recommended sight-seeing flights over the islands. As he dressed for bed, he called the concierge and made a reservation.

By seven the following morning Abel had eaten breakfast and hired a hotel cab to take him to the offices of Overfly Limited near the airport.

Business at Overfly was brisk. Five minutes after he arrived at the huge compound, Abel found himself in the rear of a six-seat Augusta helicopter. He had to pay for the vacant seats. His pilot was a lanky Spaniard with scruffy unkempt hair. The man appeared to have a hangover, not something you want to see in a man with your life in his hands. Abel tried to ignore it.

Abel sat in one of the back seats next to the tour guide, Charles Capel who told Abel he was from Birmingham, England. Capel was tall and trim and spiked his hair like a rocker. He had found Abel's decision to pay for empty seats curious, but as he confessed later, they did offer such private services to rich people. Now, he chatted away, trying to engage Abel in affable banter, assuring him of the safety and exhilaration of helicopter travel. Abel let him prattle, without saying that this wasn't his first time in a helicopter. Abel had taken helicopter tours of both the Victoria Falls in East Africa and the Grand Canyon in Arizona. Moreover, Abel wasn't in a mood to chat and said as much to Capel as they strapped their seat belts.

"All right, sport," Capel said and licked his lips. "I'll do the talking, and you can just relax."

Abel donned his headset with microphones, so he could hear the tour guide and the pilot and ask questions over the din of the chopper's engine noise.

"This is how we go," Capel said. "We are in Tenerife. We will fly north to the island of La Palma, then south to Hiero, right to Gomera and over Gran Canaria, almost a straight line to the right to Fuerteventura, and north to Lanzarote. And that would be the entire archipelago. Okay?"

"Fine," Abel said with a nod.

The pilot paid no attention to them, occupying himself with the instrument panel and then with firing up the engine.

Capel started his canned lecture once the chopper was airborne: "The Canary Islands are an archipelago of seven islands of volcanic origin in the Atlantic Ocean, off the northwestern coast of Africa ..."

Abel zoned out as he studied the islands below, looking hard for what?

"Tenerife is the largest of the islands."

Abel was thinking about Alice who might be somewhere down there, plying her trade under the authority of human scum.

Capel's tour bled in on Abel's thoughts now and then: "During the Spanish conquest, the island was divided up into nine distinct menceyatos, and each developed its own architecture and culture. Although the island is now united, its broken landscape is indicative of its diverse flora ..."

Abel watched several small craft on the water below, imagining Alice clinging to a spar, adrift after some disaster.

"Any questions?"

Abel realised he hadn't been listening and so could have no questions. He looked at his bored guide and smiled as if he'd absorbed every word, then shook his head. No questions. Abel turned his attention back to the vast stretch of water below.

After skimming across a rather calm sea with yachts sprinkled here and there, they arrived over La Palma. Capel cast a quick look at Abel and continued: "Palma, as some of us call it, is known for its spectacularly lush vegetation ..." Abel could see this for himself. He scanned the bright green jungle for signs of someone or something partially hidden. But he spotted nothing suspicious.

From there they flew south to Hiero, across to La Gomera, then to Gran Canaria. "Also known as the miniature continent ..." Capel was saying. Abel perked up when Capel mentioned the "big city bustle" of the capital, Las Palmas. *A likely place for prostitutes*, Abel thought. Certainly more likely than the other island, what's its name, which was covered in thick forest and showed little civilisation.

They next circled over Fuerteventura, which Capel identified as the second largest of the islands. But Abel immediately lost interest when he heard it was the least-populated island. Again, you couldn't get rich on prostitutes without a large supply of clients, making Fuerteventura an unlikely place to find Alice. However, when Capel mentioned that this island had a "heavy immigrant population," Abel made note of that anomaly. Perhaps she had landed there initially, then was transferred to a more populated area. It was all speculation of course, but Abel was trying to narrow his search.

"Lanzarote, a land of a thousand volcanoes, is an eco-tourist's delight!" Capel seemed to perk up as they flew over this rugged landscape, as if he'd finally found a subject that interested him. He finished his enthusiastic recitation extolling the "wonderful climate" and "lunar-like landscape," then turned to Abel. "I hope you enjoyed our tour. Now, we will return to the capital island."

"No!" Abel shook his head.

Capel looked at him, eyes widening in concern for the suddenly uncooperative passenger.

"Is something the matter?" Capel asked almost gingerly.

Abel realised he had come on too strongly. He smiled, trying to reassure his nervous host.

"I'd love to overfly the Strait of Gibraltar. It isn't very far from here, is it? It is important to me."

Capel narrowed his eyes and looked at the man as if he suspected Abel might have something other than tourism on his mind.

"That's not part of the package," he said.

Abel noticed the pilot was already making a turn back like a horse smelling the barn. He'd have to move quickly. "I'll pay whatever the extra charge is, even for the empty seats."

The pilot, who had been an uninterested party until now, turned towards them.

"The route of the chopper is recorded," he said, annoyed. "What's your interest anyway?"

Abel affected a look of great sadness. "I am a businessman who has lost the love of his life. My fiancée, she is so young and so beautiful, but I did not pay her enough attention. I have reason to fear that she came here with another man, who does not have the best reputation. I am afraid she might fall in with the wrong elements. I want only to find her, make things up with her, take her home and make her my wife. I must see all the places where she might be. Please. I beg you."

It was a huge lie, but Abel could not reveal the truth to people he didn't know. He thought his "confession" might be a way to get the pilot's attention. And it did. The pilot turned and looked at him with genuine concern.

"The Strait is becoming notorious as a place to bring in illegal young women who are then turned out as prostitutes," he said.

Abel took heart from the man's tone. It was obvious he was offended by such activities.

Abel said, "And of course the reputation of your gorgeous islands is getting stained by dead bodies from drowned immigrants who wash up on your beaches."

Finally, the pilot nodded. "I will take you, but you pay extra."

"Of course," Abel assured him. "I'll pay."

Capel had remained silent throughout these negotiations. But he stroked his temple, his eye fixed on the pilot as he made a turn north to the Strait. Abel wondered what he was thinking. Was he unhappy about being upstaged? Did he have some pressing appointment? Or was this a subject that made him uncomfortable?

The pilot interrupted Abel's thoughts.

"As a Spaniard, I worry about the archipelago becoming a popular route for traffickers. Look at that recent tragedy. Thirteen Africans drowned. The police said some of them were from Nigeria." He looked at Abel. "That's your country, right?"

"You don't sound Spanish, Mr. ..."

"My name is Aleck. Charles should have introduced me, but he still thinks I slept with his girl last week."

Capel glared at the pilot, not amused. Aleck continued. "I don't need to steal his girl. There are more ladies here than grains of sand on the beach." He laughed.

Abel couldn't tell if this rivalry was friendly or not. But he sensed he and Aleck were kindred spirits. Abel made a mental note of the pilot's name. He strongly suspected he would want to enlist the man's aid at some future time. He obviously knew the territory well, and might be willing to show Abel around, take him places Abel could not find on his own.

"I take it you've lived abroad," Abel said to the pilot, making conversation. "You have an unusual accent, not at all like a Spaniard."

Aleck laughed again. "You have a very good ear. In fact, I have lived most of my life working for Bristol all over the world as a chopper pilot. Oil fields mostly. But I retired last year. At my age, I find this job less strenuous. And it leaves me more time for the nice ladies, but only for those who like me for myself, not for my money, if you get the idea."

He winked at Abel, probably hoping to needle Capel. The Englishman finally jumped in, trying to staunch the flow of jokes at his expense.

"He thinks he's God's gift to women. If he only knew what they say behind his back. Anyway, let me give you the tour here, Mr. Abel. It's my job, not Aleck's."

Aleck grunted mockingly. "Go ahead, boy. You are paid to do that."

Capel turned to Abel, his body language attempting to shut Aleck out of the conversation. They struck Abel as two quarrelling lovers.

"Mr. Abel, if trafficking is your interest, I am wondering whether you need to see the Straits at all. The route to Fuerteventura and Lanzarote has become an alternative to attempting the currents of the Straits."

"What happened to those 13 poor souls who drowned is typical Gibraltar revenge," Aleck added. "You try to cross her, you die."

"I'm telling the story," Capel snapped. He turned back to Abel.

"It is true, though. Those victims started their journey from a beach near the town of el-Aioun, in the Moroccan-run Western Sahara, 60 miles from Fuerteventura. El-Aioun is also becoming a congregating point for people from all over Africa looking for entry points into Europe. They come in shallow Moroccan fishing boats, with total disregard for safety. It is horrible, really."

Abel was interested in any information having to do with attempts to breach the European shores from Africa, any route on which Alice might have been taken. Abel wanted to encourage Capel to disclose more.

"Why does this trouble you?" he said.

"The spiral effects are an alarming threat to our business and to the economy here. Tourism drives the economy and, of course, that is what Aleck and I live on. With dead bodies washing up on local beaches, tourism is at risk. The police become unnecessarily edgy with the growing number of migrants. And of course, many of the migrants are unable to continue because of the vigilance of the police and immigration officers. Instead of moving on to Europe, they get stuck here and become a drain on our economy."

"As they do wherever they settle," Abel said.

Capel took his lead and warmed to the subject. "We want people with money to come visit, not illegals who become penniless beggars! Summer is the worst. There are more attempts by the immigrants on summer nights. It is warm, and the water is calm. In the winter, everything ceases."

Abel took in the implications of Capel's diatribe. He tried to weed out the racist flavour and heartless attitude and distil it to something useful to his own search.

"So, Fuerteventura and Lanzarote likely have large numbers of stranded migrants?" Abel asked. He wondered if Alice was waiting in the Canaries for more favourable weather.

"You've got it," Capel said. "If you want the fun African stuff, surely that is where to go. There and Playas de Las Americas." Then, remembering Abel's lie about a fiancée, Capel apologised. "I'm sorry, Sir. I did not mean to imply that your lady friend is there."

"It's fine," Abel said. "My intention is to find my fiancée, not to exploit others. But to find her, I think, I have to know where to look."

"That is Capel for you," Aleck said. "Always opening his mouth before he engages his brain." He pointed out the chopper's front window. "But you wanted to see it, and here's the Strait."

The chopper flew over the body of water as they moved away from the coastline.

"Great," Abel said. He heard the excitement in his voice. "Aleck, can you show it to me from as many angles as possible?"

"Part of the service you are paying for. No problem."

Capel took up his narrative. "We're about a kilometre to the west of the mouth of the Strait. Look left. That's Spain. See the Rock of Gibraltar?"

Abel spotted the rock, then pointed to a town nearby. "What's that place?"

"Tarifa. Entry point for the immigrants."

Abel studied the town, thinking about what he had just heard. Then Capel pointed out the other side.

"Morocco's over there. The Strait is about 13 kilometres across at its narrowest point. Deep water. Tricky currents. You wonder why people take the risk to cross in ramshackle boats." He shrugged, then answered his own question. "Desperation probably."

Abel turned from Capel, whose cool detached observation made him sad. The landmass from both countries looked like parted knuckles, and the contrast of Western architecture on the Spanish side from the Arabian architecture of Morocco should have been thrilling. But he was numbed by the thought of anguished drowning migrants.

Capel must have read his mood because he fell silent, and the guided tour came to an end.

After a few minutes of observing the area from the circling chopper, Abel spoke to the pilot. "We can go back, Aleck."

133

All the way back to Tenerife, Abel was haunted by so many "ifs":

If Africa had more responsible leadership; if people had been less greedy; if there was proper education about the risks on the route. And somewhere in all these hypothetical questions was a very real girl in real danger.

Abel returned to his hotel room a tired and emotionally drained man. He called for lunch and soaked himself in an herbal bath soon after eating. He needed a respite from the anxiety he carried around with him. He decided that night he would take what the Islands so proudly offered: a slice of hedonistic pleasure.

He had read about the fun to be had here: *"Night time is an experience in "Las Americas" where just about anything goes. The place to head to is the central stretch of "Veronicas." This is where you'll find the best night clubs and streets packed with huge crowds of revellers who party into the early hours of every morning."*

And he also hoped with a faint ache, that he might, by some miracle, run into Alice on one of those street corners.

Abel set out just after eight p.m. for Playas de Las Americas determined to kill many birds with one stone. He had chosen La Flo Nightclub, which offered an international male and female escort service, as well as erotic massage. He had read that although the Spanish government had outlawed prostitution, it thrived in the clubs. And La Flo was openly boastful about its array of beautiful girls. Abel couldn't argue with this.

Dressed in a white silk shirt and trousers, Abel stepped into the club and looked around. He was struck by the leopard skin colours and leafy ceiling decor. After surveying the interior and getting his bearings, he chose a stool at the bar and ordered a beer.

The place was hardly jumping with action. He thought perhaps he was too early. There were only 20 customers at the long bar. But before he could finish the first tall glass of brew, the place suddenly filled up.

Abel noticed there were many girls there, all as beautiful as if they had been cast in a film. Some of them made passes at him as they swarmed the bar ordering all manner of drinks. Of the lot, there were only two Africans, but they were of exceptional beauty.

After ordering his second beer, Abel stood up so he could see the whole room, now crowded and noisy.

Almost immediately, a 20-something white woman, whose breasts spilled generously out of a tight, low cut blouse, arrived before him. Bending toward him, she asked pointedly, "You are alone?" Apparently nobody stood on ceremony here.

"For now," he said flatly.

"You are sure she is not standing you up? There are lots of us here to offer company to handsome men like you." She sat down slowly, took a sip of what looked like brandy and licked her lips. "Whoever you are waiting for, I'm better."

Abel had to admit her directness was a turn on, but he wasn't looking for a white lady. He wanted a black woman who would volunteer information. He smiled thinly at her. She took the hint, shrugged and moved on to the next man she saw.

Abel looked around for more black women, but he had only seen two. And they were engaged with some obviously turned-on burly white guys.

Abel turned around and almost bumped into the white woman who had just approached him. Apparently, she struck out with her next target, too.

"I'm still available." She smiled at Abel.

"Tough night?"

"I'll hook up sooner or later. Always do. Sure you don't want to party?"

"Maybe another time. I'm going for a massage." He started to leave.

"Well, make sure you get the erotic one," she winked at him.

"That's why I'm here, my dear." Abel turned and moved away to the entrance marked "Erotic."

He pushed past some potted plants and entered a small sitting room where three ladies waited. They offered him a nice variety: an African, a Caucasian and an Asian. Curvy in white bras and white towels tied from their waist down, they looked stunning.

"There are three massage rooms on the left," the Asian said. "You choose your kind of lady and she will take you in."

All the women were appealing, but the black lady had the most generous bust, and large breasts always took the prize where Abel was concerned. He would also get some information from her.

"I'll take this lovely lady," Abel said indicating the black masseuse. She smiled and led the way down the hall. Her legs were hot.

The room painted white was warm enough and dimly lit. Soft music drifted from some unseen speaker. Abel noticed the air smelled of mild incense. His escort suggested he take a hot bath to open the pores. It would, she assured him, make the massage feel twice as relaxing.

After his bath, he lay down on a table and shut his eyes. Abel felt soft, tender hands on his upper and lower back.

"As you breathe, imagine with each breath that you are sinking lower and lower into the table," the masseuse said soothingly.

Moments later, she stood up for something and said, "Now, I'm going to run a feather over your back. Put all your awareness into the place where the feather is touching you."

Abel gave himself over to the sensations, and for the moment all his worries dissolved. He knew, of course, that tomorrow, the hunt would begin again, but for now, he was content.

Abel left the massage table after an hour feeling very refreshed, and with a lighter head capable of focusing better. He had decided to relax instead of asking questions for a lead on Alice. He made his way to the bar, where a striptease was under way on stage. The performer was a voluptuous black lady called Black Panther.

Abel didn't find her seductive enough to watch very long. Instead, he went for another beer, and found a place to stand at the back of the club. From here he could scan the patrons, looking for black ladies. By now there were six blacks in evidence, but they were older, at least in their mid-twenties. None was Alice.

As he sipped his beer, he thought about his helicopter ride and the womanising pilot, Aleck. It occurred to Abel that such a man might be useful to him. Perhaps he would know where the prostitutes hung out and who might run them. He would try to find the man's number in the morning. For now, he was content to finish his beer in peace and return to the hotel. He felt a strong urge to lie down and sleep. It would be the last good sleep he would have for some time.

CHAPTER SEVENTEEN

Abel woke up at eight a.m. refreshed and feeling stronger than he had in some time. Certain about his plans to use Aleck as a guide, he called the chopper office before ordering breakfast.

A lady who answered on the fourth ring said Aleck was not in the office but she would find him if Abel wanted. She sounded as if she hoped he'd say no. Abel disappointed her. "That would be great," he said. "Tell him it is the man he flew over the Straits yesterday. I'll hold on."

Abel heard her sigh before putting him on hold. He must have interrupted something important.

A couple of minutes later, she came back on and said she was connecting him to Aleck. After an audible click, Abel heard Aleck's cheerful voice.

"Hey, man. You want another chopper ride? This time we leave the Brit behind."

"No. I want you to show me some of the seedier areas of town."

"You want help looking for your fiancée?"

Abel trusted this man. He thought at some point soon he would tell Aleck the truth. But not now, not over the phone.

"Her name is Alice," Abel said. "You have some spare time after work today?"

"So, I guess you like my suggestion about her being with other stranded migrants."

"Yeah, I've been giving it some thought. Makes sense. Can you take me?"

"Sure. I'll show you every hell hole we have. All shapes and sizes of women. All condemned to a lousy life."

"If you disapprove so vehemently, how do you know so much?" Abel said.

"You know the expression," Aleck said. "Know your enemy. I'll see you at seven."

"Room 313 at Vulcano." Abel clanged the receiver.

Abel took breakfast quickly and decided to spend the day talking to some of the stranded migrants. Maybe he'd get lucky.

Abel was relieved when the cab ride to the capital went quickly. As they entered the city, Abel thought back to the ride he'd taken in Lagos the day of Tunde's murder. He thought of the heavy rains and the bumper-to-bumper traffic jam. And of Tunde's ears in the plastic evidence bag. And of the heartbroken Lola. He was a world away now, but only in body. In spirit, he was still trying to wake up from the nightmare that had begun that rainy afternoon.

He should go to London soon. Armed with new information, he should ask Lola if she remembered anything that might help him, anything Tunde might have told her that didn't get into his newspaper story.

Traffic became more congested once they reached the port area of Plaza de Espana, the town's real centre. Suddenly, the streets were lively and the cars plentiful. It looked to Abel as if most of the town's population had poured into these few blocks abutting the water.

As they drove through the crowded streets, Abel admired the picturesque port, surrounded by high rocks and dotted with cruisers from all over the world.

Once he'd paid the cab driver, he strolled around the area, admiring the mix of old and modern architecture. He'd read in a guidebook that this part of town was host to many of the island's immigrants. And after taking a cup of coffee at a small café, he began his search in earnest.

Abel spent the next few hours talking to street vendors and shop clerks, school children and ladies selling bunches of flowers. He showed each person Alice's picture and retold the same lie. She was his fiancée, who'd run away. He wanted to find her and proclaim his undying love. As he'd hoped, most people wanted to help reunite the star-crossed lovers. This willingness didn't translate into any results. Nobody recognised Alice's picture.

Finally, he overheard a man's voice behind him and recognised the accent as Nigerian. Abel turned to find a young man of about 30. A ragtag sort, he wore a loose brown shirt over a pair of dirty worn jeans. The outgrowth of short white hair from his temple growing down to his chin suggested he had not shaved for days. As the man began to walk away, Abel noted he had a pronounced limp. Abel moved to his side.

"I hear from your accent that you are a Nigerian from Akwa Ibom State."

The man looked at him, surprised, then laughed.

"Yes," the man nodded. "I am Thomas Iko. And I hear from your accent you are also Nigerian."

Abel gestured to a table outside an outdoor café.

"Let me buy a fellow countryman a cup of coffee," he said. The stranger nodded, grateful, and took a seat. As Abel sat down he said, "Would you like something to eat as well?"

Thomas eased himself slowly into the chair, and coughed harshly. "Yes," he said, "but I would rather have the money to go treat myself. I am ill."

"Don't worry, you will have both!"

Thomas's eye widened with surprise. They ordered tapas and *Cokes*, and Thomas fell into silence. Abel let him rest until the food arrived. Thomas thanked Abel and wolfed it down. Abel observed this with mixed emotions. He was sorry for him, but he was just the kind of person who would tell Abel anything for a little food and some cash.

"So what are you doing here in this condition? You must be in transit to mainland Spain?"

"If I can get there. Perhaps you could help me out? I would be forever grateful."

"Well, we'll see. I'd like to hear your story first." He pushed the can of *Coke* Thomas had forgotten towards him.

He took a long sip, paused to catch his breath and began his tale:

"Truly, I am lucky to be alive. I paid 120,000 naira for a trip aboard a fishing vessel from Calabar to Spain. Of course, this is Spain, but we were assured we were going to the mainland, Madrid or Barcelona, but here I am." He swallowed, tears welling in his eyes.

Abel didn't want to interrupt his emotional outpouring and so he only shook his head slightly.

Thomas swallowed again and continued, "You wouldn't believe it, but I read Business Administration at the University of Calabar. For two years I looked for a decent job to take care of my wife and two kids. Nothing. No work. So, finally, I decided to come to Spain. I spent the last of my money for the passage. But after two months on that vessel, where I was abused terribly, here I am. I don't even have the courage to tell my wife where I am. Thank God for the Red Cross or I would have died."

"Oh, the Red Cross takes care of people like yourself?" Abel saw an opening he could not miss.

"Yes, but there is only so much they can do. Most of us work construction for a pittance. It is difficult, back-breaking work, with long hours and many accidents."

"And the women?"

"Most of them have been forced into prostitution."

"Oh, what a pity!"

"Yes, it is. Some of them look very unhappy and they cry all day, but they don't seem to have any choice." He gulped some more *Coke*.

Encouraged by the flow of their conversation, Abel ordered two more soft drinks.

They sat in silence as they were served. Thomas looked livelier and Abel felt he was getting valuable information for his modest investment. He decided it was time to ask him about Alice.

"You are lucky to be married. Some of us are not so lucky. In spite of our wealth my fiancée suddenly lost interest in me and left the country with some agent."

Thomas looked at him, suspicious.

"I have nothing to do with those men!" He appeared suddenly afraid of Abel, who put a reassuring hand on his arm.

"Of course not, Thomas. But I have been here for a while looking all over for her. And I am prepared to pay any amount of compensation to whoever is holding her. I must have her back. I love her."

Life returned to Thomas. He sat forward and seized the *Coke* can, taking a sip. Thomas saw an opportunity to make some real money. "You will pay anything to have her back?"

Abel nodded. "The traffickers who use this route must have a leader here, don't they?" He pulled out a bundle of Euros from his pocket, making sure Thomas got a good look at it.

Clearly Thomas wasn't going to pass up this chance. "Emm, you must be talking about The Lion," Thomas said slowly.

"And who is that?"

"He controls all the trafficking. He arranges for the boats to ferry migrants to mainland Spain. Of course I have never had the money to pay him for the passage."

Abel peeled off five twenty Euro notes and handed them to Thomas. "There's more if you take me to The Lion. Can you take me to him, Thomas?"

Thomas looked at him without answering. "What did you say your name is?"

"Amballo. Peter Amballo. I'm a businessman from Lagos."

Thomas closed his red, tired eyes thinking about Abel's story, which he seemed reluctant to believe, either out of fear or doubt. Clearly if he took the wrong person to see The Lion, he would be in deep trouble. Abel knew he might be putting Thomas in danger if The Lion discovered who he really was. But this was the game he had chosen to play. And he couldn't worry about Thomas.

"Who is this lucky woman?" Thomas asked, still trying to gauge Abel's true motives.

"I hear they don't use their real names, but she is Alice," Abel kissed the passport picture he fetched from his pocket and put it on the table.

Thomas looked at the photo, then shook his head: "No, I have not met her. It is so unlikely ..."

"I know. They say about 80,000 people have used this route in recent times."

"The Lion may know something about her." Thomas finally made up his mind. Money no doubt overrode any fears he might have. Money did that to people, as Abel well knew.

"And where do we find him?" Abel put the passport photo back in his pocket and signalled a waiter for their bill.

"San Marcus. South of here."

"Isn't that one of the wealthiest neighbourhoods in the capital?"

Abel stood up to hail a taxicab.

"Yes. He is not a poor man." Thomas joined him in the back seat of the cab.

After an hour's ride in the small Peugeot 206, Abel and Thomas finally arrived at their destination. The mansion, which sported panoramic views, sat on the quiet outskirts of the old market town of Icod de Los Vinos. That the Lion lived in an exclusive area did not surprise Abel. Czars of such syndicates lead luxurious hedonistic lives. As Abel took in the opulence, the shimmering pools and lush gardens surrounded by electrified security gates, he thought of the desiccated neighbourhoods where this man's whores were forced to work. Their labour paid for all this. *No*, Abel thought, *it wasn't only their labour that paid for it. Their lives were the true price.*

A tall, dark-skinned muscular man standing guard waved them through when he heard they had come on business. Abel submitted to a pat down before he was allowed inside. There was a price to pay for all this luxury after all.

"Some dude wants to sail," Abel heard the guard say to someone over an intercom. He then flung the gates open to a beautifully terraced driveway at the end of which sat a large house.

Abel left Thomas with the driver and walked inside, trying to show as much casual confidence as he could muster. The whole set-up was intimidating and was meant to be. Abel had to admit it worked.

The large tastefully furnished living room was done in predominantly blue and white-striped colours. No expense had been spared. A muscular butler served Abel coffee. He wondered if everybody on staff had to be a gorilla. As Abel looked at the man's imposing biceps, The Lion entered. He wore a blue morning robe and his eyes were blood-shot. A late night and lots of liquor, no doubt. And some great-looking young girl in his bed. Abel couldn't help but feel envious, if only for a brief moment. But then the down side of this lifestyle was staring Abel in the face. The Lion's eyes were dead. Soulless. Somewhere he had lost his humanity.

The Lion watched his guest with suspicion as he sat heavily on the sofa. He was massively built, six-feet tall with luxuriant hair, which tumbled from his temples to his chin.

142

"So what can I do for you, Mr. Amballo? My name is Roy King, but they call me The Lion."

Abel was immediately struck by the accent. Another fellow Nigerian. Were they all unscrupulous thugs? He suddenly felt ashamed that his country was being represented by such people. The Lion ran his hand through his thick hair, brushing it away from his broad, unkind face.

Abel wondered if Mr. King began growing his hair like a mane after he acquired the nickname. Perhaps he'd ask sometime when he wasn't under such a suspicious glare. Abel felt very much as if The Lion was sizing him up for lunch.

"I won't waste your time, Mr. King," Abel said and clasped his hands. "Very busy men rarely fall in love. And I am a businessman from Lagos. And I can hear from your accent we are fellow countrymen."

Mr. King waved the coincidence away as if it were a pesky fly buzzing his head.

"Yeah, but I have been in Diaspora for a long time. I operate a chain of shops here, but as you have apparently heard, I help fellow travellers." His baritone voice was flat and uncaring, matching his eyes.

Abel took a breath. "Well, it's always nice to meet a fellow Nigerian. Anyway, as I was saying, being preoccupied I wasn't devoting much time to romance. Too busy with the practical world. But I finally fell in love. But of course, given who I am and what I do, she was not happy because she said I never found time for her."

Mr. King just looked at Abel, who guessed the man was waiting for the part of the story where he got paid.

"So, she left with some guy, who is supposedly taking her to Europe," Abel said.

Mr. King obviously didn't see any problem here. He yawned, reaching for a pack of Marlboros on the coffee table beside him. He used a fancy silver lighter to spark the cigarette, then blew smoke out of his wide nostrils before finally deigning to speak.

"Why marry? I'm also busy. I am not married, but I am a happy man."

"I want to marry her and have kids," Abel said emphatically. He felt he had to match this goon in tone or he'd be buried. He was already feeling overwhelmed by the surroundings and the guy's sociopathic personality.

"Okay, lover boy, so what can I do?"

"I heard they must be passing through here, and I will pay you a thousand Euros if you can find her for me. I understand all the agents or migrants through here consult you …"

"Mmm, good homework." King puffed on his cigarette. "Who is she?"

Abel handed him Alice's photograph.

"Nice."

The way King looked at Alice's picture made Abel's hair stand on end. He was aptly nicknamed. A pure predator.

"I can see why you want her back," King said studying the photograph, the cigarette in his thin lips.

"I do. I love her." This seemed important to add. Love wasn't something Mr. King thought about or felt, but Abel wanted to put it on the table. "Her name is Alice, but of course I don't know the name she may be using now."

"Nice to know that people can still fall in love, Romeo," Mr. King said, drawing on the cigarette.

He didn't say it as if he really believed it.

"Let me check with my people." Mr. King pulled out his cell phone and dialled a number. He studied the picture as he talked. "Hey, it's me. I'm looking for a pretty girl, around 15. Scar above eyebrow. Nigerian. Have we used anyone like that lately?"

Abel was shocked by his business-like tone, as if he was checking to see if they had her in stock. On the other hand, he was excited at the prospect of this paying off. But King dashed his hopes as he hung up.

"No luck," King said as he dialled another number. "So many people pass through these days, you know." He listened to something as he killed the cigarette stub in an ornate violet ashtray.

Abel listened as the man spoke with another contact. Again, he shook his head and cut the call.

"Sorry, Mr. Amballo. She is certainly not in the Canaries. She may have been stupid enough to try the Sahara route through Mali."

That was the end of the Lion's interest in his problem.

"I hope with these calls I've earned part of your offer."

He smiled at Abel, but there was no warmth in it. And the threat was obvious. Abel reached for his wallet.

"Of course, Mr. King. I appreciate you seeing me. Very generous to help a love-struck fellow countryman." Abel counted out a thousand Euros.

King's small eyes glowed as he reached for the money, the first time sign of life in the man. He put the bills on the coffee table and stood up: "What was her name again?" Abel didn't particularly like the way he asked, but he hid his disapproval.

"Alice," Abel said and then exited the room. He could feel the man's eyes watching him as he left.

As he picked up his key at the front desk, the receptionist told him he had a visitor. Before he could ask who it was, a young lady with a beautiful athletic frame and short, close-cut hair stepped to his side.

"I'm Lillian. The Lion wants me to tell you about Alice," she whispered.

Abel wondered how they even knew which hotel he was in since he registered as Peter Abel, not Peter Amballo. He had kept a close eye on the traffic as they drove back from King's and saw no sign they were being followed.

"We should discuss this in private. Your room?" she said.

Abel nodded and Lillian turned and led the way towards the elevators. Despite being on edge, Abel could still appreciate her spectacular figure, the sway of her hips inside a tight white skirt. When they arrived at the bank of elevators she asked which floor he was on.

"Three."

The door slid open and they stepped inside. Abel dared hope that if the girl didn't know his room number, she probably didn't know his true identity. But he still didn't know how she'd found him, and that made him nervous. The doors closed and he felt the car ascend. He could smell her perfume. Like the sexiest women, she was seductive without trying. Abel had a fleeting thought she might have been sent as a gift for the night, but then doubted it. King wasn't the type.

Once inside Abel's room, the girl tried to put him at ease by plopping down casually on the sofa and smiling at him. Abel refused to sit. He had grown anxious about the reason for the girl's appearance. This couldn't be good news.

"Okay, tell me what you want," Abel finally said.

When the girl turned toward him, Abel went numb, his worst fears confirmed. In her right hand she held a lethal-looking revolver. He could see the noses of bullets in the exposed chambers. Abel doubted they were blanks.

"Sit over there." She used the revolver to point at the sofa opposite her, far enough away to prevent Abel from making a lunge for the gun, which she held easily. She looked as if she knew how to use it. Another piece of bad news. "If you don't get funny, you'll get out of here alive."

Lillian leaned over, allowing her blouse to open slightly. She had great breasts. Tanned and perfect. Abel wondered if she was taunting him or was just a swell dresser. He had to admire the outfit. But the gun kind of took the wind out of his sails.

He obediently took a seat. "And here I thought The Lion was sending you over to show me a good time." It was a bullshit line. Abel was scared to death, but he was damned if he'd let her see it. He had his pride, and with a woman this sexy you really went the extra mile to make an impression.

"Shut up!"

No sense of humour. She probably wasn't much fun in bed, either. He knew it was sour grapes, but he felt the need to buck himself up. After all, it was just him against her, the gun and that killer body. He was totally overmatched.

"My boss says nobody's heard of you. His contacts know every important Nigerian who comes here, and certainly one who can afford to stay in a four-star hotel."

"Maybe his contacts don't know everybody." Okay, he admitted to himself. It was a lame retort. "Anyway, how'd you find me?"

Lillian merely smiled at his naiveté. Then Abel remembered Susan, the lady who cleaned up his dishes and whose offer he had refused. King probably had snitches in all the hotels, women watching out for rich businessmen who might want a girl for the night. King had no doubt called around to these sources until one recognised Abel. And he was pretty sure that one had been Susan. He wondered, if he had taken her up on her offer, would she still have given him up? Probably, if The Lion frightened her enough.

"Now, Mr. Amballo, my boss says you are to leave town immediately."

"Why?"

"Because he does not want to see you hurt."

Gee, what a swell guy, Abel thought. But he figured Lillian wouldn't appreciate another smartass remark so he kept it to himself. Always bad strategy to piss off someone holding a loaded weapon.

Since Abel had apparently run out of clever repartee, Lillian continued. "And there is no reason to stay, anyway. He is telling you the truth about this girl, Alice. Nobody knows her."

This got Abel's attention. Was King trying to get rid of him because Alice was, in fact, here? It finally gave Abel some chips to play with.

"Maybe she's here, maybe not. I'd like to see for myself. After all, I love this girl. I want to marry her."

She held up her hand, the one without the gun in it.

"Please. Nobody believes your story about looking for a runaway fiancée. Whatever you are doing here, it can only lead to trouble for us. Not that you could take us down. We own this place. But you could become an annoyance if you begin poking around in our business. And my boss suspects that is what you are really doing. A cop. Perhaps you are working for an international agency. Or one of those do-gooder human rights commissions."

"Pesky things those human rights commissions. Spoil the fun every time."

Lillian's eyes grew cold, her body tensed. Abel fell silent.

"We want you to leave tonight. My boss is not a patient man."

Abel looked at her, genuinely surprised.

"Tonight?"

"There are two flights out before eleven. This time of year you can always get a seat. If you have trouble, we will help you. We know many people in the travel business."

147

I'll bet you do. Abel almost said it out, but since Lillian seemed to lack a sense of irony he held his tongue.

She got up without lowering the gun. God, what a body and so nicely draped. Abel wondered how much a night with her cost. Instead, he nodded to the gun.

"Was that really necessary?"

"Got your attention, didn't it?" She turned to leave, then stopped and looked back at him. "We have an efficient network, and if you try anything, you could become another drowned migrant floating ashore on one of our fine beaches." And she was gone.

Abel sat frozen in his seat, amazed by the whole scene. It hardly seemed real. Like some bad stage play. Even her exit line seemed scripted.

But he knew she wasn't play-acting on one score. There was little he could do to root out the syndicate. Businesses like King's could only thrive with the support of the local law enforcement agencies.

As he pondered his next move – packing came to mind – there was a knock on the door. Abel cursed under his breath thinking Lillian had returned to offer more threats. As if he didn't feel castrated enough already. It was a brilliant stroke by The Lion. Send a sexy woman to deliver the message. Total humiliation. Abel opened the door where he was surprised to find Aleck waiting.

"You look terrible," Aleck said. "That lady who just left, she took your mind off your missing fiancée?" He didn't try to hide his disapproval. Instead, he walked past a dumbstruck Abel and sat down where Lillian had been a short while before.

Abel wondered at his sudden arrival. Was he somehow connected with Lillian? It didn't seem likely, but King seemed to control everyone on the island.

"Sorry, Aleck, but you came early."

"Yeah, I can see," Aleck said.

"The truth is, she had nothing to do with sex. I went to visit Mr. King this afternoon."

Aleck sat up, alarmed.

"The Lion? You saw The Lion?"

"Yeah, and he claims my girl isn't here. But I told him a story about being a businessman looking for my runaway fiancée. I guess he didn't believe me, checked me out and figured I could be trouble. So, I'm invited to leave. Tonight. Lillian there delivered the message, gun in hand."

Aleck just looked at him, stunned. He got up slowly shaking his head.

"You mess with The Lion, you're gonna get bitten. No love bite, either."

Aleck moved to the corner where Abel's empty suitcase sat. He put it on the bed and opened it up.

"What are you doing?"

"Helping you pack, then I'm gonna take you to the airport."

Aleck pointed to the dresser. "Come on. Get cracking. This guy doesn't fool around." Aleck seemed genuinely terrified of the man.

Slowly, Abel moved to the dresser and opened the top drawer. He began putting his underwear and socks in the suitcase. Aleck moved to his closet.

"You want me to get your hanging clothes?"

Abel didn't like being pushed. He suddenly stopped packing.

"Not so fast."

"What, are you crazy? You gotta go."

"Tomorrow. I paid for this room through tonight."

Aleck looked at him, wide-eyed. "You trying to get yourself killed for a night's room rent? I know these people. They're not kidding."

"They won't kill me until they know who I really am. For all they know, I'm well connected, and killing me would bring a hammer down. No, I figure I've got at least the night."

Aleck looked surprised. "What do you mean, who you really are? You're not a businessman from Lagos?"

Abel sank onto a sofa.

"I have to trust you, Aleck, but you can't mention this to anyone. You have to swear your word."

Aleck nodded, looking puzzled and unsure if he wanted to hear what was coming.

"I'm an investigative reporter, Aleck," Abel said, noting the sincere shock on the pilot's face. "I'm doing a story on trafficking.

149

The missing girl, she's not my fiancée. She's a child I care about, and I've promised her mother I'll find her and bring her back safe."

Aleck shook his head and thought about that.

"You're going to get yourself killed, for sure, and maybe me with you," he said.

"Not if we get this done tonight," Abel said. "Who runs the prostitutes here in town? There must be some Mother Superior-type who watches over the girls, knows them all."

Aleck looked at Abel and nodded. "Mrs. Churchill. Everyone gets a big kick outta the name. She keeps the girls healthy, feeds them sometimes, listens to their problems. Most of them are so young they need a mother figure."

Abel started out of the room. "Let's go see her. If she hasn't seen Alice, I'll leave, I promise." Aleck hesitated. Abel took out his wallet. "You going to show me or do I have to find another guide?"

Finally Aleck nodded. "Knowing you, you'll ask one of The Lion's gang. I better take you." Then he led the way out of the room.

Abel found himself standing in a small, modestly furnished flat somewhere in the centre of town. The room was comfortable and homey and he could smell something baking. A couple of girls, dressed in robes, passed through on their way down a hall. This wasn't a brothel. It was some kind of way station where the girls could relax, get a home-cooked meal and find a little peace.

After a few minutes, Aleck emerged from the kitchen with an elderly woman, probably in her late 70s. White hair, kindly eyes, wearing an apron. She reminded Abel of his grandmother.

"This is Mrs. Rose Churchill," Aleck said, then stepped aside. The old woman approached Abel and offered her hand.

"Hello, son. You look troubled."

No argument there, Abel thought. He gave her his hand, which she took in both of hers. She smiled warmly, and he could see why she was someone the young girls would like.

"I'm sorry to bother you, Mrs. Churchill. But I'm looking for a young girl. She was taken from her home in Nigeria. Maybe brought here and forced into prostitution."

He handed Mrs. Churchill the photo of Alice. The old woman

carefully took a pair of reading glasses from the apron pocket and placed them on her face. She studied the picture.

"Lovely girl. This was taken just before she left Nigeria." It was a statement, not a question.

"Yes. How do you know?"

"She was already involved in prostitution. What she will find abroad is no different. You can tell a girl who has sold herself. It's in the eyes."

Mrs. Churchill handed the picture back to Abel and removed her glasses. She seemed sad. The words had carried no judgment.

"Yes, you're right," Abel said. "But I believe she can still be saved. If I can find her."

"She has not come through this house. I'd remember. I remember every one of them."

"May I ask you something? You seem to know how bad this all is. Why don't you do something."

"I am. I am offering them love. But I can't stop what is happening. Good luck. I hope you find the girl."

"She's different to most of these girls, Mrs. Churchill."

"She is in one respect. She has someone who is willing to risk his life to rescue her."

With that, Mrs. Churchill returned to the kitchen and whatever it was she was baking. Abel turned to Aleck who had been watching from a distance.

"Okay, Aleck. Take me to the airport."

First they stopped back at the hotel so Abel could collect his things and check out. They didn't talk the entire way, until Aleck dropped him off in front of British Airways. Abel got out and took his bags. Just before he stepped onto the curb Aleck asked, "What is next?"

"London. To see a friend. Then Mali. Maybe that's the route they took."

Abel thanked Aleck and disappeared into the terminal.

CHAPTER EIGHTEEN

The Marriott on Westminster Bridge Road was a hotel Abel fancied.

Abel felt safe there because it was not a place for every Tom, Dick and Harry. It was expensive! And after his experience in the Canaries, Abel above all wanted to feel safe.

Abel arrived in London and took a taxi straight to the hotel and collapsed in his room. He slept for the next 24 hours.

When he finally awoke, he ordered some food, opened the curtains and sat at the window, which overlooked the Thames. The views of the river and of Big Ben were particularly thrilling to him. He began to feel himself relax.

After eating, Abel phoned Chief Benson to give him an update and assure him he was all right. He had expected the Chief to remark on the expense of the hotel he had chosen, but instead, Benson had merely ordered him to "get a good rest."

After recounting his adventures in the Canaries, he told Benson his plans to head out for Mali as soon as he checked with Lola to learn if she had remembered anything more about the circumstances that led up to Tunde's murder. He didn't tell his boss, but he also was looking forward to assuring Lola that he was still on the story that cost her husband his life. He felt responsible somehow, since Tunde always thought of him as a mentor. But Benson told him Lola was already in London for a vacation courtesy of *The Zodiac*. Abel took her number.

He reached Lola that evening, and he apologised for losing track of her movements. They arranged to meet at a local pub for a traditional bangers and mash dinner.

Lola entered the pub looking much younger and more relaxed. She wore a dashing black leather jacket over a yellow T-shirt and black jeans. Abel stood to greet her, throwing his arms around the slender woman.

"Lola. You look ..."

"Thanks, Abel," she said quickly to stop his compliments. She sat down gracefully at the table before Abel remembered he should have taken her jacket.

"I am impressed, you staying at the Marriott on Westminster," she said. "Very luxurious."

"Courtesy of *The Zodiac*."

"I know a little about *The Zodiac* my Tunde loved so much, but there must be some additional reward for those of you who live dangerously."

Abel hoped to veer the discussion off her bitter past, so he ignored the remark.

"You look beautiful, Lola," he said. "And this ordinary t-shirt you have on ..."

"Don't start the debate of the hood and the monk, Abel." She crossed her legs. "I'd like a Guinness before listening to your story."

"Story?"

"I hear you've been all over the place looking for ..."

"Alice, but please, please don't spoil the evening. This is not your problem, at least not for now."

"Peter, we share this pain. Don't shut me out. You look so worried and tired. You've had a hard time. And I want to hear about it."

Abel could see Lola wasn't about to budge. "Okay, you win," Abel waved a waiter over and ordered the drinks.

"It's a long story, but I'll do my best," he said. "I write stories better than I can tell them."

"Start at the beginning. Leave nothing out," she said.

Abel waited until their beers arrived, then began.

By the time he finished, they had ordered and finished dinner. He sat back, drinking a third beer and regarding his empty plate. He loved English food. He didn't care what anybody said. Overcooked peas were tasty. Lola watched him, admiration in her eyes. She shook her head.

"Well, thank God for your life."

"Somehow, I enjoy the challenges, the rush of adrenaline. But as you said, I must thank God for still being alive."

"So, what do you do next?"

153

"Oh," Abel yawned. "I'm headed for Mali on Monday. That is the other popular route for the traffickers."

"I will go with you." She looked him straight in the eye.

"No, Lola. It's too dangerous."

"I don't care," she insisted. "This is my fight, too."

"No, Lola," Abel sat back and folded his arms. His father used to do the same thing when he wanted to signal the discussion had come to an end.

"You're not being fair. I have every reason for wanting to follow this story to the end."

"I know we share a common pain, but you're still mourning. Still dealing with grief. No matter what you think, you haven't recovered. I say this because I care. Believe me. Revenge is not a good reason to go on a dangerous assignment like this."

Abel knew he was echoing his boss's own wise words to him before he left.

She sat back, sulking. Abel reached over and put a hand on her arm.

"Lola, I've taken an oath to care for you. Part of that involves finishing Tunde's story. And part of that involves making sure you stay safe."

Lola suddenly looked at Abel, eyes hardening in a hatred he hadn't seen before or even suspected was there.

"Maybe it's better I don't go," she said. "If I went with you and we found these people who are smuggling children, turning them into whores, I would kill them. They would be dead by my hand. They are the reason Tunde is dead."

As shocked as he was, Abel admired her anger and her strength. And it only drove him harder than ever to follow the story. And to make sure it was told.

CHAPTER NINETEEN

Abel spent the next several days talking with police, immigration officials, UN agencies and a couple of British investigative journalists about his next destination: Mali.

After his experience in the Canary Islands, Abel didn't want to be taken by surprise. He felt he had stepped into the Canary Islands situation without preparation, and this could have been a deadly mistake. So, he was determined to do his homework, learn the lay of the inhospitable land and ferret out the players before he arrived in the country.

The information he gathered in London told him the ancient town of Gao was the principle starting point for illegal immigrants from all over Africa. Those hearty (or more likely desperate) souls who were willing to face the burning Sahara desert for a chance to reach Spain would first find their way to Gao.

If Alice had used that route, she must have travelled by land across the Benin Republic, Togo, Ghana and Côte d'Ivoire into Bamako, Mali's capital. An arduous and dangerous journey. She would have been forced into prostitution at each stop to raise money for the next leg of the trip.

Abel wondered if perhaps she could have been flown directly from Lagos to Bamako. But he told himself this wouldn't have helped Alice in the long run. Had they flown, her handlers would have made the girl work extra hard to defray the additional cost. Either way, it meant the sweet little thing would be heavily abused.

Abel arrived in Bamako a little after nine p.m., then took a minibus to the Hotel de Naboun on the outskirts of the city. Compared to the Vulcano in Tenerife, this was a downmarket, even seedy hotel. However the air conditioner, double bed and private bathroom made it liveable, at least for the night. He had a dinner of salad and French fries in the hotel's restaurant then went straight to bed. He knew his first step, and that was to find his way to Gao.

Early the following morning, he joined a group of French tourists on the long trip to Gao. As he boarded the bus, he could smell the city. The fog carried an acrid mix of dust and smoke. Despite the conditions, he found the country fascinating. And once out of town the roads proved particularly interesting. Cars, mopeds, lorries, donkey carts, bicycles, goats and sheep competed for right-of-way. The bus made constant stops to allow animals to pass.

Abel kept to himself, pretending he didn't speak French. It wasn't that he felt anti-social, but he needed to use the time to review his strategy. Still, he couldn't help being distracted now and then by the poverty of villages living along the route. As they drove, the sparse vegetation gave way to sand dunes.

Where they crossed the River Niger, Abel saw fishing piroques plying up and down the river banks, and every now and then they passed isolated villages consisting of three or four mud buildings. The river made Abel nostalgic. After all, the Niger flowed through his home country, too.

Some 14 hours after departing the capital, they arrived in the sprawling town of Gao, with its unbearably hot and windy weather.

Tired and dirty, Abel checked into the Hotel de l'Atlantide.

A man on the bus who spoke English had described the place as bad value for money. He and his group preferred to camp along the Niger. After checking into his room, Abel couldn't disagree. It was bare and dusty, as uninviting as the squalid town. When Abel inquired discreetly about moving to another hotel, he was told without irony that he was already in Gao's most auspicious accommodation. He consoled himself with the thought that at least it offered him the one thing he wanted most: security.

Shortly after unpacking, he ate some bread and sardines he had purchased in the outdoor market in Bamako that morning. Then he put on a clean shirt and trousers and took the stairs down to the lobby. He decided to avoid the elevator, which ran only intermittently and made alarming noises when it did work.

There he found several men lounging about, hiring out as guides. Abel approached the least ragged of the group and offered him a modest sum to show him around. The fellow bowed, hat in hand, and said his name was Musa.

156

Musa, who claimed to be 30 but looked closer to 50, insisted on showing Abel around the Musee du Sahel, a museum of ancient art tools and household items. They also went to the tomb of Askia, a 500-year-old structure. Situated on the northern outskirts of town, this tomb of a 16th century ruler is a classic Sahel-style building in the shape of a pyramid. It is made from dark grey mud and sports porcupine spikes that make Sahel mosques so distinctive. The wooden spikes on the Tomb of Askia are particularly big and bristling, giving it the air of a Sahel mosque. This wasn't the kind of sightseeing Abel had in mind, but he went along to gain Musa's trust.

As they walked back to the hotel near dusk, Abel decided it was time to tell Musa what he was really doing. He signalled for the guide to a stop as they walked under a nim tree. Musa looked at him, puzzled. Then Abel said, "I want to go to Spain. Which means I need to meet the best person you know who can arrange such a thing."

Musa's narrow face lit up. "There is someone at your very hotel," he said in passing English. Abel figured that was the upside of staying in the garden spot of the city. You meet the best people.

Next on the agenda was getting a look at the prostitutes who roamed the city. He hadn't seen any in the hotel, so he asked Musa where he could find them. "Woman. For sex at night," Abel said, trying to make Musa understand what he wanted. When Musa looked uncertain, Abel pantomimed the act with his fingers. That apparently did the trick because Musa lit up.

"Ye waah!" Musa exclaimed with a broad smile: "The Ghetto. Good, small, small girls. Good."

"Take me there now."

And so Musa led the way with the confidence of someone who'd done this before. Apparently lots of tours ended with this little trek.

The sight of the decrepit ghetto brothel shocked Abel. Several teenagers in skimpy clothes, some of them far younger than Alice, drank and smoked in front of the long cement block building. He counted about 20 rooms in the block, each with a steel door and window.

Abel shook his head mildly as the girls made passes at him, some even bold enough to reach out and touch his thigh. The thought that Alice may be involved in such abuse infuriated Abel, but he quickly quelled his emotions as he looked around to see if by any chance she was among them.

Not seeing her, he bought a pack of cigarettes, trying to make himself seem like just another customer. After approaching several girls, he picked one who spoke English well. The girl shook her head when Abel asked where she came from. She wasn't interested in idle chatter. All business, she spelled out her fees, which ranged from a "short one" of 10 minutes, to an hour's session, to an all-night tryst. But for that she'd have to talk to her boss.

Abel was tempted to ask the girl about Alice, but he suppressed the urge. When he finally shook his head, turning down her services, the girl moved away and approached another man and began the same litany of sexual favours and attendant prices.

Abel returned to the hotel at about 8 p.m., still angry. He would have killed anyone who pushed his sister into that kind of life.

Musa had set a meeting with the agent who could arrange passage to Spain for 9 p.m. Abel waited in the bar, drinking and silently fuming over the whole sordid scene. Just after nine, Musa entered and told Abel the man wanted to meet outside. "He says he do such business away from the hotel."

"Why?" Abel asked, in a surly frame of mind and not inclined to be cooperative. At least not without expressing some displeasure. Musa smiled.

"Man, the walls of the hotel leak."

Abel wasn't in the mood for a long walk in the dark. For one thing it wasn't safe, and after his experience in the Canaries, he was being cautious.

He met the man a block from the hotel.

"I'm Peter," Abel said.

The man was stocky and had small eyes for the size of his head. Abel thought it made him look stupid, but he doubted that was the case. The man nodded without offering Abel his hand and without reciprocating an introduction.

"I am told you wish to go to Spain."

"Yes. I want to make the next available trip."

"You are from Nigeria?" The man asked.

"Yes. And I like to know who I'm doing business with."

The man nodded, apparently conceding it wasn't an unreasonable request. "I am Robert. Liberian." Robert stopped and lit a cigarette. It was a classic stall. Abel thought he must be sizing him up. When Robert finally broke his silence, it was to deliver a rambling diatribe on the state of the world.

"Nigeria helped us during our civil war. Odd how most of the migrants here are from Nigeria. And over sixty percent of the prostitutes in Italy are Nigerians. Your country must really find out the underlying causes of this migration and do something."

Abel wondered what the hell he was going on about. This guy made his living ferrying would-be prostitutes around.

"Yes. Well, I'll look into it once I settle all the world's other problems."

Robert laughed. Good. Whatever Robert was looking for, Abel had given him. Robert visibly relaxed.

"So, you know what you want, Sir?" Robert was opening negotiations.

"We've established that already. I need to get to Spain."

"You are ready to pay for it?"

Abel thought every conversation manages to find its way here. Money. The universal knows-no-national-cultural-racial boundaries bottom line.

"Yes. If I can make it to Spain, I have employers who will hire me."

"Excellent. So many who go have no such prospects," Robert said. He apparently approved of enterprising men like Abel.

"I have no idea how this works. I'm really in your hands. Of course, I'll pay half of the fees tomorrow and the rest upon departure."

Robert shivered in the dim light then said, "Here's how it works: I arrange to hand you over to one of the Touaregs, who are the masters of the desert. They know all the routes that avoid official border crossing points, where you would otherwise be stopped and returned to Nigeria."

"I see," Abel nodded, playing the interested customer.

"The Touaregs will drive you in their truck for a fee of seven hundred dollars, American. When you get to Morocco, they will hand you over to the master smugglers who charge about one thousand Euros per person to get you across the Mediterranean Sea to Spain."

"How long does the trip take?" Abel asked.

"Two weeks to a month, depending on the kind of service you want and the Spanish and Moroccan police. But a good Touareg worth his salt is able to avoid them."

"I'm in a hurry and want an express service," Abel said. He couldn't afford to waste so much time in transit. And he figured money could speed up the process. He was correct.

"That will cost you twice the rates I have quoted, Peter. Are you ready for it?" Abel nodded. "The money's worth it."

"Yes, with a job waiting for you, of course. I will get you the best Touareg on the route. I think he leaves tomorrow evening."

But the business wasn't concluded. There were incidentals. There always are. Abel wasn't surprised when Robert brought them up as an afterthought.

"Oh, I forgot," he said, suddenly remembering something and acting all innocent. "To travel through the south-western tip of Algeria, you will need a Malian visa."

"And where do I get one of those?" Abel asked, knowing perfectly well.

"I can get you one by morning."

Who would have guessed? Abel only smiled as if he were grateful for this extra expense.

"Very good, Robert. I'll pay you tomorrow morning."

"Excellent. I'm in room two-seventeen." He handed Abel a worn business card, which looked as if he had been carrying it around in his pocket for awhile.

"I move around a lot, but you can always reach me on my cell phone. I will do you a better job than Philip."

"Who's Philip?" Abel asked, curious for more information.

"He is the Nigerian who runs human trafficking. He is really a figurehead. I am the chief operating officer. I know all the vital links."

Robert said this as if he were talking about IBM. Chief operating officer. Abel held his tongue, but he was already writing the paragraph in his future story. The one where he skewers this complete piece-of-shit criminal, exposing him for the worm he was. Abel regretted the man probably didn't subscribe to The Zodiac.

Early the following morning, Abel delivered an envelope full of money to Robert's room. He then waited as Robert went about the job of obtaining a visa and arranging for transportation. They were to meet that night at eight.

Abel knocked on Robert's door at eight sharp and was pleasantly surprised to find that Robert had accomplished everything. As they spoke, a tall, slim, fair-complexioned man in a sparkling white tunic emerged from the bathroom. Robert introduced him as Aghreb, the Touareg.

"He is your driver. Unfortunately, he does not speak much English."

"Thank you," Abel said and offered his hand.

Robert counted out $1,400 from the envelope Abel had brought that morning and handed it to the driver.

His toothpaste smile in that dusty environment surprised Abel, "Tonight," Aghreb managed to say.

"So," Robert said, "you are on your way."

Abel felt a pang of genuine fear. "I read that people die on the way."

Robert's smile dissolved.

"You see people die everywhere, even in the best aircraft. People die in the best automobiles along city roads. What happens here is that some people disobey the Touaregs, who are masters of the desert. When they tell you to cover up, you do. They ask you to drink water, you do. People die of minor things like sunstroke." He paused for effect. "In this game, you listen to the masters and you will be okay. In your case, it is the duty of the driver to ensure your safety. So, please, do not be afraid."

Abel took a breath and thought of Julius Caesar's famous words as he crossed the Rubicon. "Iacta alea est." The die is cast. There was no turning back. He turned to Robert.

161

"Okay. Let's go."

Some two minutes away from the hotel, they arrived at the departure point, an open space dimly lit by a fading streetlamp. Abel could not see much of the pickup truck because the back was covered with a tarpaulin. The driver and five other men stood some distance away counting money. No doubt they were other "facilitators."

Abel walked to the back of the truck where he was startled to see people huddled on two long seats opposite each other, luggage packed in the space on the floor.

"Get on board and let's go," he heard someone shout at him.

"You sit with the driver. You paid for a first-class passage," Robert said, pulling him toward the cabin.

As Abel climbed into the passenger seat, Robert said, "There is enough space in the back for your suitcase."

"I'll keep it with me if that's all right," Abel said, sliding the suitcase into the space behind the seat.

A short time later, the driver came over, shook Robert's hand, and got in. A second Touareg took the seat to Abel's right and banged the door shut. The two men recited a prayer in Arabic before the driver turned the key in the ignition. The engine roared to life.

The truck moved slowly through the night, past shops and cafés and men on benches playing cards. The town suddenly seemed safe to Abel, the familiar signs of any civilised society very much in evidence.

As the truck finally reached the outskirts of Gao, joining a dusty road, Abel felt isolated, as if giving himself over to a fate he could not control. These strange men on either side of him, the pathetic souls huddled in the back of the truck, all they owned squeezed into a small suitcase between their feet, it was suddenly more than he had bargained for.

Abel wondered if he would ever see his comfortable house in Lagos again. He felt as if he were on the dark side of the moon, home impossibly far away and unreachable. As the truck gathered speed, Abel leaned back and watched the speedometer climb steadily up to 80 kph, acutely aware that every second carried him farther into the vast desert.

At some point, Abel fell into a deep sleep. When he opened his eyes, the sun was just coming up over the horizon and the truck was pulling into a small remote village around an oasis.

Everybody tumbled out, stiff from the long ride. The driver spoke to them in Arabic, which, of course, nobody understood. Finally, he pointed to a body of water down the horizon.

"Boat."

Abel felt a wave of relief wash over him. Apparently, he had made it through one leg of the journey. He hadn't been murdered and dumped in the desert. Looking back, he had to laugh at himself. These were businessmen who made a living ferrying people safely to their destination. How long would they last if they murdered their customers?

Feeling silly, but giddy at the same time, Abel retreated to a small café on the water to buy some breakfast. He joined his fellow passengers, who were ordering the meagre fare available. Fish looked like the best thing on the menu, so Abel ordered a plate of the local catch.

As he ate what turned out to be a delicious unnamed delicate white fish, he flagged down his waitress, a pretty young girl with shiny earrings that dangled along her neck. Abel, as had become his habit, showed her Alice's picture. He had taken to showing it to everyone when it felt safe to do so. He also had come to expect a blank stare and a shake of the head. But this girl nodded when she saw the photo.

"Yes," she said. "I have seen her."

Abel could hardly contain himself. He asked for details, and the girl said Alice had come through about a week before with a man. When she described him, Abel knew it had to be Kehinde Lawal.

Abel kept the girl talking by offering her a large tip. She said, yes, they had taken a fishing boat across to Spain. Did she know where in Spain? The girl surprised Abel by saying she didn't think Spain was their final destination.

"What do you mean?"

"The man got a phone call when he was here. He was very upset. He asked the owner of this place about getting to London from Spain."

Abel was excited, but puzzled. What could have spooked Lawal? Who would have called? And what were they doing in London? Abel moved around asking others who understood English in the village if they had seen or spoken with Alice or Lawal. Nobody had.

But at least he had a lead now. The first hint of where Alice might be. And he knew she was alive and well. Finding her in London would be infinitely easier than Spain or North Africa. At last she seemed within his grasp. At this point Abel decided to return to Mali, rather than take risks the rest of the journey. He could be arrested or drown in the boat ride across the Strait of Gibraltar.

"My tummy, my tummy," Abel grimaced, chewing at his lips hysterically, as they boarded the truck to continue.

The driver pulled the truck to a halt and turned to Abel. "Hospital Gao? You can go Morac?"

"He means whether you want to go back to Gao to attend hospital or you think you can continue," the driver's aide asked.

"Oh, my tummy o!" Abel screamed. "I don't think I can go. Please take me back. I will go another time."

"No money back, my friend," the driver said angrily and broke into Arabic language.

His mate promptly fetched a Turaya phone and dialled a number. "Robert, your man is ill, he wants to abort the trip, so we are bringing him back.

"Yes, please, I will go back." Abel pleaded.

The driver's mate jumped down to go to explain the situation to the other passengers at the back and Abel could hear them express sympathy for him.

On the man's return, the driver spoke some more Arabic and turned the truck back to Gao. Robert was at the gate of the hotel to receive him. "What is the matter, my brother?" He led Abel back to the hotel lobby.

"I had some slight pains last night, but it suddenly developed into cramps. I need to lie down so please get me a room."

"But you have spent so much? And you nearly made it o! Unfortunately, my brother you don't get your money back."

"No, I understand. I will go and get some more money for another attempt. I have a friend in Bamako."

"Fine," Robert said, relieved. He helped Abel, who was bent over, to the lobby.

Later, in his room where Abel said he had brought some drugs with him for such emergencies, he lay quietly on the bed reviewing his next line of action. If it failed, it meant he had to look elsewhere for Alice. He reached for the photographs from the suitcase and kept them under his pillow.

An hour later when Robert returned to check on him, he could afford a smile.

"That must have been a powerful medicine. You should have taken it and continued the journey." Robert said settling in the seat opposite him. " Or was there some allergy on the truck?"

"No, it must be something I ate in Bamako, but as you can see I am feeling better now. I will go and get some more money and try again. My people must be worried on the other side."

"Yea, you said you have people there."

"You may even know him. He had been using this route but he seems to have hit gold with his last batch of migrants, so he does not come around again." He tossed the two photographs at Robert.

He raised them to the light for a close examination and burst into laughter. "I told you there is nothing here I don't know. This is Kenny, Kehinde Lawal, and this is the girl he used while they were here. Bastard, he didn't want anybody to get near her. I think her name is Alice or something."

"I don't know about the girl, but it was the Kenny guy who fixed me the job," he said slowly and sat up. "I did not believe him until I spoke with the employers myself."

"And you said he is in Spain?" Robert had another look at the photograph.

Abel felt butterflies fly around in his tummy. He had said his benefactor was in Spain and he had to be consistent. "Kenny travels all over the place. When we spoke, he was in Barcelona."

"I see." Robert rose to give the photographs back to him. "The last time people told me about him, they said he was in London, where he sold the girl off in a good deal. He took the rest to Italy."

Abel swallowed his anger and changed the subject. "So, when is the next trip? Am I likely to get another of your friends to travel with? That driver was good."

"It depends on when you come back here. And I believe you will still go for the express service."

"Sure!" Abel said, happy about the sweet returns of the money he lavished on Robert. "Give me a week, I will be back here to see you."

"Okay," Robert got up. "I must allow you to sleep. I will check you tomorrow morning."

Abel could barely sleep that night. Careful not to talk, he sent a text to Lola to announce Alice could be in London. Before Robert could get up, Abel had left a note for him and checked out.

CHAPTER TWENTY

Lola stood over Abel, laughing. "You don't like my cooking!" she said.

They were in her sister's apartment at Elephant and Castle, where Lola had been staying since her arrival in London. With her family away on holiday, she had the place to herself. Abel had been back in London a week. They had met a few times for meals, but this was the first time they had been alone. She wanted to cook her version of shepherd's pie and was testing it out on Abel.

"I do too like it," he said. "It is delicious. You're becoming an expert cook of English food!"

She put a hand on his shoulder. Physical contact. Abel felt an electric charge run through him.

There had been something between them the last few times. Although unspoken, they both felt it. Perhaps it was the highly emotional crusade they shared that created the attraction. When Lola had invited him over for dinner, Abel was excited, but nervous. Lola was beautiful, and Abel a normal male with high levels of testosterone. He often joked that the only thing he could not resist was temptation.

This evening, she wore blue jeans below a tight-fitting red t-shirt, her hair neatly woven in cornrows. She allowed her hand to linger on his shoulder.

"You haven't given me an update on your progress," she said.

Abel patted her hand in a paternal way and indicated she should sit opposite him. He wanted to put some distance between them. As much as he was attracted to her, he didn't think the timing was right to begin anything. And besides, his investigation had yielded big results, and he was ready to move on them.

"Since you told me Alice could be here, I've been using a journalist friend to help me track her down." She looked up at him and saw a face plastered with doubt, "you know I will do everything to support you …"

"Yes. He was helping you check out the various houses of ill-repute and massage parlours. Have you found her?"

"We think it's possible. There is an African girl who works in a place off South Audley Street behind the Hilton. Someone who said he had been there identified her picture. But I won't be sure until I see her myself."

"You should talk to the police. Have them check it out."

Abel shook his head as he took a bite of the shepherd's pie. "No. The last thing I want to do is tip off the people who have her. I don't trust the police, even here in London. The only way these places stay in business is by paying off the cops."

"Then what are you going to do?"

"Go in as a customer. See if it's really Alice. If it is, I'll sneak her out of there."

Lola smiled. "Sure you're not just lonely and looking for a nice evening?" She reached across and placed her hand on his. The meaning was clear to him.

"Lola, you are a beautiful woman. But Tunde's death is still an open wound for both of us. We should not fall into something neither of us is prepared for. So let's move slowly. Tonight we have business."

Lola nodded. "Of course. How soon are you going?"

"Maybe tonight. Can you help me?"

She nodded, anxious to be of service. "Whatever you need."

"I want you to plait my hair. I need a disguise. If Alice sees me in front of the others, and recognises me, she might give the game away before I'm ready to move."

Lola got up and moved behind him.

"All right. How do you want it?"

"I think in the cornrow style you're wearing. After you finish, we'll need to pick up some clothes."

An hour later, they returned to her flat with Abel's outfit. He had decided to dress up as a stoned-out reggae musician. And when they finished, he looked the part: a silky shirt, loose-fitting pants and a long, black winter jacket. The outfit was completed with a pair of dark, wrap-around glasses.

Lola smiled at him. "You look cool." She moved to him and kissed his cheek.

"Good luck, Abel. Come back to me, safe."

Abel's first stop was at an ATM, where he used his company credit card to get cash. He'd been spending lavishly and restocking his funds frequently. He hoped when the bills began arriving, they wouldn't elevate Chief Benson's blood pressure even more.

He located the massage parlour in a small nondescript building off South Audley Street. He walked confidently up to the lone receptionist, a tall lanky Jamaican, and registered as Roy Brake. He was dismayed to see he had to queue behind six men to have his turn. The place was popular, even mid-week.

As he took a seat, he tried to look more laid back than he felt. He was almost shaking in anticipation. Alice could well be behind these walls. As happy as he was at the prospect of finding the girl, it depressed him to think she had wound up here servicing overweight pasty Englishmen.

After about 45 minutes, he approached the lady of about 22, who tried to look tough with a straight face. Abel suspected she could only be working for the owner of the parlour.

"I've been waiting a long time. Don't tell me you only have one lady here," he said and pouted his lips impatiently.

"I'm sorry, Sir. We have three women, but our customers all seem to like Nanny, the African," the lady whispered.

This gave Abel hope that he'd found Alice. "That's okay. I'll wait for Nanny. She must be something special."

The lady gave him a tolerant nod, although Abel could see disapproval in her eyes. He didn't blame her. Abel returned to his seat.

Apart from the two hefty men at the gate, he hadn't seen a security person on the premises. Abel decided they must rely on cameras. A potential problem if he wanted to spirit Alice out of the place.

After another half hour, the lady finally called Abel. "Go straight up to the second floor. Third bedroom on the left."

Abel headed up the stairs, almost breathless. His heart beat quickly and he broke out in a sweat. He had no idea what Alice's reaction would be if he actually found her.

Abel counted three doors on the left and stood before the third. Music played somewhere down the hall behind one of the other doors. Abel put on his sunglasses and knocked. After a beat, a young girl whom he couldn't see clearly in the dim light, made worse by his shades, opened the door and let him inside. Before he could get a good look at her, she turned away and disappeared into an adjoining bathroom.

"Get undressed."

Abel didn't recognise her voice. Maybe it was Alice, maybe not. He looked around the room, which was furnished sparsely. A double bed and a mirrored wardrobe were pretty much it. The wardrobe door stood open and he could see a shelf housing various sex toys.

After a minute, the girl, obviously high on something, re-entered. She wore only a white bra, covering orange-shaped breasts, and white panties. Her eyes were glassy as she swayed back and forth. Abel stepped forward so he could see her better.

It was Alice. His knees went weak as he studied the girl who obviously did not recognise him. This didn't surprise Abel. He figured they probably kept her so high she couldn't tell you which continent she was on.

"I'm two hundred and fifty pounds an hour. I don't do massage. You want that, hire one of the other girls. I do foreplay and sex only. People who have been with me come back."

Abel could hardly believe that this was the same girl. Tears stung his eyes. Somehow after all the miles and all the pain, it was heartbreaking to see what had become of her. He wondered if there was anything human inside this shell left to save. What would her mother think when she saw her?

Alice had grown impatient. "So, are you going to undress? Time is wasting."

It was strange. When Abel had rescued her that night in Lagos, she had been so full of life, so seductive. Now she was offering a body devoid of a soul. Who would want to make love to such a creature? Did the men who came here really not notice? Didn't they care?

She started to undo her bra. Abel reached out and stopped her.

170

"Alice, don't." She looked at him blankly, as if he had spoken in some strange unexpected language. Abel took off his sunglasses.

"Alice listen carefully and don't say anything. I'm Peter Abel. Remember me? From Lagos?"

She stared at him as if listening to a faint voice spoken from far away. Her memory searched for the answer.

"I have come to take you home."

"Peter Abel ... I don't ..." Suddenly tears appeared in her eyes. "Yes. You cooked me dinner." The kind gesture made so long ago was still alive in her and this gave Abel hope she could be saved.

"Yes. That's right. You spent the night in my guest room. I need to get you out of here." Abel went to the wardrobe and dug out some jeans and a shirt. He tossed them to her.

"Come on." But Alice wasn't clear-headed enough to make the connection between the clothes and her need to put them on.

"Dress!"

"No. It's all right. I'm going away from here. Tomorrow. To Washington, D.C. That's in America."

"Then we really need to get out of here quickly." As Abel began to help the girl into the jeans, he worried about the security cameras. He glanced around the room and as he feared, there was one in the corner over the door.

Abel was struggling with a pant leg when he heard heavy footsteps running down the hallway. Before Abel could react, three hefty men in uniform burst inside.

"Get her out of here," ordered the shortest of the three.

Abel stood up. "Hold on. You can't take her anywhere. I've got agents outside and you guys are fucked. Now stand back!"

Abel figured his only hope was to bluff. For a second, the guards froze. Abel took the initiative and grabbed a robe from the floor, then flung it around Alice's shoulders. No time to dress her now.

"If you're a cop, I want to see some ID," the guard finally said.

"Come downstairs. My men will show you a dozen IDs. Look, we don't want you. We want the people who sell these girls. She's a material witness. You let me take her, we'll turn a blind eye this time."

The men seemed to be considering the proposal as Abel steered

Alice towards the door, hands on her shoulders. Just as he reached the open door, a middle aged woman he suspected to be the owner of the parlour appeared. She was the Madam, who must have bought Alice.

"He's no cop, you fools. He's a journalist. Hello, Mr. Abel."

Abel stopped in his tracks. How the hell could she know?

"Word gets around when someone is snooping about our business."

Two more security guards appeared at her side. One grabbed Alice by the arm and led her away down the hall, leaving Abel alone with four very angry Neanderthals.

"Take him downstairs to the basement," the Madam ordered.

"Wait!" Abel said. "How did you know?"

"We've been expecting you. For days."

Abel shook his head, signalling that he did not understand.

The man who brought the girl here, Lawal, he had been warned that you were looking for him, and he, in turn, warned us."

The truth hit Abel in a rush. The phone call Lawal had gotten in the restaurant in the desert, the call that upset him so. That had to be it, the warning. And Abel was willing to bet a week's salary that the alert had come from The Lion.

He wanted to ask something more, but the Madam had turned on her heel and was disappearing after Alice.

Abel remembered Lillian and her gun and thought he'd hit a very bad streak with the opposite sex. And as he was led by the arms toward the other end of the hallway, he wondered if this was to be his last night on Earth. For some reason, the fact that his final meal was Lola's shepherd's pie seemed grossly unfair.

When they reached the basement, one of his escorts shut the door. The leader of the team didn't wait long before smashing Abel in the jaw, sending him crashing into some old furniture.

The man grunted and pulled Abel up. His knees were weak, and he had a cut streaming blood from his chin.

"What do you want?" Abel managed to ask.

"Nothing," the man said as he kicked Abel's feet out from under him, which sent him sprawling on the floor. Abel realised with growing horror that the only thing they wanted was to stomp him to death.

They all jumped in, kicking Abel with their heavy boots. He tried to protect his ribs to little effect.

Several kicks later, the leader stopped his minions.

"Keep an eye on him, Von. I'm going to ask the Madam what we do with the body," he said and left with the two other men who were still panting.

As soon as the door shut, Von started kicking him again. Apparently Von wasn't going to wait to find out what was next on the fight card.

Abel groped behind him for anything with which to fight back. He found a broken leg of a chair with some nails protruding. When Von's black boot came down again, Abel thrust the nails as hard as he could into his attacker's knee.

"Aoo!" Von moaned, bending over to hold the torn knee.

Abel took the opportunity dig the nails into Von's eyes with all the strength he had left.

Von yelled and crashed into the furniture. Bleeding from the eyes, he tried to stand but he tumbled over a fallen stool and collapsed to the floor in agony.

The weapon still in his hand, Abel stumbled from the basement and made his way up the staircase to the first floor, where he found a window. He pushed it open and climbed out.

Abel made it to South Audley Street, where traffic was heavy. After a few seconds, he spotted a taxi and waved it down. He fell into the back seat and said simply, "The nearest hospital."

Once admitted, Abel called Lola who arrived a half hour later. She was there when Abel was brought to his private room, patched up and looking terrible.

Later the police interviewed him. They said when they raided the massage parlour it was empty. They traced the owners through the recorder's office but were certain it would lead them only to a dummy front company. The people who had beaten Abel and run off with Alice were no longer in England. Of that, he could be sure.

After they left, Lola held Abel's hand and stroked his bandaged head. She was sorry it had all turned out this way. Abel smiled at her.

"It didn't turn out so badly," he said. "I know where they have taken Alice. And as soon as they release me, I'm on their trail again."

"Where?"

"Washington, D.C."

"But why would they take her there?"

"That is what I'm going to find out. They have not seen the last of Peter Abel."

And then, as Lola sat by him, he closed his eyes and fell asleep.

CHAPTER TWENTY-ONE

Abel walked gingerly through Reagan National Airport. He hadn't fully recovered from the injuries he had received at the hands of the whorehouse thugs. His ribs were still sore and his back ached. The long transatlantic flight hadn't helped.

Still, being in Washington energised him.

It was the seat of government in the last superpower on earth, a nation wealthy enough to serve all of its citizens well. And yet even here, shoulder-by-shoulder with the opulent and impressive federal city, the extremes of wealth and poverty, or order and chaos, stared one another directly in the face.

On one side of town was the White House, a symbol of world power and national wealth. The Washington Monument glimmered in the sun as well as in the long reflecting pool on The Mall. Lincoln, carved in pristine white, sat grandly in his chair.

Only a few blocks away, within sight of these landmarks, lived the "other" America, the one with the worn project apartments and worn-out houses. These neighbourhoods were, at once, sustained and devastated by the drug and sex trades. Cynicism and distrust infused young blacks, who had watched their parents struggle to make an honest living yet never escaped the systemic poverty.

These disenfranchised youths served as bag carriers, drivers, and in some cases, cannon fodder for the drug lords. They viewed the ostentatious mansions, parks, and monuments with resentment. They all shared a Washington, D.C. address, but that's about all they had in common.

Alice, the child prostitute, was shuttled between these two starkly contrasting worlds. She would be kept in the ghetto but sent off to work in the land of privilege as she serviced congressmen, lawyers and rich businessmen, Abel thought painfully.

After checking into the Chevalier D.C. Hotel, an impressive work of architecture in the heart of the political metropolis, Abel pulled out his black address book. He had one solid contact in the city, a freelance journalist named Maxwell Elliot.

Elliot had remained freelance his entire career. He didn't like the idea of attaching himself to any single media outlet. In recent years, some members of the media had mutated from voracious journalists, hell-bent on revealing the truth, to corporate shills with ties to big business.

It was this maverick trait that made Abel believe Elliot would be helpful to him. The reporter picked up and immediately recognised Abel's voice.

"Don't get too many calls from people with a Nigerian accent," he said, laughing, and greeted Abel warmly. The two men had met a couple of years before when Elliot was in Africa doing a story on the almost unchecked spread of AIDS. He'd concluded, to nobody's surprise, that were this a European or an American problem, it would be getting a lot more attention and money.

"Where are you, Peter?" he asked. "Stateside?"

"Just got in," Abel told him. "Some city you've got here."

"It's even more fascinating under the surface," Elliot said.

"That's exactly why I'm calling you," Abel said.

Abel and Elliot arranged to meet at a place called Murphy's the next morning. It was a quiet coffeehouse off the beaten path, a place that was too out-of-the-way for tourists, but too expensive for the locals. Nicknamed "FYI" by its regular patrons, Murphy's had become the unofficial meeting place for people trading information.

Abel glanced up from his coffee cup to see the powerfully built Elliot push his way through the door. It had been quite a while since Peter Abel and Maxwell Elliot were in the same country, let alone the same room. Even so, Abel had no difficulty recognising his American counterpart. Elliot was only about five feet seven inches tall, but he had the broadest pair of shoulders Abel had ever seen. Although he had a touch of a "beer belly," he didn't seem overweight. He looked strong enough to hold his own in any altercation. It flashed through Abel's mind that having Elliot on hand during his London dustup might have been helpful.

"Welcome to D.C.," Elliot greeted as he approached the table.

"Thank you," Abel replied. He couldn't hide his mischievous

grin.

"Is something funny?" Elliot wondered.

"Sorry," Abel said, "but I think that's the same hat you were wearing when I first met you ten years ago."

Elliot took off his porkpie, examined it, and then set in on the table.

"It's part of my persona," he explained. "Without it, I lose my journalistic allure. I was thinking about having it attached with stitches, but it wouldn't be the same."

The two reporters huddled inside the booth, the lighting so dim that they had to lean across the table to see each other's faces. Abel relayed as much information as he could about Alice's situation.

"What do you think?" Abel asked. "Can you point me in any good directions?"

Elliot had listened, deeply interested, as Abel spun his tale. He scratched his chin. "I know one woman who used to be in the trade."

"She got out? I didn't think that was possible," Abel said.

"She got old. That's how you get out," Elliot responded. "But she keeps in touch with people, hears things. And she's made a career of trying to help young girls escape the life."

Abel thought this was exactly the kind of person he needed to speak with. Elliot made a call and arranged a meeting for later that morning.

"That was quick," Abel said, surprised.

"Mirabelle likes to help when she can. And the prospect of making a little cash was enough to clear her calendar."

When they arrived at Mirabelle's decrepit apartment, it became obvious to Abel that Elliot's remark about clearing her calendar had been totally facetious. Mirabelle turned out to be a sickly woman, who admitted up front she was constantly in and out of rehab clinics. And that made her the exception. Most ex-hookers were unapologetic junkies.

Mirabelle greeted them wearing an old cloth robe. Even though it was past noon, she had made no effort to bathe or dress herself since she got out of bed. Abel could see she had once been a striking-looking woman with a lush figure and blonde hair. Now, her hair was thin and straggly, her figure gone to seed. She was heavy and puffy and her skin was yellow.

As they talked, Mirabelle brewed coffee.

"Runners bring in girls from all over the world. I came from Denmark. They treated us real nice until they got us hooked on drugs. Then we can't afford to leave. We're slaves for the pimps because we need them to feed our habit."

Mirabelle served them coffee in cracked cups, but it smelled good enough. Abel watched her, feeling pity for this wasted life in front of him.

"And when you get older?" he asked.

"Well, when us girls get old - as human beings tend to do - we're not as valuable. The johns only want pretty young things, you know, especially the high rollers. The pimps stop giving the older girls the good dope and start feeding them bunk, the fake stuff. The girls get the shakes and the rest of the horrors. They don't generate income, so the pimps kick them out. After that, they just vanish."

Mirabelle sat down and joined them.

"But you're here."

"Yes. And I'm trying to do what I can, but I'm not much good at being a saviour. Shit, I can barely save myself."

Elliot sat forward. "My friend is looking for one specific girl. Her name's Alice. He has a picture."

Elliot nodded to Abel who showed Mirabelle the picture he had been carrying around with him all over the globe. She squinted at it.

"So, this girl," Mirabelle said. "What's her name again?"

"Alice. The last contact I had with her was in London."

Mirabelle clearly knew something. "I don't know the girl. But if the network who owns her moved her from Nigeria, through Europe, and then to the States, she must be a money maker."

Abel nodded. "Apparently she's popular wherever she goes. Is that why they brought her to D.C.?"

"No doubt. See, this is a town with money. Lots of money and very weird taste. Kinky sex. Sick, really. But it's full of politicians. What do you expect? Your Alice is, what? Fifteen?" She studied the picture.

"Yes."

"Okay. Someone that young who's that good, it's like finding a star. You get your stars to the spot where they can generate the most cash. Washington is the place."

"How do I find her?"

Mirabelle studied Abel. "You sure you want to find her, Peter? Because these folks aren't gonna appreciate your gallant knight routine."

"I already found that out."

Elliot chimed in. "Peter was almost beaten to death the last time he tried to rescue the girl."

Mirabelle laughed, not at Abel's pain, but at the irony. "Man, I woulda done anything for a guy who'd tried to save my ass. Where were you fifteen years ago, honey?"

"Can you help me find her?" Abel asked, not wanting to derail the discussion. "The information's worth good money."

Mirabelle looked at him, offended. "Now you're making me feel cheap."

Abel looked at Elliot who had assumed this is what she was after. She caught the look.

"Oh, I get it. Elliot here has a low opinion of me."

"Not at all, Mirabelle."

"I'll tell you what I know. You can pay me what you think it's worth. Fair enough?"

Abel, feeling slimy, nodded.

Mirabelle wrote something down on a pad of paper. She handed it to Abel.

"Call this number. Ask for Dennis, Luud Dennis," Mirabelle explained. "Say you're the assistant to a visiting African dignitary and your boss needs a little entertainment. Tell him he's homesick. Maybe that will convince him to hook you up with an African girl."

"Then I'll actually become the dignitary, right?" Abel asked. Mirabelle nodded. "That's the game, sure."

"Who is Dennis?"

"He runs the most profitable stable of girls in D.C. Most of them come from abroad. If your Alice was high-priced coming out Africa and Europe, she'll work for Dennis. That doesn't mean he's got her, but it's the best place to start."

Abel folded up the paper and stood up. He reached into his pocket and pulled out some bills. He counted three hundred and handed Mirabelle the money.

"I want you to know, I take twenty percent and put it away for any girl who needs help. I use it to buy bus tickets, plane tickets, new clothes, new hairdo for a disguise. I'm not a whore anymore."

Abel put a hand on her shoulder, moved by the woman's attempt to attain some dignity. "I never thought you were, Mirabelle. Thank you. And God bless you."

Mirabelle shook her head. "Too late for that. All I want from Him now is to quit throwing shit my way."

After dropping Elliot off at his apartment and agreeing to keep in touch, Abel booked himself into a different hotel – one that would more likely serve as the lodging location for a visiting African dignitary. Elliot had suggested the Hotel Cornelius, located only a few blocks away from the Capitol building.

After settling in, Abel unfolded the paper on which Mirabelle had written Dennis's number and called him. Giving the same false name he used when checking into the hotel and speaking as his own assistant, he requested an evening of bliss for his employer with a girl from his homeland, with a special order for a girl in the age range of 15 to 17. He didn't dare ask specifically for Alice, for fear of making the man suspicious.

"I'm sure I can be of service to your employer," Dennis replied, all business. "You can meet her in the hotel bar at eleven. Are you the one handling the fee for services?"

Abel rolled his eyes. Fee for services? Did this guy really think he was running a legitimate business?

"Yes, I'll handle the fee."

"Cash," Dennis stated flatly. "American dollars only."

The conversation ended with an assurance the girl would be to his boss's liking.

At precisely 11 p.m., Abel entered the hotel bar. As he looked around, praying Alice would be waiting for him, he was approached by an attractive young African girl wearing high heels and a cocktail dress.

"Good evening, Mr. Aboku." She greeted him softly, using the false name he had given her pimp. "Mr. Dennis sent me."

Abel forced himself to smile. His heart sank.

"Let's get a table."

He guided the girl to a corner table where they would have maximum privacy. She was a far cry from the everyday streetwalker, yet her youthful features didn't match the maturity of her fashion statement. Abel studied her face. He recognised her features to be Sudanese, but her swagger was undeniably American-influenced.

The girl studied Abel's face in return, confused by his expression. "Is everything all right?" she asked quietly. "You look disappointed."

Abel shook his head and let out an uncomfortable laugh. "Nothing is wrong," he assured her. "I was simply expecting someone else."

"Had you requested someone else?"

"Not exactly."

The waiter came by and they ordered drinks, the girl a Tom Collins and Abel a double scotch. After the waiter departed, the girl put a hand on his arm and leaned closer to him. "I'm sure I can help your employer forget about everyone else."

"Look, I'm sure you could under ordinary circumstances. But the truth is, tonight, it's just me, and I just want to talk," he said.

The girl sighed involuntarily, as if she were preparing for an unpleasant but necessary task. Abel caught the attitude. He also saw the resignation in her manner. Apparently she felt it was her job to "entertain" him and if that meant tedious conversation, that's what she'd put up with.

Or perhaps she was reacting to his disappointment. Abel internally admonished himself. What made him think that out of all the prostitutes in Washington, D.C. he could just summon Alice by asking some faceless pimp for an African woman?

But he knew that in certain circles, large cities like D.C. had a way of turning into small towns, if one were to ask the right questions.

"What's your name?" he began.

"Marcy," the girl said flatly.

"How old are you, Marcy?"

181

"Twenty."

Abel looked at her. *Right*, he thought. *If this girl is twenty, I'm seventy-three.*

She was seventeen at the most, but probably younger than that. This kind of life tended to make young ladies age quickly – and this girl still seemed very young. But he had more important matters to pursue.

"Marcy," Abel continued, "I won't need your usual services tonight."

Marcy was about to protest, but Abel cut her off.

"Not to worry," he assured her. "You'll get paid for your time. In fact, you'll receive a very generous gratuity if you can help me."

Marcy looked interested. "What do you want to know?"

"I'm looking for a girl," he told her. "She is very much like you. In the same line of work, shall we say."

"I know lots of girls."

"This one is from my country." He showed Marcy the photograph.

"Alice. She's fifteen and originally from Nigeria."

As they sipped their drinks, Marcy told him she knew Alice. She said Alice worked for Dennis. But then she fell silent. Abel took the hint, reached into his pocket and pulled out his money clip. He peeled off a $50 bill and handed it to Marcy. She snatched it out of his hand and slipped it into her dress. Abel held up the money clip.

"What else can you tell me?" he pressed.

"I'm not sure how long she's been here. Not long, I don't think. I haven't really spoken to her. From what I can tell, she's been introduced to some very important clients."

"Of her own free will?" Abel asked.

Marcy winced. "Nobody is here willingly." Abel realised Marcy was right. It was a stupid question.

"Sorry. Look, I need to find her. It's very important."

"The most I can say for sure is that Dennis watches her closely. She is of great value to him or someone he knows."

"So, she won't be leaving town anytime soon?"

"That's up to Dennis. She'll only disappear if he chooses to make her disappear. And that could happen if he runs into some

182

kind of trouble."

Abel pulled open his money clip, peeled two hundred-dollar bills off the roll, and handed them to Marcy. Once again, she snatched the cash out of his hand.

Abel paid for their drinks and stood up. "I think we're done for tonight," he said.

Abel walked her to the lobby, thanked her for an informative evening, and headed for the elevators. The girl left without comment. Abel had no idea if she was insulted or relieved he hadn't slept with her. It was probably all the same to her.

By the time he had reached his room, he'd made a plan. If Alice was Dennis's "girl of the moment," she'd be servicing his most powerful johns. Somehow, Abel had to get a look at Dennis's client list. No easy feat. It was bound to be his most carefully guarded possession.

Abel picked up the phone beside his bed and punched out a few numbers.

"You've reached my voice mail," Maxwell Elliot's recorded voice garbled. "Leave a message and make it quick."

Beep.

"Max, it's Peter Abel. I have a lead, and need to talk to you. There's a great story here for both of us if you can help me. Call my cell as soon as you pick this up." Abel left his number and hung up.

Now all he had to do was wait for Elliot's response. Abel wasn't patient by nature and this waiting for a call-back was the thing he hated most about journalism.

He finally climbed into bed and tried to read a paperback he'd picked up in the London airport. It was a thriller about Vegas gambling and a security expert who busted cheaters. He liked the breezy style and the feel of authenticity. But he couldn't concentrate.

Abel found himself reading the same paragraph a fourth time. When he still didn't know what it said, he gave up and turned out the light. But he couldn't sleep either. He looked at the clock around three and was tempted to call Elliot again but thought better of it.

When he was finally about to drift off, a siren broke through the night air. Abel cursed under his breath. This always happened when he travelled to large cities. Hospitals, fire companies and police, seemed to do their best business when everyone else was trying to sleep.

At six o'clock Abel gave up. He got out of bed, threw on some clothes, went for a walk.

After wandering aimlessly for an hour, Abel decided he needed something to eat. He entered a diner and took a booth near the front.

By the time his breakfast of eggs, ham and orange juice had arrived, he had finished the morning *Post*. Abel fretted about how he was going to get at Dennis's client list. He was counting on his fellow journalist to help him. If he didn't come through, Abel was sunk.

Abel glanced up just long enough to notice the diner staff gathering to watch the TV mounted in the corner above the cash register.

The busboy pointed up at the screen. "This stuff doesn't usually happen in this neighbourhood."

"Yeah, it does," the hostess countered. "It just doesn't get reported much. It's bad for tourism."

"Turn it up," the waiter said.

The hostess reached up and adjusted the volume.

"The body was discovered in the early hours of the morning near the service entrance by a truck driver making a delivery to the hotel," the reporter announced.

Abel was suddenly alert. He recognised the hotel immediately. He had been lying awake in a bed in one of its rooms barely an hour earlier. And he recognised the alleyway as the one behind the hotel. Paramedics were wheeling a gurney down the alley with a covered body strapped to it.

"The young woman had been seen in the hotel lobby earlier that evening," the reporter continued. "Hotel workers identified her as a regular visitor, but so far investigators have been unable to officially confirm her identity."

Abel slumped back in his booth and rubbed his eyes. He was sure the dead woman was Marcy. And he was sure her murder had something to do with their meeting the previous night.

His heart ached for the poor girl. She had done nothing wrong.

Why did these thugs have to kill her? Was this supposed to be a warning to him? Were they preparing to do the same thing to Alice?

What he saw next stunned Abel. His face, a grainy image, filled the TV screen.

"Investigators have released this videotape taken by a hotel lobby security camera late last night," the reporter explained.

The image being beamed across the country — and perhaps other parts of the world — was one of Marcy walking alongside Abel through the hotel lobby. Able knew it had been recorded as they left the bar.

"The young woman was seen with a tall, thin man believed to be in his mid-thirties," the reporter continued. "A hotel employee said he was a guest of the hotel, however, he was not in his room when police raided it just moments ago. Several objects, some said to have shown evidence of blood, were allegedly found among the man's belongings."

"Damn!" Abel muttered under his breath. He checked his pocket for his passport and was relieved to find it. It held his true identity. His shoulders sagged as the truth hit him.

The whole encounter had been a setup. He should have insisted on meeting the girl in his room. He'd been told to meet her in the bar so intruders could salt his room with her blood, and he'd walked right into the trap.

"Records with the hotel desk do not confirm the man's identity, and investigators believe he was registered under a false name. Police describe this man as a 'person of interest' in this young woman's murder and are actively searching for him."

Abel's first instinct was to jump out of his seat and charge for the door, but that would have been dangerous and stupid. He was barely two blocks away from the scene of a crime for which he was the prime suspect. The last thing he could afford to do was appear guilty.

He nonchalantly pulled his hat down lower over his face and took another swig of coffee. He waited until the news broadcast switched to a story about some disaster in South America before leaving money for his meal on the table and exiting as surreptitiously as possible.

He carefully wove his way into the human traffic that was moving along the sidewalk, melting into the throng of congressional staffers rushing to early breakfast meetings.

CHAPTER TWENTY-TWO

"Hey, Peter! I saw you on TV this morning. Next time, make sure they get your good side." Maxwell Elliot chuckled. At the other end of the phone connection, Abel cringed.

"I'm glad you find it so funny," he said with an edge to his voice. "I'm a goddamned murder suspect. I'm in hiding for God's sake."

"I wouldn't sweat the cops in this town, Peter. They couldn't find their ass with both hands."

Abel shook his head. He was as cynical as the next reporter, but right now he wouldn't mind some sympathy.

"Look, I spent the night hiding in some Motel 6, so I'm in no mood, Maxwell. I need your help."

"No shit."

"When can we meet?"

Abel could hear Elliot fumbling around with some papers.

"Hold steady there, Abel," Elliot encouraged. "Let me get a few things together for you. Meet me outside that coffee shop in half an hour. And try not to get shot."

"Thanks for the advice," Abel muttered. He could hear the sarcasm in his tone. If Elliot heard it as well, it didn't bother him.

Abel could hear Elliot laugh as he snapped his cell phone shut.

Abel's hands were beginning to ache in the morning cold as he made his way to the coffee shop. As he approached the entrance, he spotted Elliot standing on the sidewalk. He was surprised to see him dressed in a business suit.

Abel shook his head in mock admiration. "You dress up just for me?"

"I always put on my so-fines when I aid and abet a murder suspect." Abel gave him a look and Elliot shrugged. "I figured we might be less conspicuous if we both looked like businessmen." Elliot studied Abel's rumpled suit, which he had worn now for the better part of two days. "Although that suit doesn't exactly sell the concept."

"You want to buy me a change of underwear I'm all yours."

"Undies are a little personal. Maybe a new tie."

Before Abel could think of a smart rejoinder, Elliot headed off down the street. "Come on. We need to find a less conspicuous place to talk."

Ten minutes later they were in the quiet corner of a local park. Across from them, asphalt basketball courts already were taking a pounding from groups of kids either skipping school or waiting for a drug deal to go down. Or maybe looking out for a scout from the NBA. Abel and Elliot sat on a bench near some broken swings and a sandbox no mother in her right mind would let her kid get near. Abel looked around, uncomfortable.

"Nice spot."

"Cops avoid it. I figured that might be an advantage considering your circumstances." Elliot pulled some papers out of his ratty briefcase. "Dead hooker's last name was Tripps," he announced.

"Marcy Tripps," Abel repeated, memorising it.

Elliot handed him a four-by-six colour photograph. "At least that's the name she went by. I managed to find a little bit on her. Father was Sudanese. Mother was Jamaican."

In the picture, Marcy was standing beside a short portly Caucasian man with a bad comb-over. The guy had to be three times her age.

A siren wailed somewhere nearby and Abel turned, startled. He and Elliot shared a look. The siren belonged to an ambulance, which flew past unmindful of them. It occurred to Abel he might not be the only fugitive in the park.

"When was this photo taken?" he said.

Elliot flipped it over and pointed to the date on the back. It was about six weeks old.

"Who's the man?" Abel said. "Dennis?"

Elliot shook his head. "That's Congressman Jason Schroeder, from Kentucky. He's one of those Moral Majority types. Made his bones opposing gay marriage and supporting the military. He's a Vietnam vet – sort of."

"Sort of?"

"National Guard." Elliot said. "The closest Schroeder ever came to Southeast Asia was stir-fried noodles at his local Thai restaurant."

Abel's eyes narrowed as he continued staring at the photograph. "What's Mr. Moral Majority doing with a high-end prostitute?" Abel knew the answer, but he was curious to hear Elliot's version of it.

"He's doing the same thing that any other holier-than-thou hypocrite would do," Elliot said, deadpan. "Saving her soul."

Abel grunted. "Where'd you get this?"

"Private detective. Worked for Schroeder's wife. I guess the happy couple worked it out because they're still married, and I think Schroeder still manages to see Ms. Tripp."

"How come his political enemies haven't splashed this all over the *Post*?"

"Man, for a reporter you are one naïve dude. Look, Democrats, Republicans, Independents. They all swim in the same sewer, all drink from it. They all have secrets. Someone starts a pissing contest, everyone goes down. You understand? Everybody knows everything about everybody else. Nobody talks. It's one cosy club. One. As in undivided by issues affecting the public good. They might take swings at each other on political stuff, but it's bullshit. You know. Theatre for public consumption. In the end, they're rich and privileged, and they run the country for their own benefit and the benefit of their friends and benefactors, and this red-state-blue-state stuff is all crap. The rest of us saps just think we have a choice when we vote. You never read Gore Vidal? The man's a prophet. Only he's Cassandra because nobody believes him."

"That's cynical, even for an American journalist," Abel said. "Surely, there are a few honourable people serving your country."

Elliot thought about that for a moment and then nodded as if it violated his wishes.

"Yeah, there are," he said. "But they only get so far before they hit the glass ceiling. They never grab the brass ring. Never. Those who have too much to lose see to it that the ring stays within the conspiracy."

"So, what's your stake in this?"

"I don't know how much you've heard about this in your part of the world, but American spirituality has been hi-jacked, mostly by guys like Schroeder, who sell God as a commodity for their own gain. You've got your story, the human trafficking stuff. This one is mine. I've been looking to bring down Schroeder and his pals for quite a while now, the ones who get the faithful in America to vote for them on the claim they're doing the Lord's work, when they're doing exactly the opposite. The guys who imply their actions are dictated by the will and the word of God, when in fact they were dictated by the sources of their campaign contributions. The ones who only walk in the front door of a church for a photo opportunity. I'm still getting my evidence together. This photo is just one piece of it."

Elliot let out a frustrated sigh. "I was hoping to talk to Marcy about Schroeder, but I could never get close enough. Dennis keeps his girls under lock and key."

"Boy, it happens in Nigeria too. Politicians flaunt religion on telly, and God must be shaking his head in regret. It is a story I will look at someday, but for now, it is Alice." Abel took the photo back from Elliot and looked at it again. "Marcy said she knew Alice. And that Alice works for Dennis."

"I have informants who say Schroeder's taste runs to girls like your Alice. Young African women with fat bums. I hear he has no patience for elaborate foreplay which our women insist they must have for full sex."

Abel studied Elliot. "Then he might be sleeping with her."

"That wouldn't be a bad guess. She's hot new talent. Dennis is gonna sell her to his best clients."

"What now?"

"Schroeder's careful when his wife's in town. But she's on a trip with other Congressmen's wives now. Some goodwill tour of Mexican schools. Chances are, he'll be playing while the cat's away."

"You know his schedule?"

"I do my homework. I'm just as eager to bring this asshole down as you are to save Alice. He's giving a speech tonight at the Mayflower Hotel. My guess is, after the speech, he retreats upstairs and has a little fun."

"That sounds like a long shot."

"Oh ye of little faith. I checked with my source in the hotel. Someone in Schroeder's office booked a room. Under as assumed name, of course."

"What room number?"

"He won't tell me. He's already shitting a brick about giving me this much. But if we know Schroeder's going to be there for the night, we can trail the guy right to his room. Provided we can avoid the bodyguards."

"For Schroeder?"

Elliot shook his head and pointed at the photo. There was another figure walking a few paces behind Schroeder and Marcy. "One of Dennis's men. Always shadowing the girls when they work."

Abel's eyes hardened. "He might have killed Marcy because she was with me. How could they know who I was?"

"You told me it was no secret you were in town," he said. "Someone tipped him off."

"Damn!" Abel muttered under his breath. "They must've known it was me from the start. When I described the girl I wanted, someone who looked like Alice, I gave myself away."

Elliot shrugged. "If it went down that way, then Marcy was a sacrificial lamb."

"You mean, they planned to kill her when they sent her to me?"

"Sure. It's why they arranged for you to meet her in the bar. Got you on video with the victim-to-be."

"That's a lot of trouble to go through for a foreign journalist."

"They probably think you have bigger targets than you actually do," he said. "You just want to save your Alice. They think you want to take down their entire operation."

"If it would save those girls from this filthy life, I *would* take down their entire operation," Abel said.

"You're what we call in the States a real Boy Scout." Elliot said with a laugh.

Abel looked at the only friend he had in the entire country and thought how different they were. Elliot hadn't been this much of a cynic when they met. Perhaps years of investigating crime,

191

corruption and deviance produced his bitter, rawhide façade. Abel found himself suddenly uncomfortable with his friend. Maybe Abel had allowed himself to get too emotional about his pursuit of a story, the way Elliot got overly emotional about his investigation. Chief Benson's words echoed in his ears. A reporter out for revenge is not good at this job.

As Abel pondered this, Elliot put the pictures back in his briefcase and got up. "Come on. We need to get you a shower and a clean change of clothes before tonight."

"You really think Schroeder will end up with Alice?"

"He won't be with Marcy," Elliot remarked, "unless he has an unknown fondness for necrophilia."

"Jesus, Maxwell."

"You have to admit, it'd make the Schroeder story much more interesting."

Abel just looked at him. "Where exactly is the Mayflower Hotel?" Abel said.

"Not necessary. I'll take you there."

Abel shook his head. "I'm going alone. You can't be involved. If things go bad I won't have you on my conscience."

It was a noble gesture, but Abel wondered if it wasn't being selfish. He was getting tired of Elliot's cynical remarks and edgy attitude. And in any event, he worked better alone. On the few occasions where he'd had a partner, he never felt comfortable, and things had gone badly, perhaps inevitably. This time, with his own life at stake, Abel needed to be able to control everything, make his moves and not feel responsible for someone else.

Elliot didn't argue. He gave Abel the address and the time and place of Schroeder's speech.

"After the speech and dinner, maybe around eleven, Schroeder will head for the room. That's when you make your move."

"Thanks, Maxwell. I appreciate this. Do me a favour? Call my cell if you come up with anything more."

Elliot nodded. "No problem. Just remember. You share what you learn. I still have my story to write. Got it?"

Able nodded.

"Okay, before I send you on your way, let's attend to your

hygiene."

Abel smiled at the jibe. He had to admit, he'd be grateful for a shower and a fresh outfit.

After a visit to the local YMCA where he showered, Abel emerged to find Elliot had somehow found him an entire change of clothing. Elliot told him the underwear and socks came from a local department store and the suit and shirt from the Goodwill.

"Thought underwear was too personal," Abel teased.

"I did it out of self-interest. You were pretty ripe. You'd never make it ten feet inside that hotel tonight before security jumped all over you. Then I'd have no story."

"You got heart, my friend."

Elliot wished him luck, reiterated the request for an update on Schroeder once Abel had secured Alice, and departed.

It qualified as the longest day of Peter Abel's life. There was no way to find Alice safely until late that night when Abel planned to slip into the hotel where Congressman Jason Schroeder was scheduled to speak, eat and, Abel hoped, enjoy some female entertainment. There was no guarantee, of course, that Schroeder was meeting a hooker, and even if he were planning that, his companion might not be Alice.

Despite Elliot's dismissal of the Washington, D.C. Police Department, they continued to hunt him. Abel knew when it came to politics and power, all countries, democracies, monarchies, Communist regimes and dictatorships were exactly the same. The local police were going to protect the powerful. It's just how things worked in this world.

Now who was getting cynical? Abel thought.

Yet he had no doubt that powerful forces were putting out the word that he was dangerous and needed to be apprehended quickly. And not necessarily alive.

It also occurred to Abel that getting arrested might be the least of his worries. The syndicate who ran these girls had already slaughtered Marcy without a second thought. If he was their target, and he certainly was, they were probably in a race with the police to see who could get to him first.

Either way, chances were if he tried to throw up his hands in the middle of a crowded street and surrender, he'd likely still get shot by someone claiming they saw him going for a weapon.

These circumstances forced Abel to remain suspicious of anyone who looked in his direction. Every time he caught a pair of eyes glance his way, he wondered if they belonged to a member of the syndicate. Or were they informants? Or police investigators? Or simply people going about their business with no interest in him whatsoever? But if they were ordinary citizens, did they recognise his face from the news broadcast, and if so, would they reach for their cell phones and call the police?

One woman who walked past Abel, suddenly pulled out her cell phone, quickly punched in a number, and appeared to speak nervously. Abel's heart was in his throat as he carefully turned his head to get a better look at her. After a few moments, the woman flipped her phone shut and slipped it back into her pocket without looking back. Abel felt foolish but relieved.

He had read about paranoid people and all their crazy fears, and now he found himself highly sympathetic to them. And who knew? Maybe they had damned good reason to be paranoid. Maybe he did.

Abel found a quiet place to ponder his fate and make plans, the local library. It was perfect. He found several books on the Washington. D.C. area so he could familiarise himself with the city, then settled into a seat among the stacks.

He needed to make a contingency plan if Alice did not show up that night. He'd have to find Dennis, her pimp. But how? He had no idea what the man looked like or where he was located. He didn't even know if Dennis was in Washington. Or for that matter if Dennis was his real name.

From the sound of his voice, Abel guessed Dennis was a white man in his forties. The man had coughed a couple of times, not from a cold, but a deep chronic smoker's cough. One small clue. Lots of people smoked, but not, perhaps, as many in the United States as overseas. He accepted the cough for what it was, a clue, and better than nothing.

Abel hoped Alice would appear that night at the Mayflower. Otherwise he would have to look for Dennis with the police looking for him, and that seemed an impossible task. He couldn't even think of a disguise he could adopt to any certain advantage.

Abel shook his head at this idiotic train of thought. He was getting woozy and losing his focus. His energy was definitely at an ebb. He wanted nothing more than to find a nice warm bed and take a long nap.

The thought flashed through Abel's mind that perhaps he should give up this mission and get the hell out of Washington.

He didn't know why that notion occurred to him. He'd done this sort of investigation plenty of times before in his homeland. He wasn't new to danger. Whenever bad guys felt threatened, they fought back. They'd already tried to shoot him once, when they ambushed his car back on the bridge. The danger had followed him and would continue to follow him until one side prevailed.

This was an international problem. Abel knew he had nothing to gain by fleeing. Even if he left the United States and didn't make another move against Dennis and the rest of the syndicate, the people who wanted him dead would continue to hunt him down wherever he went. They would assume, even if he stood down now, that he would take up the cause again someday, never giving up his mission. That was his reputation. That was his vulnerability. He was stubborn.

Thus, he made a solemn pledge to himself. He was not leaving the United States without Alice.

CHAPTER TWENTY-THREE

About ten that night, Abel made his way to the posh Mayflower Hotel where Elliot told him Congressman Schroeder would be.

He slipped in through the service entrance with an unsuspecting member of the laundry crew. Abel realised his professional clothing wouldn't allow him to pass for a hotel employee, so he had conjured up an alternate identity all by himself, without Lola.

"How busy is the shift this evening?" Abel asked the crew member as they approached the service entrance.

The woman, dressed in a housekeeping uniform, looked at him oddly. "It's normal, I guess," she said.

He smiled at her. "I'm with the Department of Health and Safety," he told her. "I'm just doing a routine inspection."

The woman nodded indifferently. She was a maid earning minimum wage. If the hotel got dinged for health violations, that wasn't her problem.

"I bet you find lots of shit. The pigs who run this sty oughta be in jail."

Abel knew that was sour grapes from an employee who felt ill-used. He had read in the Library that the Mayflower had an excellent reputation and had it for decades.

She opened the entrance door and disappeared inside. Abel followed her. The woman, totally indifferent to him, had vanished, leaving Abel alone.

He found himself at the head of a staircase with only one option: down. Abel took the stairs into the bowels of the building. A few hotel employees were scattered about, folding linens and filling service carts with cleaning agents, sponges, rubber gloves and fresh towels.

Abel wandered down the corridor, trying to appear casual as he glanced around. He reached another metal staircase, which clearly suggested a passage from the workers' area up to the "other" world, the place with the heritage, high ceilings, wall-to-wall carpeting, and sparkling chandeliers for the guests to enjoy.

Abel took a moment to reflect on his surroundings. This was, after all, the hotel where the legendary FBI director, J. Edgar Hoover, ate lunch every day in the dining room. He wondered if Hoover's table had a sign over it, or a nameplate on the surface. Washington liked that sort of thing.

But Abel had work to do. He wanted to scout out all entrances and exits, as well as the placement of the security cameras. If he had to run with Alice, he had to know the lay of the land.

He passed quickly through the lobby and moved towards the rear of the building. He saw exits which led to the main thoroughfares around the hotel, but that wasn't what he was looking for.

He searched farther, peering through doorways into offices and meeting rooms. Finally, he approached a large double door. He pushed it open cautiously and found exactly what he wanted: a warehouse area. It stored furniture in various stages of repair, large drapery rods and rows of service carts. At the far end, Abel saw his escape hatch, a large rolling door already halfway up, a rope handle dangling from a hook at the centre. Abel made a mental note of it and walked back down the corridor, counting exactly how many steps it was between the warehouse and the edge of the lobby.

As he approached the lobby area, Abel noticed a uniformed security guard patrolling the corridor. The man was not looking in his direction, but just the sight of him reminded Abel once again that he was a fugitive. He paused for a moment and adjusted his suit jacket before nonchalantly walking into the lobby.

Abel started worrying that Alice would not be the Congressman's date. It was just too easy. But if it turned out to be another girl, Abel wanted to create an opportunity to ask her where Alice was. Getting information from a hooker would be infinitely easier than hunting down the elusive Dennis.

As Abel considered this option, he made his way down to the floor where several banquet rooms were located. Elliot had told him that Schroeder was speaking in the Oak Room. Abel saw it dead ahead of him. A man in a tuxedo was just exiting, talking on a cell

197

phone. Abel managed to get a peek through the open doorway. He saw Schroeder on the dais eating dinner. Probably rubbery chicken, overcooked broccoli, cold potatoes and gooey cherry cobbler. Classic banquet fare. If there was any justice in the world, Schroeder would get ptomaine poisoning from the chicken and die a painful and horrible death. Preferably while he watched Abel waltz away with Alice on his arm.

Now that he had located Schroeder, he needed to find a place where he could watch the Oak Room's entrance. Abel chose one of the comfortable chairs scattered at random around the open areas of the hotel. Usually, they were placed by columns and hidden behind large potted tropical trees. It struck Abel as ridiculous. Some plant that belonged in the West Indies stuck in a climate where it snowed. At any rate, the out-of-place trees provided Abel with some cover. At that moment he was grateful for the stupidity of American excess.

A half an hour after taking up his spot, the banquet apparently broke up because people began streaming out of the Oak Room.

Finally, Abel caught close sight of his target. Congressman Jason Schroeder, a short, balding, portly man in a tuxedo, exited the room and headed up the stairs towards the lobby. Abel followed at a discrete distance.

Schroeder nodded a weary but friendly greeting to the bellman and then shook hands with a man who was passing by. Abel wondered if that man was connected to Dennis and if he would be delivering the girl-for-hire to Schroeder's room.

As Schroeder moved towards the bank of elevators, Abel walked up beside him and looked at the numbers on the elevator display. This was the patented elevator passenger's posture. Schroeder didn't even look over, which relieved Abel.

When one of the elevators finally reached the lobby, the doors slid open and a few passengers spilled out. Schroeder, along with three others, stepped inside. Abel casually joined them. At the last second, a man wearing a tailored business suit slipped inside. The timing of his arrival put Abel on edge.

Using his peripheral vision, Abel watched Schroeder push the button for the ninth floor. Another man pushed seven.

"Push eight, please," a woman in the back requested.

Schroeder nodded and obliged. Now it was Abel's turn. He reached over and pushed number ten. The man in the business suit twisted his neck to get a look at the panel, but he did not press a button. This didn't make Abel feel any more secure. He tried to study the man's expression, but he was giving away nothing. Not a guy you wanted to play poker with.

The elevator stopped at the seventh floor, then the eighth. That left Schroeder, Abel, and the poker player.

When the bell rang signalling they had arrived at the ninth floor, Schroeder sighed and waited patiently for the doors to open. When they finally did, he exited and took a right turn down the hall.

With the presence of the mystery man, Abel couldn't exit behind Schroeder and was prevented from holding the elevator until he could see which room he entered.

Abel felt an involuntary chill. The other man was standing much too close to him. The ride to the next floor seemed as if it took forever. When the doors finally opened, Abel decided to wait and let the man in the business suit exit first. But he didn't move. Abel looked at his profile, trying to read his face. Something wasn't right.

They stood with the elevator doors opened onto the tenth floor for a few seconds, neither one of them moving. Finally, Abel took the initiative and stepped out into the hallway. The other man followed.

Abel was not sure where to go. His plan had been to take the stairs down one flight to tail Schroeder on the ninth floor, but his unwelcome companion's presence prevented that.

Finally, Abel turned and headed for the far end of the corridor. He expected to be followed, but instead he heard the man speaking in a low voice. Abel reached the end of the corridor and turned, but the man had disappeared. This shook Abel. Was he talking to some compatriot on a cell phone or two-way radio? Was he relaying Abel's position? Or was Abel being paranoid again?

Abel stood at the end of the hall and looked out of a window that provided a ten storey high view of the city. The night was dotted with lights from shops, offices and monuments. Abel wasn't sure what he should do next. He wanted to run down the stairs and catch up with Congressman Schroeder, but he was afraid that would present too much of a risk.

The man who had ridden the elevator with him was not with the police. If he had been, he simply would've arrested Abel on the spot. He considered that he might have been a private bodyguard for Jason Schroeder, but he quickly dismissed that possibility. Schroeder had no way of knowing Abel was tailing him. The only person who knew that was Maxwell Elliot. For a moment, Abel wondered if Elliot had ratted him out. Not likely. Elliot was too much of a hardcore journalist to cave in to pressure from a political figure. Then again, maybe he had no choice. Elliot had been pursuing Schroeder for more than a year. Perhaps someone had turned on Elliot.

Finally, Abel admitted he was avoiding the obvious, perhaps because it was too terrifying. The mystery man had to be a member of the syndicate. They were the ones who knew Abel was hunting for Alice.

If this were the case, though, why wasn't Abel dead?

Of course. Too many witnesses around. There were other people who'd seen Abel standing with the mystery man. He could be identified. Which meant they must be waiting for him to leave the hotel to make their move. They were watching him. And apparently, they wanted Abel to know they were watching.

Why? Again, the answer seemed obvious. If Abel knew he'd been spotted, he'd have to make a run for it. And that's when they'd have him.

Abel found the stairwell and walked down one flight. His teeth were grinding as he fought off the unrelenting desire to burst onto the ninth floor and bang on every door until he found Jason Schroeder. Dennis's girl, be it Alice or someone else, would arrive soon. The more Abel thought about it, the less likely it seemed that Schroeder would be having a dalliance with Alice. It might have been in the cards earlier, but if the syndicate knew where he was, then word would have been sent back to Dennis to keep Alice away from the hotel.

Once he reached the lobby, Abel checked out every major exit. Strange men, men who might or might not be part of this, seemed to be everywhere.

Abel was glad he had done his due diligence. He manoeuvred his way down the rear corridor until he reached the warehouse. He then weaved his way around the errant pieces of furniture until he reached the roll up door.

"Hey!" a deep male voice shouted. "What do you think you're doing?"

Abel glanced back to see a man wearing coveralls and a tool belt snarling at him. Abel ignored the carpenter's grumblings and continued toward the door. It was still only rolled up halfway, but Abel managed to exit the building by crouching underneath it.

The cool air smacked him in the face so harshly he had to catch his breath. He wasn't quite sure where he was in relation to the main hotel entrance. There was very little light shining in the area, and Abel bumped his knee on something he couldn't identify as he tried to get his bearings.

He shuffled up against the building until he rounded the corner and found himself in a parking lot. He saw a large sign prominently displayed: *LOT C: PARKING FOR HOTEL EMPLOYEES ONLY. GUESTS PLEASE USE LOT B.*

The lot was half-full, and there were no signs of people coming or going. He was about to take a step away from the building into the light when he saw something that was curiously out of place.

Most of the hotel's employees were housekeepers, bellmen, waiters, busboys, and other service people who drove modest cars as befitted their low economic state. The cars parked in the lot reserved for employees reflected this. Among the compacts, hatchbacks, old-model vehicles, and practical pick-up trucks, Abel observed one vehicle that didn't fit the mould. A long, black, four-door Lincoln Town Car. This didn't belong to a dishwasher or maid.

Abel's heart pounded. He heard sirens in the distance. He was sure the syndicate had alerted the D.C. Police to his whereabouts at the hotel. And if he tried to run, he was certain they had men stationed all around it, hiding somewhere in the dark, silencers and scopes at the ready. He'd be taken out with one shot. Another Washington casualty in a city with an astronomical crime rate. Who'd care? Who'd even notice?

All this made Abel determined to make his move now. What did he have to lose?

He pressed his back against the wall of the building and shuffled toward the opposite end of the parking lot. He then slipped behind one of the parked cars and crouched. Moving between them, Abel made his way toward the Lincoln. He stopped in his tracks when he heard voices coming from the hotel's service entrance.

"Goodnight, Maggie!" a man's voice called out.

"Goodnight, Tony," Maggie responded. "See you tomorrow, bright and early."

Abel turned towards the door and saw a woman walking into the lot. A male silhouette, probably belonging to Tony, appeared in the lighted doorway. He seemed to be watching Maggie carefully, as if to ensure that she reached her car safely. Abel cursed silently and crouched lower, praying to the fates that he wasn't hovering behind Maggie's car.

To his great relief, Maggie stopped beside an old banger, a Toyota. A moment later, the headlights were aglow and the car pulled out of its space.

Abel's eyes widened. Although he had been startled by Maggie's initial appearance, he was now pleased that she had come by. The headlights of her Toyota swept across the Lincoln. In doing so, they revealed the silhouettes of two figures. One was in the driver's seat and one in the back.

Abel cautiously worked his way across the lot, making sure he kept out of sight. When he was still two cars away, the driver's side door opened and a man threw his legs out onto the pavement. The light inside the vehicle revealed that he was talking on a cell phone.

"How much longer?" he growled, irritated.

Abel moved in closer in an effort to hear more clearly.

"Damn!" the man muttered. "Should I bring her back?"

Abel listened intently for the response. He squinted and stretched his neck, desperately trying to get a better look at the person in the back seat. He could tell it was a woman, perhaps a young girl, but she was positioned just far enough out of the light to remain anonymous. Then she turned her head slightly and Abel swallowed hard. He'd know that profile anywhere. The girl in the car was Alice.

"Why not?" the driver barked into the phone. "Can't someone else take care of this guy? How hard can it be?"

Abel cupped his hand around his ear to channel the conversation more clearly. A moment later, that was unnecessary. The driver had bounced to his feet and was pacing from one end of the car to the other.

"So, what the hell am I supposed to do now?" he growled. "I can't sit out here all night! This isn't good for business either. The Congressman's gonna be pissed. So is Dennis. Fine, you can explain it to him."

Abel held his position behind the parked car. When the aggravated driver took a few steps towards the Lincoln's front grill, Abel quietly moved in closer, edging around to the trunk.

The driver's pacing became more erratic as he muttered into his cell phone. Abel felt his heart racing. He had a plan, but he would have to move quickly, and any hesitation or misstep would be fatal.

"Well, how'd he lose the guy? He was right there! Okay. Okay. Let me know. But I'm not waiting all fucking night."

With that, the driver snapped his cell phone shut and muttered a string of profanities.

"What's going on?" Alice said. If there was any doubt before, now Abel was sure. It was her voice.

"Shut the hell up!" the driver snapped. "I'm dealing with enough shit."

The man's aggravation had gotten the better of him, and that gave Abel the upper hand. Abel made his move.

He lunged out from behind the Lincoln's trunk and caught hold of the driver's ankle, sending his large body crashing to the ground. The back of the man's head smacked hard against the pavement. It hit with a sickening thud.

As the dazed man tried to sit up, Abel snapped his head onto the pavement again. When he felt the driver slump, unconscious, Abel got up and jumped through the open car door into the driver's seat. He reached for the key and started the car. Alice screamed from the back seat.

"What the fuck's going on? Who are you?"

"Sit back and hold on. It's Peter Abel!"

"Oh, Jesus," Abel heard her exclaim.

But before he responded, the driver regained consciousness. His head wound was bleeding heavily but he managed to reach inside and grab the collar of Abel's jacket.

Abel jerked his body sideways, struggling to break free of the man's solid grip. With one violent pull, the driver inadvertently tore part of the collar off. The momentum sent the thug falling backward. Abel used this split-second opportunity to shove the car into drive. The car lurched forward, the driver's door still open. The thug, determined to reclaim his vehicle, shoved his right arm through the door and attempted to grab anything that was within reach.

Abel steered with his right hand and swatted at the driver's arm with his left. He cranked the steering wheel hard counter-clockwise, making a sharp enough turn to snap the car door back toward him. The door slammed the driver in the shoulder and he cried out in pain, but he still held on.

Alice continued to shriek in the back seat. Abel ignored her. He grabbed the door handle and yanked it towards him, but the driver's arm prevented the door from closing. Abel pulled and released the door several times, violently cracking it against the driver's forearm. When the thug was holding on only by his hand, Abel saw his opening. He yanked the door one more time as hard as he could, catching the driver's fingers in the door jam.

The driver screamed in pain as the bones in his fingers splintered. Abel released the door, and the driver fell backward in anguish onto the pavement. Finally free of the man, Abel slammed his foot on the accelerator and the tyres screeched as the car bolted out of the parking lot.

"Oh my God!" Alice screamed. "What are you doing? Where are you taking me?"

"I'm getting you the hell away from those people."

Alice whimpered, clearly distraught. Abel was having trouble manoeuvring the large car through a city with which he was completely unfamiliar. He had no idea where he should go, and had he been able to identify a safe place, he wouldn't have known how to find it. He wanted to get out of the main city to some quiet spot. He turned off whatever main artery they were on and found his way to a deserted side street. They parked in front of a badly kept house. It struck Abel that they had wound up in one of Washington's famous dangerous drug-infested neighbourhoods. Only moments before they had been in a district with bright streetlights and high-end restaurants.

Abel turned off the car's headlights and concentrated on catching his breath. Behind him, Alice continued to whimper. Abel knew the driver was probably screaming on his cell phone at that very moment, and that everyone from the cops to the syndicate killers would be hunting the Lincoln. He would have to ditch it then take Alice to safety on foot.

Abel got out and opened the rear door. He grabbed Alice's arm.

"Hurry," he ordered. "We've no time to waste."

"No!" Alice cried, sounding more like a wounded animal than a young girl.

"Alice, you must come!" Abel pleaded. "We need to get away from the car before they discover it!"

"I'm not coming with you!"

"Alice, you've got —"

"Leave me alone!"

Totally desperate, Abel leaned inside the car, grabbed Alice's body with both hands, and wrenched her out of the vehicle. He carried her in his arms, as she kicked and cried. Eventually, he found what he believed to be a safe hiding place behind a gas station dumpster.

Abel carefully lowered Alice's feet to the ground, but he still held her close to his chest. She started to yell, but he quickly put his hand over her mouth to stifle the noise.

"Shush, Alice!" he whispered. "Someone will hear you and think I'm kidnapping you."

"You are!" she hissed back at him. "I don't want to go with you. Let go of me!"

Through the dim light of a distant street lamp, Abel caught sight of Alice's face. It was worn and haggard, like that of a person who had been through more than she could handle.

"Alice, look at me," Abel said quietly.

Alice turned to face him, but their eyes did not meet. Abel tried to match his gaze with hers, but she was unable to focus. He could see by the streetlights that her pupils were dilated, and her head shook with unnatural ticks. She was clearly under the influence of some kind of drug, maybe multiple drugs, though Abel was at a loss to identify which ones.

"Alice, I've come to take you home," Abel said, keeping the message simple for her fried brain. "I will take you back to your mother."

Alice thrashed in his arms. "No!" she yelped. "I know you killed Marcy!"

Abel felt his heart breaking, but he had to maintain his composure. The influence of the drugs was evident in both her face and her voice. She had been completely brainwashed, robbed of her free will. She seemed to have lost all signs of the vulnerability and compassion that had made her so special, so unique. Abel could only pray they were still inside her somewhere.

"No, Alice," he insisted. "I did not kill Marcy. Yes, I did meet with her, but I wasn't the one who killed her. Men from the syndicate killed her because she agreed to help me find and protect you."

"Then they will kill me too," Alice said, a growl in her voice. "If they find me with you, they will kill me for sure."

"Alice, I'll take you away from here, to a place where you'll be safe," Abel said. "Just come with me. I promise I won't let anyone hurt you."

"You're a liar!" Alice said.

Abel was ready to make one more plea, to say whatever it took to convince Alice that he wanted to save her from all this grief. She didn't give him a chance. Suddenly, with one hard push, she freed herself from his grip and bolted down the street. Abel instinctively chased her, but the darkness served as his enemy. Running as hard as he could, he tripped over a discarded object on the sidewalk and went crashing face down to the concrete.

He could taste the blood from his split lip seeping into his mouth and his shin burned. Despite that, he struggled back to his feet and continued running, but then staggered to a halt.

Alice had disappeared, and he had no clue which direction she had gone. He listened carefully for a moment, hoping to catch the sound of running footsteps, but the only sound to be heard was that of the cars rushing down the avenue on the other side of the building.

Abel leaned against a chain link fence and wiped the blood from his lip onto the cuff of his sleeve. His torn jacket hung in shreds from his shoulders. He rubbed his eyes and choked back tears. He could not remember feeling so utterly devastated. He had lost Alice, not just physically, but mentally and emotionally as well. The darkness and evil had devoured her. She was merely another stolen soul added to their long list of conquests.

As Abel dabbed again at his bloody lip, he wondered what he should do next. He was in a strange city, being pursued by a powerful syndicate of vicious thugs and wanted by the police. His instincts told him to run, that he had done all that he could do, and now Alice's fate was no longer in his hands. All he had to do was to call Maxwell Elliot, who could set up a connection that would get him safely out of the United States and back to Africa.

But the haunted look on Alice's face, the vacancy of her eyes, gnawed at Peter Abel's soul. He had come so far and endured so much. He was in this way too deep.

CHAPTER TWENTY-FOUR

Abel spent most of the next few hours walking the streets, wracking his brain for a new strategy. Alice's mind had become fogged by drugs, no question, but she was controlled by fear. Her handlers had done an expert job on their charge, rendering her helpless. This made Abel's mission much more complicated. Saving Alice from this evil group was hard enough. Now he had to save the girl from herself. A nearly impossible task and one over which he had only marginal control.

The hours refused to pass. Every time Abel checked his watch, the time seemed not to have changed. The syndicate was on his tail, likely more determined now that he had overwhelmed one of its thugs and made off with an expensive car and a prize commodity – Alice.

At first, Abel had sought refuge in a 24-hour diner, but sitting in the booth made him feel conspicuous. Abel was convinced the few people who were in the place were looking directly at him. He could understand why they might take a second look. His tattered jacket and swollen lip were bound to encourage curiosity and suspicion.

His heart nearly stopped when two uniformed policemen came through the front door. The cops hung around waiting for their coffee and sandwiches, chatting casually with the manager about the recent Redskins' loss.

The ice cold fear of discovery did not prevent Abel from smiling when he heard them jabbering about quarterback sacks and first downs. He had seen a little American football on television when he travelled the world, but it was still a game he didn't fully comprehend. It wasn't anything like World Cup football. In fact, players didn't even move the ball with their feet. It was more like rugby — with crash helmets. To most of the world, it was a very strange ritual, but for Americans, it was a passion.

For a moment, Abel put his prejudices aside and wished he were part of whatever normal world the cops and the manager inhabited. All they had to worry about was the point spread and some field goal kicker who couldn't hit the side of a barn from the inside. He felt as if he were on another planet. In this case a planet inhabited by ghouls and monsters, and one where death was imminent.

Finally the cops left, juggling their paper coffee cups and bag of sandwiches. Abel felt himself exhale as if he hadn't been breathing the whole time. He got up and left soon after, having had enough of American society for the time being. He needed to be alone.

Once outside in the cold night air, he wrapped his torn jacket tightly around his body. He had a hundred questions and no answers. Where did Alice run? Would she go back to the syndicate or would she go into hiding on her own? She was clearly an addict, and she would have to feed her habit. She wasn't experienced enough in the real world to score on her own, but that didn't mean she wouldn't try, putting herself in serious danger in the process. She certainly had no money of her own, and that meant she would have to sell her body to a john or directly to the dealer to score.

Alice could exercise her second option and return to the syndicate, where drugs would be readily plentiful with much less exposure to danger. No, that wasn't right. Going back to the syndicate carried very severe risks of a different kind. They might simply murder her to get rid of a potential problem. They had no qualms about killing Marcy to frame Abel; they would be no less reticent to kill Alice to get Abel off their backs.

Even if Alice recognised this risk, she might be desperate enough to take it. Or maybe at this point she didn't care if she died. It wasn't much of a life she was leading. Even as drugged out as she was, Abel thought Alice realised that much.

Abel was wearing down. He badly needed a place to crash even for a few minutes. He considered finding a nightclub, a place where there would be a crowd of people, many of them intoxicated or high, and the lights would be dim enough to shroud him. Such a place likely would be blasting music, but given his circumstances, he would have to take any safe port he could find.

As he struggled to decide which direction to go, Abel was

startled by the piercing ring of his cell phone in his jacket pocket. His cold fingers fumbled it as he tried to get control of the device and open it. It continued ringing even after it hit the concrete. Abel quickly knelt down and flipped it open.

"Hello?"

"You've had an exciting night, haven't you?"

Abel rubbed his eyes and let out a tired laugh. Maxwell Elliot's voice had never sounded so good.

"Either you're psychic, or you have an amazing pipeline of information," Abel remarked.

Elliot laughed. "Nah, I just connected the dots. My contact said Schroeder left the hotel very upset right after the banquet. That could only mean one thing. He didn't get laid. Dennis would never have let one of his girls stand an important client up, so I knew you must have trashed his evening's fun."

"Yeah, guilty as charged. Listen, have you heard anything else?" Abel said.

"You don't sound happy, so I guess Alice isn't with you," Elliot said.

"You're very insightful," Abel said. He then gave Elliot a quick run-through of the evening's frantic events.

Elliot snickered on his end of the line. "You know, Peter, you have a habit of rubbing people the wrong way. Then again, that's what makes for a good journalist. If you're not pissing someone off, you're just not doing your job. Where are you?"

Abel looked around. "Ah ... I'm not really sure."

"Give me some landmarks."

"Well, there's a Seven-eleven on the corner."

"C'mon, man, there's Seven-eleven's on every corner," Elliot said. "You can do better than that."

Abel spun around, searching for a more distinctive sign. "There's D.C. Auto Repair and...what's that say? ... Phil's Bar and Grill."

"Go to Phil's," Elliot ordered.

"It's closed, Maxwell," Abel reminded him. "It's three o'clock in the morning."

"Go stand in the parking lot," Elliot insisted. "I'll be there in five minutes."

Abel's phone went dead.

When Elliot picked him up, he made Abel hunker down on the floor in the back.

"I'd rather not chance us being seen together tonight," he said. "I've got enough enemies in this town. I don't need to take on your enemies too."

After a few minutes, they pulled up in front of an old apartment building. Elliot went in first and Abel slipped in a few minutes later.

Abel followed Elliot into one unit and looked around. "Nice," he said in his best tone of sarcasm.

The place was very small and only had the most essential furniture – a desk, a chair, and a mattress on the floor.

"It's a pit. You don't have to be polite," Elliot said.

"It's not the street which makes it a palace as far as I'm concerned."

Elliot laughed and pulled a laptop out of his backpack, set in on the desk, and booted it up. He gave Abel a soft shove and pointed him toward the mattress.

"Sleep," he ordered. "You look awful."

Abel didn't argue. He was dead to the world in seconds.

"Have a nice nap?"

Elliot's voice roused Abel from a fitful sleep.

"What time is it?" Abel wondered.

"Seven in the a.m.," Elliot replied. "Come here and look at this."

Abel rubbed his eyes and walked over to the desk to get a look at Elliot's computer screen.

"I got some info from my insider," Elliot said. "Schroeder's scheduled to take a boat ride on the Potomac this afternoon."

Abel scratched his head. "Isn't it a little cold for sailing?"

Elliot laughed. "Nobody sails, Peter. This is probably a sixty foot yacht with a games room below decks."

"So, what's he doing there?"

"Well, he doesn't have any official business, so my guess is he's gonna make it a pleasure cruise. And since you messed up his fun last night, maybe he'll try to make up for it today or tomorrow. He has to make the best out of his wife's absence. She returns in three days."

"Do you think Alice will be there?" Abel asked.

Elliot shrugged. "I got sources, not psychics."

Abel grabbed his coat and started out.

"Relax. They don't leave till this afternoon. You have time to sleep and to eat one of my famous egg sandwiches."

Abel made a face involuntarily.

"Hey, most people don't make that face till after they've tasted it."

With that, Elliot headed for the fridge and Abel took a seat.

Even at one o'clock that afternoon, the breeze off the Potomac cut through the old windbreaker Abel had borrowed from Maxwell Elliot. He'd finished breakfast - not half bad he had to admit – then left Elliot behind. Again, he didn't want to be responsible for anyone else.

Abel huddled behind a shed on the pier and waited. Elliot had given him the name of the boat and the slip number where it was moored. It was an impressive ship, the kind of vessel only the super-rich owned. It wasn't any good for commerce. Its only purpose was play. Abel considered the self-indulgence behind such a pointless expenditure.

He called Elliot to report that he had found the yacht and nodded when Elliot admonished him to be careful. Good advice and probably impossible to follow.

He watched as crewmembers and service people scrambled about the gigantic yacht, clearly preparing it for important passengers. Abel had been stationed at his post about half an hour when a stretch limousine rolled up to the dock. The chauffer stepped out, walked to the back of the vehicle, and opened the door. Out stepped Congressman Jason Schroeder, dressed in what Abel thought to be nautical wear for people who weren't particularly nautical: a blue windbreaker over a red cable-knit sweater with white trousers and deck shoes. The only accoutrement missing was the fake Captain's hat, although Schroeder had managed to remember the mirrored sunglasses.

A well-dressed man came down the gangway to greet the

congressman and escort him onto the vessel. During the next few minutes, Abel watched several other expensive cars pull up and expel equally expensive men and women, who also boarded the yacht.

Finally, Abel got what he wanted. A Lincoln, very much like the one he had commandeered the night before. He watched, transfixed, as two men climbed out of the front. Abel recognised one as the thug he'd fought with the night before. He didn't recognise his face, but he noted telltale bandages around his left hand and a white gauze wrap around his head. Abel took some satisfaction in the damage he'd inflicted. On the other hand, he wished he'd done more so this guy wouldn't be on the scene. He didn't need a thug out for revenge. And this guy would want Abel's blood.

Abel heard the other man call his thug, "Rudy," so Abel now had a name to go with the unpleasant face.

As Rudy opened the rear car door, out stepped two elegantly dressed women, or more precisely, young girls.

The second one out was Alice. They wore expensive outfits that were designed to be flattering on women twice their age. To Abel, the young girls looked tawdry, inappropriate and exploited. Alice didn't seem to know it the night before, though. She was too scared to fight for her freedom. Or too stoned. Or both. Abel noted that she didn't look any the worse for wear. Hell, he was relieved she was alive at all.

After everyone had boarded the vessel, Abel inched his way closer to the gangway. Taking advantage of a short interval when it was unguarded, Abel quietly scurried onto the yacht.

Once on deck, he slipped to the lower level where the serving crew was bustling around the kitchen. Abel knew he'd have to stay hidden. This wasn't some huge hotel with a staff of hundreds. This was an intimate group and any stranger would stand out immediately.

Abel felt the vibration of the giant diesel engines when they started up and swayed as the yacht moved away from the dock and made its way out into the Potomac. The water was choppy, and Abel worried about getting seasick. He wasn't much of a sailor.

As the guests socialised in the main cabin upstairs, the crew continued running up and down from the kitchen. Abel sneaked around and inspected the yacht. There were two smaller rooms at the back of the lower deck, and a bathroom on each floor. Abel slipped into one of the small rooms because the windows allowed him to see who was moving about. He noticed Rudy and the other thug walk by every few minutes as if patrolling the area.

After a few minutes, Abel heard voices from the adjoining room. When he put his ear to the wall, he heard a female giggle followed by an older man's voice. Abel guessed Schroeder was ready to have his way with at least one of the young ladies.

Abel dreaded what he had to do next. Despite his bold act of sneaking on board, the next move was just plain crazy. Abel was counting on surprise and the Congressman's basic unwillingness to become involved in anything that required murder. Abel figured if he made it clear he only wanted the girl, then maybe they'd let him off the yacht alive. It wasn't much of a plan, he had to admit, but he couldn't think of a better one. And besides he was eager to get back on dry land. He was feeling queasy already.

After glancing out of the window to make sure nobody was in sight, he slipped out of his door into the adjacent one.

What he walked in on might have been comical had it not been so pathetic. Sitting on the futon was Schroeder, shirtless, while Alice and the other young girl, both naked, rubbed his shoulders. The corpulent bare-chested Schroeder was hardly a pretty sight.

"Excuse me, Congressman," Abel said quietly, "but I believe these girls are underage."

Schroeder jumped up startled and grabbed his shirt. "Who the hell are you?" he said, his voice a high-pitched screech.

"Mr. Abel!" Alice cried. She threw a robe on to cover her naked body. Abel took her by the hand. "I promised your mother I would take you home. Your mother! Alice, your mother! She has been crying all day, every day since you left. She may die!"

Abel turned to Schroeder. "I'm not out to hurt you, Sir. I want this girl. I'm taking her home, and I'm asking you to help me."

Schroeder was dumbfounded. He just stared at Abel, mystified as if he couldn't believe this was happening.

Before the congressman could regain his power of speech, the door opened. Rudy stood in the passageway, gun in hand. He smiled at Abel.

"You're dead," he said.

"Now, just a minute. I can't be involved ..." the Congressman said, sputtering. But Rudy cut him off.

"You won't be. Go upstairs."

As they were talking, Abel reached into his pants pocket deftly and turned on his micro-tape recorder. He wasn't sure how he would get out of this predicament, but he hoped that recording it might somehow help.

The other thug arrived. He stepped into the room and grabbed Abel by the shoulders and tore off his jacket. He went through the pockets to make sure Abel wasn't armed. The only thing he came up with was Abel's cell phone, which he casually tossed across the room.

Abel worried the man would find the recorder if he patted him down, so he spoke up. "I'm not armed. I'm a journalist. The only thing I carry are pens and note pads."

It worked, sort of. The second man smashed Abel across the face and dragged him out of the room. But he'd forgotten to pat down Abel's pants.

"Wait!" Alice cried. "Please don't hurt him! He's not here to cause trouble. He's a friend of my mother's."

The men laughed.

"Your mother is probably the only friend this guy has left," Rudy said. "Now you go back inside, keep your mouth shut, and wait for us. If you get in our way, you'll wind up like Marcy."

The men continued to manhandle Abel, but Alice tried to impede their path. Rudy grabbed her arm and flung her back into the room. She landed hard on the wooden floor, rubbing her sore shoulder.

Rudy turned to Schroeder, who hadn't moved a muscle this whole time.

"Go on, Congressman. You don't want to see this."

Schroeder finally left. The other girl put on a robe and ran out right behind him. Abel watched them go. So much for the Moral Majority.

He was shoved into the adjoining room, and the door was shut.

Left alone, Alice had a moment of panic. Her confused brain

could not think what she should do. Fear gripped her. Then she saw Abel's cell phone where it had been dropped in the struggle. What was the number she should call? How could she call the police? Poor Alice, in a strange and foreign country, her minded clouded by drugs, could not remember that 911 was the magic number. She pressed a button on the phone and then waited in despair. The button was redial and Elliot answered, heard what was going on and called a contact at the FBI. He lied, telling the FBI agent that the yacht was full of gunrunners. The agent alerted the Coast Guard. The question was, would it arrive in time?

"Who sent you here?" Rudy demanded of Abel. "Who told you about the yacht, and who else knows about it?"

Abel knew that no matter what answer he gave, Rudy was determined to kill him, so he simply held his ground and stared. If he could find someway of disarming the man, he could put up a good fight. Once he did that, he'd find his way back to shore, swimming with Alice strapped to his back if necessary.

"Are you Dennis?" Abel asked the second man, stalling for time.

"No," the man said. "Dennis wouldn't waste his valuable time dealing with scum like you."

"Scum like me?" Abel remarked. "I'm not the one trafficking fifteen-year-old girls out as sex slaves to perverted politicians."

The man laughed. "It's all just business, pal. There's a demand, and Dennis is smart enough to fill it. Now If you want to save your ass, you'd better tell us who told you about the yacht and anything else you know."

"If I do, will you let Alice go?" Abel asked, hoping he could at least save her life.

"Not our decision. She belongs to Dennis," the man responded.

"Then call and ask. If he agrees, I'll tell you everything. He might even slip a murder charge."

"He didn't kill Marcy," Rudy said.

"No. You did."

"What of it? You couldn't prove that even if we let you live. Which we won't."

"The girl for what I know. Otherwise, go fish."

Rudy slammed Abel's head against the wall viciously.

"You're fucking dead. And so is the girl, once we're done selling her."

Rudy stuck the barrel of his gun into Abel's ear. Abel figured that was the ballgame. He was dead.

At that moment, an ear-piercing siren blasted through the air. Startled, Rudy jumped back.

"What the hell is that?"

The second thug peered out of the porthole. "Coast Guard cutters! Four of them."

Abel's would-be murderer spun around, trying to catch sight of the boats. Abel seized the moment, picking up a heavy metal paperweight off a table. He smashed it over the first thug's head. The man fell to the floor. Before Rudy could react, Abel grabbed his wrist and tried to wrench the gun from it.

"Come out on the upper deck with your hands in the air!" A voice boomed from a loud speaker outside.

As Coast Guard officers prepared to board the yacht, Abel and Rudy continued to wrestle. A shot rang out from the handgun, and the bullet lodged in the wall. Abel pounded his fist against Rudy's already broken fingers, causing him to shriek out in pain. The gun fell to the floor with a loud rattle.

The other man recovered from the blow to the head and made a lunge for the gun. Abel shoved him aside and grabbed the pistol. He was panting with exhaustion as he pointed the weapon at the two defeated men.

"I guess we'd better go out on the upper deck," he said.

Once the Coast Guard and the local police had the situation under control, Abel approached the officer in charge.

"My name is Peter Abel," he stated. "The Washington D.C. Police Department wants to question me regarding the death of Marcy Tripps. I believe I have all of your answers right here."

He handed the man his tape recorder. A crew of officers took the thugs into custody, and the Coast Guard and police boats escorted the yacht back to the dock.

Abel cooperated with the agents, telling them everything he knew about Dennis's operation and the murder of the young girl, Marcy Tripps. Alice also cooperated, and with her help they hunted down and arrested Dennis and his business partners. They were to be charged with many things, including the murder of Marcy Tripps. Schroeder and the other guests aboard the yacht professed to know nothing that had been going on below decks, but Alice and the other girl ratted out Schroeder. He was taken away in handcuffs, charged for starters with contributing to the delinquency of minors. More serious moral charges would be added later, the police said. Abel wondered how all that would play back in the home district.

After spending the rest of the day answering questions, Abel and Alice signed statements and were released.

When Alice and Abel stepped out of the police station, they were met on the steps by Maxwell Elliot.

"You must be the famous, Alice," Maxwell said.

"Yes," she answered as she shook his hand.

"This girl saved your life, Peter," Elliot told him. "She called me, and I called the Coast Guard. She's very brave."

"I know. Alice told the police about contacting you on my cell phone. I've expressed my gratitude."

A cold breeze shot through the air and Abel threw his arm around Alice's shoulders. "I'd have given you my jacket, but those thugs pulled it off of me," he said.

"Wasn't that *my* jacket?" Elliot asked.

"Ah ... yeah, as a matter of fact it was," Abel said with a laugh. "I guess I owe you one."

"You owe me more than that. You owe me a story."

For the first time in months, Abel felt truly relaxed. He kept his arm wrapped around Alice's shoulders as the two of them followed Elliot to the parking lot. Before they could enjoy their moment of glory together, a harsh voice blasted through the air.

"Elliot, you moron!"

The three of them spun around to see a tall, thin, good-looking man in a suit come running towards them.

"How's it going?" Elliot replied nonchalantly.

The breeze blew the man's jacket open to reveal the gun nestled in his shoulder holster and a badge clipped to his belt.

"How's it going?" he asked back. "It's going lousy! You said there were *gunrunners* on that yacht. My men have been all over it.

They have searched every tiny crevice. Do you know what they found? Some plates of fancy pâté, caviar, bottles of expensive Champagne, and a bunch of hard-core porn in which men are firing, but not bullets."

Elliot bit his lip to keep from laughing.

"Peter Abel. Alice Udor. This is Chase Watkins of the FBI. He's the one who called in the Coast Guard."

"Under totally false pretenses!"

"Hey," Elliot laughed, "I had to tell you something."

He then reached into his pants pocket, pulled out his car keys, and tossed them over to Abel. "You two can take my car. Now that this is cleared up, you'll probably be allowed back in your hotel room. I'll catch up with you later. My man Chase and I need to have a little talk."

Abel nodded and led Alice over toward Elliot's car. "Hey, Maxwell!" he called back. "Thanks ... for everything."

Elliot smiled and waved.

As Abel and Alice pulled out of the parking lot, they could see Elliot and Chase walking along the pier. Chase was clearly irate, waving his hands and pointing. Elliot simply listened and nodded.

Abel looked over at Alice, shrugged, and then pulled the car out into the traffic.

CHAPTER TWENTY-FIVE

"Nice work," Elliot said as he looked up from his reading. "Is this your first by-line in the *Washington Post*?"

Abel sat at a table in the corner of the hotel room, the newspaper spread out before him. "As a matter of fact, it is," he said. "Front page no less. I like the way it looks. Except for the photo." Abel pointed to a picture of Jason Schroeder being dragged off the yacht, cuffed hands in front of his face. This caused his shirt to rise up enough to expose his ample girth. "That's an image I didn't need to see while I was trying to eat my breakfast."

Elliot laughed out loud. "Have to take the good with the bad, my friend."

Abel wished he could enjoy his front-page success more fully, but then there was Alice. For the moment she was resting comfortably in bed, but she had awakened several times during the night, sweating and shaking. Abel couldn't be sure if she was suffering from nightmares, or if she was having withdrawal symptoms. Since she hadn't had a fix for her drug habit in more than 10 hours, withdrawal was the likely cause. Abel was concerned how she might react once she was fully awake.

Elliot interrupted Abel's thoughts. "When are you giving TV interviews? I heard someone from *Larry King Live* called."

These Americans, Abel thought. All they think about is becoming famous. Even though he didn't want to talk right now, he felt he owed Elliot basic courtesy. In fact, he owed Elliot a lot more than that.

"I haven't dealt with the TV media yet," Abel answered. "I told the hotel staff that Alice and I wouldn't be talking to anyone for now. Anyway, they seem more interested in Jason Schroeder and his prostitutes than in this human trafficking business."

Elliot exhaled a sigh. "That's par for the course," he said. "Especially since Schroeder got elected by selling himself as part of

220

the Christian right."

"They should get over this adolescent preoccupation with sex and focus on what matters," Abel said, his voice grumbling with disdain. He was feeling less sanguine by the minute as the prospect of having to deal with Alice's addiction came closer.

"Horny congressmen are fun, man. What's not fun are teenage girls forced into the sex trade. Hits too close to home. People think about their own little girls falling into that life, and it scares them. This is America, man. People don't want reality. They want fantasy. You think network news could survive if they kept airing real stories? Fairy tales. They give the masses what they want."

Abel looked at the photograph of the congressman and felt vaguely ill.

"Somehow I doubt people really want to see this guy's beer belly," he said.

But in truth, Abel understood what Elliot was saying. Salacious stories weren't the exclusive preserve of the American media. He'd seen it all over the world. The British made it an art form. In the United States, all network television outlets – broadcast and cable – and most of the country's newspapers were owned by large corporations with stockholders. You had to keep the stockholders happy, and you did that by making money and turning profits. A major component of that for the printed word was selling newspapers, not only for the money direct sales brought in. The more newspapers a company sold, the higher the advertising rates it could charge. Same for television. The more viewers a show drew, especially in that 19 to 49 demographic age group, the higher the advertising rates went. And scandal sells. That was the bottom line.

Abel felt a rising anger at the way corporations had consumed the world, and how this philosophy, devoid of morality, focused so narrowly and collared everything. But then he realised that blaming corporations for their behaviour was no more sensible than blaming a shark for eating a seal. It's what they do. It's what they were made to do. The difference, of course, was that God had made a shark. Man had made corporations. And he had made them in his own self-image: greedy, voracious, self-serving.

What a world, Abel thought, shaking his head. He should be

happy this morning. Instead, he felt the weight of so many problems yet to come. And so many problems that would never be solved. Not by him. Not by anyone.

So, the only sensible thing to do was to keep his head down, keep moving forward and keep trying to do the right thing.

Alice interrupted his musings when she rolled over in the bed and groaned softly, pulling the fluffy comforter up around her shoulders. Abel watched her closely, his heart racing and his throat tightening.

"Maxwell, I really need your help with Alice," Abel said. "I don't want the press seeing her. Not like this."

"No problem," Elliot responded. "I can help the two of you slip out of the hotel and get on a plane back to Nigeria this afternoon."

"We can't do that just yet," Abel said. "She hasn't had a fix since we left the yacht yesterday. I don't know what to do about that."

"Don't worry," Elliot assured him. "We'll take her down to Bethesda Medical Centre. I'm sure they can find a spot for her in their drug rehab unit."

Abel rubbed his eyes. "I'd rather get her out of town."

"How far out of town?"

"As far away from Washington, D.C. as possible."

Elliot looked at him. "You're not thinking these guys would still come after you two?"

"I don't know what they'll do. But the farther away we are the better."

"There are plenty of places she can go for rehab," Elliot replied. "Regular hospitals and private facilities. The Betty Ford Clinic is in California."

Abel waved him off. "Forget it. Too expensive. Too exclusive. Too high-profile."

"Okay. I know of one in Canada."

Abel responded to that notion. "Another country. That's perfect."

"I'll check into it. But you still have to deal with the immediate problem. That girl will need a fix *right now*."

Abel shook his head. "This is your city. How would I know about that kind of thing?"

222

"You wouldn't. Let me make a few calls. I'll see what kind of short-term treatment we can arrange for her."

Abel nodded, grateful for the help. He was feeling over his head, dealing with a drug addict in a strange country. It was all overwhelming. He thought things would get simpler once he had Alice in hand. It dawned on him how wrong he was. Their journey home was only just beginning.

Bentley Medical Centre, a small, private health-care facility, was located in Chevy Chase, Maryland, an upscale suburb of Washington, D.C. Elliot called in a favour with a former addict to get Alice admitted there. The man was only too willing to help Elliot. After all, the reporter had saved his life with a series of articles on street people. The addict's picture had accompanied one of the stories. His brother, with whom he had long ago lost contact, spotted the picture and followed up. Ten days later, he was in a clinic. Now the former addict was an administrator and counsellor at the clinic. This Dickensian tale had turned out well for all concerned, since he arranged to get Alice admitted quickly and anonymously.

It was a good thing, too, because Alice had been in a frantic state when she woke up in the hotel. A doctor from the clinic arrived to help sedate her for the ride to Chevy Chase.

Once they had checked Alice into Bentley, the doctor told Abel she would be put through a three day emergency detoxification programme. This would allow her to function somewhat normally until she could be put into long-term rehab.

Abel breathed easier once Alice was admitted. Just the sight of the girl sleeping comfortably, free from the control of narcotics, the abuse of the sex trade, and the brutality of the syndicate, made all his other problems seem manageable.

As Alice rested, Abel sat down with Elliot to arrange their next move. He would spirit her out of Washington into Canada. The long trip home was to have many detours.

CHAPTER TWENTY-SIX

Elliot had arranged for Alice and Abel to travel by train into Canada. Once in Ottawa, Alice was checked into a private facility that not only treated her physical drug addiction, but provided counselling. Abel knew that was as important as physical therapy. After all, Alice needed to recover her dignity in the wake of the deep and ongoing trauma she had suffered. Without self-respect, there would be no impetus for her to kick her drug habit. In short, Alice needed help learning how to be a human being again. How to feel something other than fear, loathing and disgust. It was a long road, but Abel was certain the girl had the strength to travel it.

Abel was happy to see improvement in Alice's physical health almost immediately, but he knew that after everything she had been through, her recovery would be an ongoing process. In all likelihood, one that would require a certain amount of care and maintenance for the rest of her life.

Being young, tenacious, and determined, Alice was encouraged by the early results of her treatment. But she had to be reminded that many patients suffered setbacks along the way and that she shouldn't regard any problems she might encounter as failures on her part.

While visiting with her one morning, Abel found Alice in a wonderfully exuberant mood.

"I've made a decision about my future," she declared. "I've thought long and hard about it, and I finally reached a conclusion. I know what I want to become."

"What's that?" Abel wondered.

"A nurse!" Alice said proudly.

Abel was genuinely surprised. "Is that right?" he asked. "That's wonderful, Alice. How did you arrive at that decision?"

Alice's face was beaming. "The nurses here inspired me," she said. "I've watched what they do and the way they handle their duties. They help so many people. I would like to do that. I think I would be an excellent nurse. I understand people. I know what it feels like to be sick and not have control of your fate. I think I could make a big difference in people's lives. What do you think?"

"I think you would be an outstanding nurse, Alice," Abel agreed.

Alice appeared concerned. "It requires quite a bit of schooling, though. I would have to attend university and get medical training."

"You can do that," Abel said, trying to be encouraging. "You're very smart. I'm sure you'll do very well."

"Could you help me arrange to do it here in Canada?" Alice asked. "I won't be leaving the clinic for quite a while, and I'd like to start as soon as possible."

Although Abel was pleased Alice was thinking so positively about the future, he was concerned she might be moving too quickly. But Alice assured him she had checked with her counsellors, and they were all for her plan.

"For the first time in my life, I have a goal, something special that I really want to achieve." She seemed so excited, Abel could only support her wishes. He planned to check with the counsellors anyway, just to make sure this was the best course for Alice.

Alice surprised him with her next question.

"Will you stay here in Canada, or are you going back to Nigeria?" The question was so direct and so unselfconscious that Abel had to think a minute.

"I suppose I will stay, for a while anyway." Abel was about to ask the reason Alice had brought this up now, but he suddenly realised her motivation. She needed help with the details of getting into school. And she needed money. Abel was pleased in an odd way that Alice was thinking so far ahead. It was a sign not only of maturity, but also of a healthy mind and ego.

"I promise you one thing, my dear. I won't leave until you are settled in school and know how to pay for it."

Alice smiled broadly at him. "Thank you." Then the smile disappeared.

"What is it?" Abel said, seeing the sadness on her face.

"You suddenly reminded me of my father. Not the one you

met, but the father I once knew when I was a little girl. Before he changed."

Abel felt her grief, as if someone had died. And in fact, that was the case. The kindly caring parent had died and been replaced by a monster.

Able spoke carefully. "You never really told me about what happened with him."

Alice took a moment, then shook her head. "I've been talking to the counsellors about him. Part of my treatment. I don't really want to go into it if you don't mind."

"Not at all."

"But you probably know anyway. Where once he hugged me and kissed me on the cheek, he suddenly began putting his hands on places they didn't belong. And then he demanded more. I tried to resist, but he was too strong. Of course once it happened, he just kept coming back. And since I had already lost one struggle, I couldn't hope to stop him. So I just let him do what he wanted. It was better than him forcing himself on me. It hurt less. And was over faster. By the time I was handed off to other men, I had so little self-respect left, it hardly mattered anymore. Anyway, I decided if men were going to use me, I'd use them back. I did manage to extort many fine gifts. But the price was very high."

"I'm so sorry, Alice," was all Abel could gather himself to say.

Alice brightened, as children will, shedding the sad thought and replacing it with something more delightful. "I love you, Peter. With all my heart."

Abel's eyes felt moist as he looked at the girl. His heart swelled with a kind of love, something he hadn't felt since he played happily with his younger sister. It was different than the feeling he had for his wife. It was more parental, more elemental, more connected to an instinct to protect and to nurture. Men, he thought could indeed feel such things.

"Of course you must go back," Alice said, with startling maturity. "Your work is in Nigeria. You have responsibilities there. You can't leave *The Zodiac* stranded forever."

Abel smiled and nodded. "Sad but true."

"I will miss you," Alice said softly.

And he knew he would miss her, too.

Abel went to work, securing Alice's schooling. After a series of telephone calls, e-mails, faxes, and migraine headaches, he managed to have Alice's school transcripts sent to Canada. The doctor who ran the treatment facility wrote a glowing letter of recommendation, casting her as an inspiring success story. This and her own native intelligence and charm got her accepted at several universities.

Abel, having no children and therefore never having gone through the application process with his own offspring, couldn't believe how complicated the whole thing was. In the middle of one harried phone call, applications spread out before him and Alice. Abel had realised with some irony that he had managed to acquire classified information from government sources and wise guy informants with a lot less hassle.

The one last hurdle to be overcome was money. It always came down to that, Abel thought. The fact that money had gotten Alice into the sex trade in the first place only highlighted the trouble it endlessly created for the world. On the other hand, money spent on her schooling insured her future, and that was a good thing.

The university Alice most wanted to attend had offered her only a partial scholarship. Abel used the Internet to research charitable organisations and benefactors that might come to Alice's financial rescue. After all she had been through, it would have been tragic for her dreams to be grounded by a lack of funding.

Abel logged onto the website for an organization called Youth Justice International, which subsidised recovery programmes for children who were enslaved by international drug runners, sex traffickers, and illegal labour cartels. YJI's home base was located in Seoul, South Korea, but they had branches all over the world. Abel contacted their office in London and sent them an early draft of the story that he was composing for *The Zodiac*.

"Are you *the* Peter Abel?" the counsellor asked. "The one who broke the sex trade story in the *Washington Post*?"

Abel was flattered and humbly replied, "It's nice to know that you are familiar with my work."

"We are very familiar, Mr. Abel," the woman stated. "Your reporting has been a help bringing attention to the very things we are trying to combat. And we understand you are based in Nigeria."

"Yes," Abel said. "It's where the whole story began."

"Well, Nigeria is a big window to Africa where so much of this trade takes place. We would love to help your friend Alice in any way that we can."

And that's how it all happened. Within days, Alice was granted a generous stipend and her bills, both medical and educational, were covered.

Once Alice was settled, continuing her medical treatment and registered to begin her university studies, Abel bought a ticket home.

He took Alice to dinner on his last night in Canada. They shared a warm friendly meal and remembered the first night they met and how she had spent it in the guestroom of his house.

"I remember our first night vividly. You were so sweet that day and I still wonder how you were able to resist me," she said and leaned back. "That was the beginning of my turnaround, Peter."

"No," he said. "You went through hell after that."

"But the way you treated me that night never left my mind. I knew it was possible to meet kind men. I knew you were in the world. I think it kept me alive."

"Chief Benson," the man's voice answered the phone.

"Hi, boss! Remember me?"

There was a pause on the other end of the line. "The voice sounds familiar," Benson said. "I could swear you sound just like Peter Abel. He used to work here."

Abel laughed into the phone. "I didn't fall off the world, boss," he clarified. "I just swung from the edge of it for a while."

The boss laughed. "You settled the girl in school?"

Of course Abel had been in touch over the weeks with Benson. His good-natured boss had allowed him to stay in Canada and finish what he started. Not professionally, for the articles were well under way. But personally. Benson knew his reporter needed closure as much as the girl he saved.

"Are you coming home soon, then?" his boss asked.

"Yes. I'll be back in a couple of days. I don't suppose you still have a job for me at *The Zodiac*, do you?"

"I'll have to check."

With that, the men laughed and said their good-byes and Abel ran to catch his flight to London, which had announced its final boarding call.

CHAPTER TWENTY-SEVEN

"So, this is what you've been up to. It's a good series, Peter. Well worth the time and expense." Abel's boss raised his head from the copy in his hand and smiled.

Abel should have felt good about the stories, which would run on consecutive days over the next week. But he knew the trafficking in children for sex would not stop because of anything he wrote. People would pay attention briefly, there would be an outcry from the public, politicians would say the right things, and the police might even arrest a few bad guys. But in the end, it would be business as usual. The demand for the sex trade was too great and the people who worked in it too unscrupulous.

In prior cases, Abel's stories had served as a catalyst that set investigative wheels in motion. Results were rapid. Corruption was cleaned up, criminals were arrested, victims were compensated, and entire hierarchies, some powerful and longstanding, came crumbling down. This time Abel felt the results wouldn't be so rapid, but he knew he was making an indelible point.

"You don't seem particularly happy," the boss said.

Abel shrugged. "I managed to help Alice get out," he said. "And that was well worth the effort."

Benson studied Abel, and Abel could see the concern on Benson's face.

"Yet, something is troubling you," Benson said.

Abel wasn't sure how to put it into words. He slumped into a chair and stared between his knees at the carpet under his feet. He sighed.

"Did you know," he said, "that in the end, Alice saved me? If Alice hadn't taken it upon herself to call Elliot, you would be attending my funeral instead of reading my by-line."

The boss scratched his chin and grinned. "This isn't your first brush with death, Peter," he remarked. "Are you suddenly getting a taste of your own mortality?"

For the first time since he'd gotten back to Africa, Abel allowed himself to laugh.

"No," he said, "It's not that, not exactly anyway." He shook his head and shrugged. "Well, yes, maybe it is that. But I also can't help thinking about all the other girls just like Alice who are still out there, the ones that came before her, and the ones that will never be saved."

"Well," Benson said, "Take the small victories where you can, and don't worry about what you can't control. At any rate, the paper will make out well."

Abel looked at him, surprised. "The paper?"

"Forgive me if I think like a businessman for a moment, but this story has everything. Sex, crime, worldwide locales, power, and more. It's unbelievable. We will sell a hell of a lot of papers with this. And we need to, given what your expense account looks like."

"Duly noted." Abel was reluctant to agree, but Benson had a point. "But I would object to selling this story with even a hint of titillation."

"That never crossed my mind," Benson said, slightly defensive. "I will see that our marketing department does not sell your series for its prurient interest. Fair enough?"

Abel nodded.

"Will you be paying a visit to Alice's mother – or to her father?"

Abel headed towards the door. "I'll be seeing her mother," he said, "at least for the time being."

As Abel waited on Mrs. Udor's doorstep, he felt a sense of pride, despite the work left undone. Here was the one concrete accomplishment he could point to. He had saved this woman's daughter.

Alice's mother smiled broadly when she saw Abel. "It is so wonderful to see you," she said, hugging him impulsively. "I have received so many letters and calls from Alice. My goodness, she sounds happy! She and I are both grateful for everything you've done for us."

"It's my honour and pleasure," Abel responded with a slight bow of his head.

Mary invited Abel inside her humble home. The place was clean and well-kept, even if the furniture was old and the carpets worn. The surroundings reflected the woman perfectly. She was tidy in her manner of dress and her hair was done in neat cornrows. Signs of pride. But she could not hide the age which her daughter's ordeal had added to her appearance. Her face betrayed deep lines, the dark circles under her eyes had become permanent fixtures, the result of endless worrying and sleepless nights. And her hair had turned completely white. Like the furniture in her home, Mary Udor was old and worn.

Even Mary's voice sounded damaged. She spoke in a soft, raspy whisper. "I spoke to Alice last night," she said, her voice crackling. "Right now, she is learning CPR and emergency first aid. She was talking about recognising symptoms of a heart attack and how to tend to a patient who has a broken limb. I've never heard her so excited about anything. She seems mature and professional. I'm so proud of her."

"So am I, Mrs. Udor."

CHAPTER TWENTY-EIGHT

"Welcome home, Sir," Ikomma said as Abel entered the house. "I'm sorry I missed you last night. You have been gone for so long. Had I known you would be coming in, I would have turned back your bed for you."

"I appreciate that, Ikomma," Abel replied. "I got in very late."

"You should have awakened me." Ikomma seemed disturbed Abel would not let him perform what he considered to be his duties. "Can I interest you in some lunch?" Ikomma seemed determined to do something for his employer.

"As a matter of fact, you can," Abel answered. "My appetite is catching up with me."

Before Ikomma headed for the kitchen he handed Abel a slip of paper. "I took this message this morning. I thought you would want it right away."

Abel looked at the paper and felt a surge of adrenaline. "Mrs. Picketts called?"

Ikomma nodded. "She was very eager to speak with you. She said she is at her sister's in Isolo. I wrote down the address," he said.

"I thought she was in London."

"She just arrived back. I don't know if she has returned permanently. There was some grapevine talk that she might be planning to return to Europe for good. Word has it that she is having a difficult time adjusting to life without Tunde."

Abel nodded. "Lola and Tunde were devoted to each other," he said. "I'd better get back to her."

Once Abel reached her, Lola Picketts immediately asked if he could come see her that afternoon. Ordinarily, Abel would have put off their meeting since his mind was very much on finishing the newspaper series. But this was Lola, Tunde's widow and a woman to whom Abel was deeply attracted. Whatever was in their future, Abel wanted to see her.

Much to Ikomma's distress, Abel snatched a sandwich off the side board and said he'd eat it on the way to Lola's. Ikomma disapproved, not of the meeting with Lola, but of the hasty lunch. He felt his employer needed to begin taking care of himself. He was clearly exhausted from the past few weeks, and he had lost weight. But as Abel reminded him good naturedly when he had scolded, "You're not my mother, Ikomma." And he was out the door.

Abel and Lola hugged as they greeted each other on the doorstep of her sister's flat. Lola led him inside.

"Would you like a cup of coffee?" she said.

"That sounds great. The stronger the better. Don't take this personally, but I might need something to keep me awake. I have a lot of work ahead of me, and I'm already running a sleep deficit of more hours than I care to count."

"Don't apologise," Lola insisted. "I remember what it was like when Tunde was wrapping up a story. It's not surprising that you're exhausted, given what's happened to you the last few weeks."

"Yes," Abel said. "This series has taken a bigger toll on me than any story I've ever done. Perhaps it is because of the physical strain in the US."

They sipped their coffee as Abel told her about his adventures in the United States and Canada.

"Wow, nice to have you back in one piece," she said, genuinely impressed. "Now, I understand why you couldn't call."

"I'm glad to be back in once piece," Abel said. "Did you enjoy London?"

"It was better when you were there," she said. "You took my mind off my loss. When you left, I had nothing any more to distract me from thinking about Tunde. Worse still, when the calls didn't come."

"I'm sorry to hear that."

"Things got better as time passed," she said.

"You're still a young woman, Lola, not to mention beautiful and smart. There are so many opportunities for you out there. You have so much to offer."

Lola smiled and patted his forearm. "Bless you, Peter. You always know the right thing to say. All this time, I've been wondering what I should do next. Should I take on a new profession? Should I travel? Should I throw myself into volunteer work? I just don't know."

"Perhaps you could do a little of all three?" Abel suggested.

Lola nodded. "Like you said, there are so many opportunities out there." She gently caressed his arm. "Peter, my heart belonged to Tunde for so long. The hardest part for me now is the loneliness. You live alone. Don't you ever feel the desire to share your life with someone?"

Peter nodded. "I've struggled with that many times," he said. "Then I get a new assignment, and I find myself married to *The Zodiac*. I'm not complaining, mind you. Every time I pursue a lead, I feel a burst of energy that just overwhelms me. I don't know how to describe it."

They gazed into each other's eyes for a moment. There was an electrical charge between them, but it was broken a few seconds later when Abel dropped his eyes to the floor.

"Lola, I can't be sure what's going on between us, and I don't want to guess for fear I might reach the wrong conclusion."

A nervous smile appeared on Lola's face. "I don't want to sound forward," she said, "but I was hoping you and I could see each other. Casually. But who knows what might develop between us."

Abel was only slightly surprised. For as long as he had known her, Lola had always demonstrated a great deal of affection for him. It was all very sweet and endearing, and Abel had similar feelings towards her.

"I've had time to mourn for my husband," she said. "I will always love Tunde, but I would like to have another man in my life. Tunde loved you like a brother. I think he would be very pleased if the two of us ended up together."

Lola waited for Abel's response. So many thoughts were racing through his mind that it took a moment to gather them. Lola suddenly dropped her head in her hands.

"My goodness," she exclaimed, "I've made a complete fool of myself, haven't I?"

"No, Lola," Abel said. "You haven't made a fool of yourself at all. On the contrary, I am enormously flattered. You are an amazing woman in so many different ways. I have no doubt that I could someday fall completely, hopelessly, head-over-heels in love with you."

"Someday?" Lola questioned. "You mean not now?"

Abel noticed her eyes become watery with tears. She quickly turned away and wiped her face.

"Lola, you deserve a man who can be there for you," he said, "one who can build his life around you. I simply cannot be that man right now. You said it yourself. My work is my passion. It demands all of my heart and soul, not to mention almost every waking hour of my days. I won't make promises I already know I can't keep. That wouldn't be fair to either one of us."

"But I know the life, Peter. I lived it with Tunde."

"And maybe that's where hope lies for us. There is already a level of understanding. We're already friends. That part, the hard part of getting to know one another, we've already gotten past."

Lola sat back and sighed. Abel thought she understood, but the revelation didn't seem to provide her with much solace.

"Please don't feel rejected, Lola," Abel pleaded. "I'm not pushing you away. I'm trying to be honest and fair. Let's continue to be good friends and see what happens as time goes by."

She nodded and smiled through her tears. She said nothing more as she picked up their empty cups and carried them off into the kitchen.

As Abel watched her go, he wondered if he wasn't making a mistake, throwing away a chance to spend the rest of his life with someone for whom he cared deeply and was attracted to on every level.

"Mr. Abel! Mr. Abel!"

Abel was jarred awake by Ikomma's voice followed by his hand shaking Abel's shoulder.

"What's going on?" Abel groaned, barely half awake. "What time is it?"

"It is four o'clock, Oga," Ikomma said. "I need you to wake up."

"Four o'clock in the morning?" Abel said. "What in the world is happening, Ikomma?"

Ikomma held up Abel's robe. "There is a telephone call for you, Sir," he informed him. "It is your boss. He said it is an emergency and he must speak to you immediately."

Abel threw the covers off of his legs. He slipped into his robe and walked down the hall to his study.

"What have you got, Boss?" Abel said into the telephone.

"Sorry to wake you, Peter," the boss said, "but I knew you would want to know about this. Alice's mother was admitted to hospital about two hours ago."

"Admitted for what?" Abel said, feeling his chest tighten.

"I only spoke to an administrator, who didn't know any details. She called the paper because Mary Udor named us as her emergency contact. It could be serious, Peter. They brought her through the casualty unit."

"Damn!" Abel muttered. "I begged her to go to a doctor. In fact, I was going to make some calls tomorrow to arrange it."

"She's been sick?" the boss asked.

"I couldn't tell if she is suffering with a specific illness," Abel said, "but she looked very unhealthy the last time I saw her. And she acknowledged that she wasn't well. I'd better get down to the hospital and find out what the story is."

"Give me a call when you get some information."

Abel hung up and ran back to his bedroom. Ikomma had already set out a suit of clothes for him.

"I had a feeling you wouldn't be going back to bed," Ikomma said.

The streets were almost empty at that dark hour of the morning, so Abel drove over the speed limit and even went the wrong way down a one-way street to get to the casualty unit as quickly as possible. He parked his car haphazardly and dashed through the automatic doors, searching for the duty nurse.

Abel found her at her station.

"I'm Peter Abel from *The Zodiac*. Mrs. Udor named our paper as emergency contact."

The nurse looked at his press credentials and nodded.

"Apparently the police got a call from a neighbour who said Mrs. Udor was screaming very loudly. The neighbour was reluctant to go over and check on her, for fear there might be danger. The policeman who brought Mrs. Udor in said there was a history of violence with the husband and guessed the neighbour was afraid he would be there."

Abel grimaced. He wasn't sure how many of the neighbours knew Mr. Udor had syndicate connections. Some of them probably suspected it and didn't want to risk getting on his bad side.

"The police found Mrs. Udor on the floor of her bedroom," the nurse said. "They think she might have fallen out of bed. She was in a great deal of pain. She couldn't walk. She could barely move at all."

"Had she broken some bones?" Abel asked.

The nurse shook her head. "The attending physician ruled that out after examining her and sending her to X-Ray."

"Do they have any idea what else it might be?" Abel said.

"You'll have to ask the doctor, Mr. Abel."

After a few minutes, Abel found the doctor. He introduced himself and asked about Mary Udor's condition.

"Mrs. Udor is suffering from acute arthritis," the physician explained. "It is present in most of her joints and even within the vertebrae. Frankly, from the photographs, I'm shocked that she hasn't been admitted to casualty before. The pain would have to be excruciating. She must have a high tolerance to it."

"Can she be cured?" Abel wondered.

"At this stage, I would say no," the doctor answered. "At the moment, we have her resting comfortably with the help of morphine and other painkillers. That's really all we can do for her. The condition will not reverse itself, and there are no treatments. Medication will only be given to provide some pain relief, but eventually, that will cease to be effective as well. This is a very tragic circumstance."

Abel felt sick. "May I see her?"

The doctor led him to a room at the end of the long hall.

"She may be a little groggy," he said. "She is very heavily medicated right now."

Abel found Mary lying in a hospital bed, an oxygen tube clipped to her nose to assist her breathing and an IV attachment delivering fluids and medication. She opened her eyes when Abel approached her bedside.

"I said I was going to make a doctor's appointment for you," he said with a forced smile. "It looks like you went ahead and did it on your own."

"Have you spoken with the doctor?" she said.

Abel nodded.

"Then you know there isn't much hope for me," she said softly.

"There is always hope," Abel said, perhaps more so to convince himself than the woman before him.

"Mr. Abel," Mary said, "I want to see Alice. I need to see her. Is there any way you can make that happen?"

"Of course, I can make that happen," he assured her. "I will call Alice today, and my paper will arrange for her to fly to your side as soon as possible."

Mrs. Udor closed her weary eyes and smiled. "Thank you, Sir. Thank you so much."

Abel waited to call Alice until it was eight o'clock in the morning in Edmonton, Alberta.

"Dear Lord," she said, "has it really gotten that bad? Mum has been in pain for so many years, but she has never complained. She never wanted to be a burden on anyone. I wish she had gotten help sooner."

"You mum wants to see you, Alice," Abel told her. "Right now, that's the only thing she wants in the whole world. We'll pay for your plane ticket."

"Please tell her I will be there, Mr. Abel," Alice said. "I will take the first available flight."

"I will be at the airport to take you to Yaba Medical Centre," Abel said assuredly.

"Thanks for being there for me, Mr. Abel," Alice said

And so it was that Alice left Canada. The last leg of her long journey, and of Abel's, was about to come to a close. And even though he had the ending for his series in mind already, subsequent events would force Abel to alter the last instalment radically.

CHAPTER TWENTY-NINE

Abel met Alice at the Murtala Muhammed airport shortly after seven at night. He saw immediately that the scared, frightened, and abused child he left at the medical clinic in Canada had been replaced by a confident young woman.

Abel had always perceived Alice as a beautiful girl, but what he saw before him now was altogether different. Alice radiated a healthy glow. Her skin had a rich, natural hue, and her eyes, which had once been vacant and disconnected, were now full of emotion and life. Even her manner of walking was different. Instead of a shameful hunch, she now carried herself with a genuine sense of dignity and pride.

"Welcome home, Alice," Abel said softly. He extended his arms and she fell into his warm embrace. "It must seem like years since you've been home."

Alice apparently was not ready to reminisce about her homecoming. She had more pressing things on her mind.

"Please take me to see my mother, Mr. Abel," she said.

"I'm afraid we can't see her tonight," he said. "Visiting hours end about now. If it were an emergency, I'm sure I could get one of the security staff to let us in, but there is no urgency. Your mother is not in immediate danger. The doctors are administering analgesics to relieve her pain. She is probably sleeping quite comfortably."

"That's good to hear," Alice responded. "I don't want her to endure any more pain. She has been living with it for far too long."

Abel understood that Alice was speaking of pain that extended beyond Mrs. Udor's physical condition. He felt certain the medication Mrs. Udor was receiving wasn't powerful enough to relieve her emotional agony.

"I will take you to her ward first thing in the morning," Abel said, smiling at Alice. "I'm sure her spirits will rise at the mere sight of you."

"Thank you. I can't wait to see her again. I've spoken to her on the telephone from Canada, of course, but it seems like forever since we've actually been together."

Abel led Alice through the maze of travellers out to the parking lot.

"You've had a long day," he said. "I'm sure you're ready to get comfortable in a nice warm bed."

"That sounds so wonderful," Alice said.

"I've had Ikomma make up the guest room bed for you. I thought it would bring our story full circle," Abel said, recalling the night he met Alice.

"That's very kind," Alice said, "but there is a room waiting for me at the Congrieve Hotel."

The hotel was located just two blocks from the hospital, which would certainly make it convenient for Alice. It also was the preferred lodging place of visiting dignitaries and affluent businessmen. Some of them were the same kind of people who commissioned the services young girls run by the syndicate. Abel immediately became suspicious.

"Did *The Zodiac* set that up for you?" he said. "No one at the newspaper mentioned that to me."

"Oh, no," Alice said. "This was arranged by the people from Youth Justice International. My counsellor at the clinic called Edmonton, and they contacted the branch in Accra, which made this arrangement. They wanted to find me a place as close to the hospital as possible."

Relieved, although still somewhat apprehensive, Abel pulled his car into the traffic and headed in the direction of the Congrieve Hotel. A voice in the back of his head told him he should book a room for himself just to keep an eye on Alice. But after a glance at the young woman sitting in the passenger seat, he immediately changed his mind. This was a much stronger Alice than he had chased across the globe. He could tell by her demeanour she would sooner die than go back to that horrific life. She had become her own saviour.

Abel escorted Alice through the lobby. The clerk at the front desk checked her in and provided her with a room key.

Alice turned to Abel. "I'll be fine if you want to go home and get some sleep. The bellman can bring my suitcase up for me."

"I'd like to see you up to your room, if you don't mind," he said.

Alice laughed. "Maybe 'father' isn't the right term for you. More like Mother Hen." Abel laughed at her description and couldn't deny it was accurate.

"I appreciate all you've done for me, Mr. Abel," she said, "but I'd really like to go to bed now."

Abel nodded, slightly embarrassed.

"Of course," he said. "I'll allow you some privacy. Come down to the lobby at eight o'clock tomorrow morning. I'll meet you there and then we can go over and visit your mother."

At eight o'clock sharp, Peter Abel arrived at the Congrieve Hotel. He was very pleased to find Alice sitting on a sofa waiting for him. She wore a pale blue blouse and a mid-length skirt. It was very stylish and age-appropriate, not like the blatantly sexual apparel the syndicate made her wear. Abel knew that after everything Alice had suffered, it was impossible for her to return to a state of innocence, but he was grateful to see her embracing her youth.

"Have you had breakfast this morning?" Abel said.

"Yes," Alice told him. "The hotel sent a tray up to my room. Can we go to the hospital now?"

Abel nodded and escorted her out to his car.

Mrs. Udor was resting comfortably. She tried to sit up as Alice and Abel entered her room.

"Oh, mum!" Alice said, her voice unsteady. "I've missed you so much."

"I've missed you too, baby," Mrs. Udor replied in a tired whisper. "I'm so glad to see you."

Her eyes scanned her daughter's body from head to toe. "Oh, my dear!" she gasped. "You look wonderful! You have no idea what a beautiful sight you are to my sore eyes and sore body."

Abel stood back, happy to witness the reunion. He was touched by the pride in Mary's eyes as she gazed at her daughter. Alice leaned over and kissed her mother's cheek. She worked hard not to let her emotions get the better of her. Abel could tell she wanted to cry, but

242

she was determined to hold back her tears and not frighten or worry her mother.

As mother and daughter visited, Mary fought to stay awake. The heavy medication made it difficult for her to keep focused for long periods. When Mary's energy did flag, Alice patiently pulled a stool up to the side of the bed and gently held her mother's hand. Abel found the gesture touching and thought Alice certainly had the right temperament for nursing.

"I'm sure you have quite a bit of work to do, Mr. Abel," Alice finally said. "Please don't feel you have to stay here all day. I just want to spend time with my mum. You can leave, and I will walk or call a taxi when I need to go back to the hotel."

"No, please. Allow me to give you a ride back. Just call my cell phone," Abel said as he handed her his business card.

Alice thanked him, and Abel bid his goodbyes.

Alice called him at about four o'clock in the afternoon to come and pick her up. As they left the hospital parking lot, Alice seemed distant and distracted.

"Is everything all right?" Abel said.

Alice looked at him from behind a pair of dark glasses she had purchased in the hospital gift shop.

"My mother has aged so much since I last saw her. Losing me, my father divorcing her, and leaving her in poverty have taken a heavy toll. Thank God my siblings were there to keep her company."

"Yes, it has," Abel said. He had hoped Alice wouldn't notice the drastic change in Mary, but of course how could she not?

"I want to see my father."

Abel turned to her, shocked.

"I don't think that's a good idea, Alice. What could come of it?"

"I want him to see that I've survived. I want him to know he didn't destroy me."

Something in Abel's gut told him to fight this idea. Maybe it was Alice's tone, or the fact that she kept her dark glasses on, hiding her eyes. Abel couldn't tell what was really going on inside her head. He tried to stall.

"I don't really know where he lives ..."

"Yes, you do. Or you can find out. Your paper will know." When Abel didn't answer her, Alice turned and looked at him, dark glasses still in place.

"If you don't take me, I'll go on my own."

Abel knew he had no choice. Letting her go on her own was out of the question. So he called the paper, got an address and drove Alice to her father's new home. It was a new apartment block in Apapa, an affluent part of town. As they pulled up in front, Alice studied it.

"This is it?"

Abel nodded. He could sense something in Alice harden.

"And my mother still lives in our old place? That dump?"

"Yes."

Alice got out of the car. Abel moved beside her as they walked up the steps to the front entrance and checked the mail boxes for Winston Udor's name. He lived on the top floor, 4-A.

"Are you sure you want to see him, Alice?"

"Yes," was all she said.

A few minutes later, the door to 4-A swung open and there stood Winston Udor, looking much more prosperous than he had the first time Abel met him. His bald head was still prominent, but he was dressed in a silk shirt and shiny black pants. He gazed out at them puzzled.

"Yes?"

"You don't recognise your own child?" Alice said, removing her dark glasses for the first time.

Udor registered shock, his eyes going wider, his back stiffening involuntarily. He smiled then, but not spontaneously. What he truly felt was anyone's guess, but Abel figured it was fear.

"This is Peter Abel. A friend."

"Yes, we've met." So, Udor remembered him after all.

"Aren't you going to invite us in?"

Udor nodded, finally. "Of course. I'm happy to see you."

He tried to hug Alice, but she backed away. "Don't touch me."

Udor obeyed and held open the door. After Abel and Alice entered, she looked around taking in the surroundings.

"You've grown into a lovely woman, Alice."

Alice turned on him, her anger simmering. "No thanks to you."

"Can we put the past behind us, please? We both made our share of mistakes."

Alice gaped. Abel couldn't believe Udor could be so callous and, apparently, neither could Alice.

"Mistakes? Selling your daughter into slavery is not a mistake."

"You were already selling yourself, Alice. Let's not forget that you started that of your own free will. You became a prostitute long before I arranged for you to go overseas. It was for your own good. So you could have a better life. The girls here who sell themselves all die young. Look at you! Look how you've thrived. It is thanks to me that you are what you are today!"

The audacity of the man was truly breathtaking, Abel thought. He had the strongest impulse to smash his face in with his fists, but he held his temper.

"Mr. Udor. She's only alive today because she got out of the life you sold her into."

Udor turned on Abel, regarding him cynically. "And I suppose you didn't take advantage of this girl yourself? Don't tell me you haven't taken your pleasure with her, Sir."

"He has never laid a hand on me!" Alice shouted at her father. "He saved me. Got me off drugs. Got me back into school. I owe him my life."

"And I'm sure you'll show the proper appreciation." Udor smirked. He was incapable of thinking in any other terms. In his universe, men took sexual advantage of women or girls. Nothing could convince him that anyone acted differently. Abel decided not to try. He wasn't worth the effort, frankly.

They were interrupted by a woman's voice. They turned as a pretty young woman entered. She looked as if she'd been sleeping.

"I heard voices, honey. Who is it?"

"This is my daughter, Alice and her 'friend,' Mr. Abel."

Alice turned to the woman. "You are his new wife?"

She nodded, somewhat taken aback. "Yes. I am Emily, and I'm pleased to meet you. I was hoping to be friends with Winston's children."

Suddenly, a baby's cry came from the other room. Emily

turned.

"Oh, dear. The baby's awake," she said and hurried from the room.

Alice looked stunned. She turned to her father. "Baby? What baby?"

"Our baby. Emily's and mine."

Alice looked as if she was going to be physically ill. Emily re-entered, a small baby in her arms. "Meet your half-sister. Becca."

"Sister?" Alice was clearly alarmed. Abel watched as she approached the innocent child lying peacefully in her mother's arms. "My God," was all Alice said before turning and leaving the apartment. Emily looked after her, then spoke to Abel.

"Her father told me about Alice's drug issues. I can see she's a disturbed young lady. But I want her to know I'm here if she ever wants help. We are all family."

Abel had no idea what to say to this woman whose future he could so easily predict. But it was the future of the child in her arms Abel was most concerned about. And he knew Alice was thinking the same thing. Abel nodded to Emily.

"If you want to know more about Alice," he said, "read the series on her in *The Zodiac*. It will begin next week."

Once back in the car, Abel watched Alice, whose breathing was short as she tried to regain control of herself.

"Alice, try to relax."

"It all came back to me, just seeing him. All the feelings of disgust and fear and humiliation. Then to see that baby, that poor little thing so helpless in the same house with him."

"I know. And as time goes by you might be able to help the child. For now, there's nothing to be done."

When Alice looked at Abel, her eyes were different. Something of the hardness which was once there had returned, and the joy he'd seen earlier in the day was gone.

"Perhaps you were right, Mr. Abel. I shouldn't have seen him."

Alice agreed that she would focus on her mother, devote her time to Mary and try to put her father out of her mind. At least for the time being.

For the next three days, Abel met Alice at the Congrieve Hotel and brought her over to the hospital to visit her mother. Then Abel drove to the offices of *The Zodiac*, where he spent many hours putting the final touches on his series. The storm which gathered that first day after visiting Alice's father seemed to have passed. Abel had feared the experience might send Alice back to drugs, if not sexual slavery. Once an addict, the temptation to retreat into a drug-induced haze to obliterate pain was hard to resist. Much to Abel's relief, Alice seemed to harbour no such impulses. Another hurdle had been overcome.

On the fourth day, early in the evening, Abel sat at his desk agonizing over the third installment when Taylor, the crime editor, burst through the office door.

"Mr. Abel!" Taylor exclaimed. "The boss said to come get you. You won't believe what has happened!"

Abel instinctively jumped out of his chair. "What's going on, Taylor?"

Taylor drew in a deep breath and tried to regain his composure. "Mr. Winston Udor, the one who appears in your article? He has been murdered."

"Couldn't happen to a nicer guy," Able blurted out before he realised he needed to attend to the gravity of the situation.

He wasn't shocked by the news. As the saying went, "People who dance too close to the fire are destined to get burned." Udor was a depraved and contemptible man who made himself wealthy by doing business with other depraved and contemptible men. None of these criminals had any loyalty to anyone or anything other than their own interests.

"Do they have any suspects?" Abel said. He was thinking of interviewing whoever it was for his series.

"Yes." Taylor said. "Mr. Udor's daughter."

Abel wasn't sure he'd heard correctly, at first. Then the news hit him.

"Alice!" he said. "Are you sure?"

Taylor nodded. "She's being held in the police station in Apapa."

Without another word, Abel pushed his way past Taylor and dashed out through the office door.

CHAPTER THIRTY

Abel drove his car at breakneck speed to Apapa. His thoughts raced back to the last encounter with Winston Udor, and Alice's shock and anger at discovering she had a half-sister. He remembered the hard look in her eyes. It must have been at that moment that Alice decided to kill the man.

Arriving at the police station, he almost hit a police vehicle as he cranked the steering wheel toward the parking lot. He jumped out of the car so quickly that he only shut the driver's side door halfway before he charged for the front door of the building.

"I'm Peter Abel," he said through his panting to the officer at the front desk. "I need to see Alice Udor."

"I'm afraid that's not possible, Sir," the officer said.

"I'm from *The Zodiac*," Abel said, not willing go give up. "It is very important that I see her immediately."

"Miss Udor is currently being questioned," the officer said.

"Does she have legal counsel present?" Abel said. "She's only fifteen, sixteen."

The officer held up his hand in gesture that told Abel to back off. "Yes, Sir, legal counsel is present," he said. "As a matter of fact, the attorney was sent by *The Zodiac*."

Abel stood back, completely amazed. The publisher hadn't wasted any time. He was relieved. The newspaper's legal team was one of the best in Nigeria. They would ensure that Alice's rights would not be violated.

Even so, Abel wanted to hear the story directly from the girl.

He called his friend Fakorede, but it was of no use. Abel cut him off apologetically when he launched into a boastful reverie of arrests of people he had made over Tunde's murder.

Winston Udor's funeral took place at the Yaba cemetery, along the University of Lagos road. Abel decided to attend the service, not as a mourner, but as a researcher. He wondered what he could learn

248

from those who came to see this man's body forever given to the earth.

A minister stood next to the casket and read from the Scripture to the very small collection of mourners gathered around. Emily was present, a veil covering her face, and her head bowed slightly. Abel felt badly for the widow's pain and relieved for her at the same time. The naïve young woman who would never know the life she and her child had just escaped. She didn't realise how lucky she was to have a beautiful baby to rear in a healthy, happy and safe environment.

They acknowledged one another with curt nods. Her cool attitude toward Abel suggested Winston had made up lies about Abel's motives, and no doubt coloured him as a ruthless, heartless reporter out to sensationalise stories without regard for the damage he did to innocent people.

The only thing Abel accomplished by attending Udor's funeral was a certain morbid satisfaction in the man's demise. He was seen out of this world by a very small collection of people, none of whom, except for Emily, appeared to be moved by his passing. In fact, Abel wondered if some of them had come just to make sure the villain was actually dead.

Abel hoped that when his time came, whoever attended his funeral would be more attentive than this group of people, who were clearly bored by the minister's words. Perhaps it was because they so ill-fitted the occasion.

As he was driving back to his office, Abel's cell phone rang. He looked down at the display and saw it was his boss. Abel put on his headset and answered the phone.

"Hi, boss."

"Hi, Peter. How was the funeral service?"

"Quiet," Abel said. "Small."

"Maybe his friends and family couldn't get the day off work," the boss said.

"Good riddance," Abel said. "So, what's going on?"

"I've got some good news. Our legal department got you cleared to meet with Alice."

Abel's spirits immediately soared. "I'm going straight there," he said.

"Good. Because I don't know how long this sudden display of good will towards us will last. Legal had to arm-wrestle pretty hard."

"I thought you and the Commissioner were such good buddies," Abel said, teasing him.

"Just get over there, boy," Benson said and hung up. Abel smiled at the exchange, then made a sharp turn towards the prison.

A uniformed officer escorted Abel to a dimly lit room at the end of a long, grey hallway. He took a seat at a table across from Alice, her chin up and her head held high. Her face showed no signs of shame or fear. Rather, she radiated a sense of defiance and confidence. As he sat there, Abel couldn't decide if that was good or bad.

"You must remain on this side of the table," the officer said. "No touching, and no note passing. You have a right to know that your conversation is being monitored, and we have a right to terminate your visit at our discretion."

Abel nodded, and the officer stepped outside.

"Why did you do this, Alice?" Abel said sternly.

Alice's face twisted into an expression of surprise. "You're asking why?" she said. "You saw that innocent child! You know what he'd have done to her."

Abel held out his hands, instructing her to lower her tone. "Of course. That's not what I meant. But you could have saved that child without killing the man."

"How?"

"I could have worked to take your father down, get him put in jail to get him reformed, or something."

Alice shook her head. "I didn't want to wait."

"So, this was revenge?"

Alice shrugged.

Abel sighed. "I can understand why you would want vengeance on your father, but you've sacrificed your own future to do it. Alice. Your father had stolen your childhood. Now he's going to steal the rest of your life as well."

Alice was unmoved. "He can no longer steal anything from me," she said. "And now, he will not be able to harm my sister. When I looked at that child, I saw not only a baby, I saw my own flesh and blood."

Abel was nervously conscious of the investigators who were watching them from the other side of the glass. They had heard every word Alice had just said, and they were certain to use those words against her.

"But what about you, Alice?" he wondered. "You don't want to spend the rest of your life in prison."

She smiled broadly at him. "I won't spend my life in prison," she said as a matter of fact. "The truth is on my side."

"Alice," Abel said, "the truth is that you committed murder."

"I will be vindicated," she said confidently. "When your series appears in *The Zodiac*, the world will know what a brutal man my father was. They will learn he had another daughter who would suffer the same fate I did, and they will agree that I was justified in shooting him with his own gun."

Abel felt a shock run through him. Was it possible Alice was using him? Using his paper to get off without serving any jail time?

"Alice, nobody sympathises with you more than I do, or wants to help you as much. But I don't want to feel as if you're using me. My job is to report and to enlighten."

"No, Mr. Abel. When you came after me, your job became something else. It was to save me. And that is what you will do. I have every faith in you. And I think if you write the story honestly you will, indeed, save me. I am not asking for anything. Just tell my story. It is, after all, what you do."

Abel understood the power of the press better than anyone, but he was not completely convinced that his words could save Alice from a prison sentence. Nor was he comfortable with the notion that maybe they could. The paper was not meant to replace a court of law.

Despite these misgivings, Alice was right. His job was to tell her story. If in doing so he saved her, so be it.

Before he could ask anything else, the uniformed officer stepped back into the room. "I'm sorry, Mr. Abel," he said, "but I have been told your time is up."

Abel nodded and rose from his chair, then turned towards Alice. "I will do everything I can," he told her.

Alice looked back at him wearing a confident smile. "I am at peace with what I did, Mr. Abel. I know you will not fail me. You never have."

Back at the office, Abel worked feverishly to compose an addendum to his series. He incorporated the story of Alice murdering her father, being at peace with herself, saving her new sister from a terrible fate. He described the horror and humiliation Alice had suffered at her father's hands.

The more he worked at the series, the stronger he came to feel that Alice was right. She did what needed to be done. What she had to do.

Finally, as he saved his work to a computer disk, Abel said a silent prayer. "Dear God," he thought, "do not let me fail Alice now."

The boss read his pages as Abel paced the office, his nerves completely on edge. "I know it's unusual, this crusading point of view. But I believe in her, Chief. Sending her to jail won't help anyone, and it will deprive the world of a productive citizen. A nurse no less."

Now that the piece was in Benson's hands, Abel couldn't help but feel defensive. It was one thing to write it, vent on the page; it was quite another to show it to the world. And as usual, once another set of eyes was gazing on his work, Abel became much less certain of its timeless brilliance.

Benson smiled at him. "Don't worry, Peter. You've got *The Zodiac* behind you. We support what you're doing. Our legal team is defending her, after all. We will press this issue until Alice is free."

Abel nodded. "The truth is, the police are probably just as pleased Winston Udor is dead as Alice is."

Benson nodded. "Of course they have to maintain a certain air of decorum. They don't want people to think that women won't be prosecuted if they shoot their fathers or husbands."

Benson laid the pages down. "In the end, our legal people will have to make a case for her. Extreme emotional distress. Self-defence. But I think it's a strong case. And with our series, public opinion will be in her favour. Of course everything is politics. No judge is going to preside over the persecution of a martyr. Nobody wants to play the role of Herod."

"I hope you're right, Boss," Abel said. "I really hope you're right."

With the publication of Peter Abel's series, Alice Udor instantly became one of the most famous women in Nigeria. Her story was picked up by other news media, and the police were overwhelmed with requests for interviews with Alice, as well as with the policemen who had arrested her and the counsel that would be prosecuting her. CNN reported the story on its *Inside Africa* programme. And thanks to the online edition of *The Zodiac*, Alice's story travelled all over the world, and soon human rights organizations, international political figures and concerned world citizens publicly demanded that Alice Udor be exonerated. She was seen not as a killer but as a saviour and avenging angel.

The trial was short and conducted in a pro forma way. Alice was acquitted. *The Zodiac* photographers were there to capture the moment when she walked out of the courtroom, a free woman.

"I only have one thing to say," Alice said to a large cluster of media microphones and tape recorders held in front of her face outside the courtroom. "I wish to express my gratitude to the court that acquitted me and to the people all over the world who supported me. It is humbling to think so many cared so deeply."

Alice paused, emotional and tearing up. "And I wish to extend my deepest thanks to Peter Abel and *The Zodiac* for making sure the world heard my story."

Alice began to walk away when someone shouted, "What will you do now, Ms. Udor?"

Alice turned and smiled, suddenly looking as young as her 16 years again.

"I'm going to spend time with my mother, then return to Canada to complete my nursing studies."

"Will you ever come back to Nigeria?"

"Yes," she said, simply. "This is my home. I will be back to set up a branch of the Youth Justice International."

With that, she stepped away from the microphones and walked to Peter Abel, who waited for her his car engine already running. As she got in the car, Abel drew her attention to an official of the

National Agency for the Prohibition of Trafficking in Persons, who was addressing journalists.

"…We have been following this case and we have decided to talk to Ms. Udor over a number of things later today," he adjusted his tie. "In fact, we are going to offer her a scholarship for the rest of her education in Canada and also rehabilitate her mother."

At that, Abel turned to Alice with a broad smile. "I am happy for you, Alice."

"It's all to your credit, Mr. Abel," she said, and shut the door.

Abel drove her directly to the hospital.

When they entered, Mary Udor sat up in bed. Her face beamed when Alice entered the room.

"Oh, my beautiful daughter," she said. "I knew you would be all right. Something told me that you would find the strength to pull through."

Alice leaned over and gave her mother a warm embrace. She then glanced up at Abel, who remained in the doorway.

"Thank you, Mr. Abel," she said. "*The Zodiac* driver will take me to your office later. Right now, I want to be alone with my Mum."

Abel nodded, and quietly walked down the hall.